Dark Angel

Dark Angel

"A Jack Madson Novel"

RON FELBER

BARRICADE
BOOKS

Published by Barricade Books Inc.
2037 Lemoine Ave., Suite 362
Fort Lee, NJ 07024

www.barricadebooks.com

Copyright © 2016 by Ron Felber
All Rights Reserved.

No part of this book may be reproduced, stored in a retrieval system, or trans-
mitted in any form, by any means, including mechanical, electronic, photo-
copying, recording, or otherwise, without the prior written permission of the
publisher, except by a reviewer who wishes to quote brief passages in connection
with a review written for inclusion in a magazine, newspaper, or broadcast.

Library of Congress Cataloging-in-Publication Data

Names: Felber, Ron, author.
Title: Dark angel : a Jack Madson novel / Ron Felber.
Description: Fort Lee, NJ : Barricade Books, [2016] | Series: Jack Madson ; 3
Identifiers: LCCN 2016002884 | ISBN 9780942637878 (softcover)
Subjects: LCSH: Serial murder investigation—Fiction. | Secret
societies—Fiction. | Conspiracies—Fiction. | GSAFD: Suspense fiction.
Classification: LCC PS3606.E3847 D37 2016 | DDC 813/.6--dc23
LC record available at *http://lccn.loc.gov/2016002884*

"For you have mistook me all this while."
—Richard II
Shakespeare

This book is for Mickey

BEFORE
THE
BEGINNING

Wewlesberg Castle
North Rhine-Westphalia, Germany
February 1945

With Allied forces converging on Central Europe, Josef Mengele calmly smoked a cigarette preparing to escape Nazi SS headquarters—an eerie 12th century castle studded like a gemstone above the village of Wewlesberg—headed for the jungles outside of Sao Paulo, Brazil. In his right hand he clutched a chrome-plated carrier, fist wrapped white-knuckled over its handle. The static-laced voices of frantic radio transmissions cut in and out over the yowl of Focke Wulf Condor engines warming outside as Wagner's "Ride of the Valkyries" rampaged over Sennheiser speakers.

His study, lined ceiling-high with bound copies of the latest medical journals from around the world, had become a sanctuary from the war's distractions. Now, he was forced to flee again: first, from the comforts of his laboratories in

Auschwitz to this backwater colony of Westphalian dunces; now, to Amazon jungles populated by tribes of brown-skinned primitives, living proof of Nietzsche's Aryan master race theories!

The Angel of Death ground his cigarette fiercely into an ashtray embossed with tiny swastikas, a gift from the Fuhrer, himself. His thoughts diverted from stomping boots fast approaching to wondering if his Mauthansen colleague, Aribert Heim, had made it out of Germany when a detail of *Waffen-SS* burst through the double doors, Gewehr carbines raised shoulder-high.

"*Sofort kommen!*" Lieutenant Geiger demanded stern expression turned diffident by the stony coldness of Mengele's gaze, adding the words "*Bitte, Herr Doktor.*"

Escorted by a phalanx of Security Mengele strode beyond the castle's fortified doors into the glacial cold recalling that not many years before he and Heim had been rivals. But no more, he gloated, fingers tightening around the carrier's handle. Heim, whose stock and trade was prosthesis surgery, had failed to impress even those working in his own discipline with his crude attempts at transforming humans into weapons through robotics while Mengele's superiors had immediately grasped the military applications of his bio-engineering experiments. What he saw as scientific breakthroughs, they saw as devastating new weapons. So, money was lavished upon it as he pushed to complete what they'd begun calling PROJECT REBIRTH: Hitler's dream of *schlach maschines*, an army of genetically engineered *trans-humans* that would rain the Furhrer's wrath down upon Stalingrad killing any living thing they encountered because that is what they had been programmed to do.

Mengele's eyes lifted skyward, wind-driven snowflakes freezing on his face and brow as they boarded the plane. What he felt was beyond pride. In his hands he held the most revolutionary weapon, not only of the Third Reich, but of science itself. Few men in history could claim what he could: *Mengele had changed the world!*

"This weather, is it dangerous?"

"Low hanging clouds. The pilot will fly over it," Geiger shouted back over the engines' drone. "Herr Doktor Mengele, I need to store your case."

"No!" he recoiled. "This case will stay up front with me and the other officers."

"There are no others, Herr Doktor. Just you and all of this equipment. Besides, it will be safer packed in storage."

A vein in his head throbbed prominently.

"You forget yourself, Lieutenant," he admonished. "The case will stay here with me."

Probes of moonlight pierced the shroud of storm clouds that enveloped the Swiss Alps as the Wulf Condor plowed on into the night. Mengele sat up, jolted from dark reveries about his wife and children, friends and colleagues, all of them dead or in flight from the enemy, reassured by the touch of chrome on his fingertips as he cradled the carrier delighted at what could only be described as a harbinger of future success: rays of moonlight, shot like lasers through the plane's O-shaped window, were reflecting off the case's mirrored surface; touched, as if by God's own fiery hand, to clarion the arrival of the Fuhrer's brave new world. But even before the anomaly fully registered in his mind, the Condor bucketed, violent, like a patient convulsing, then dropped a full twenty meters.

"Sicherheitsgurte! Anziehen Ihre Sicherheitsgurte!" the pilot

shouted craning his head around to Mengele, Geiger, and his subordinates.

Shit! Fuck! Was there a torture equal to this feeling of helplessness? Mengele anguished. But more than acknowledging the morbid fear of flying he'd concealed since childhood, he understood it. Control is what he lived for. Control is what he needed to patch together the divergent forces that battled for dominance within him. At times he suspected even the prisoners had witnessed symptoms of the fissure that divided his many parts. Who would it be today, the kike scum wondered as he selected subjects from amongst the thousands arriving in cattle cars each week: the doting Uncle Josef offering sweets to his favorite prisoner-twins or the clinically detached Angel of Death, more serial killer than scientist? But from out of those black waters of possibility, he fortified himself with the knowledge that it was he—Josef Mengele, loyal disciple of Adolf Hitler and pioneer in the newfound science of genetic engineering—who emerged victorious.

"Are you okay?" Geiger asked leaning across the aisle to him. "You needn't worry, Herr Doktor. Wenzel is a wizard with these planes."

"*Ja,*" Mengele retorted, face ashen but heart pounding with resolve.

To bring to bear his skills and learning, to soldier on when the others—Himmler, Goering, even Rommel—had fallen by the wayside through sheer force of will and an unshakable belief in the Reich: this was his destiny and his honor. Thanks to him, all of them would again be united, he vowed, to reshape the world. Of course, he would survive this and any other peril. God would not allow it to be otherwise.

"Sicherheitsgurte! Kopfe zwischen die Beine!" the pilot shouted, words accentuated by a flash that ripped through the sky like a machete. "Engine One out! We've been hit by lightning!" he cried out swiveling around to them for the last time. *"Prepare to crash land!"*

* * *

Mengele's sensation once he understood that he was still alive was not panic nor pain but a sense of tranquility; a quiet so profound that he wondered if he'd been rendered deaf by the accident. Despite the gusting wind and feeling of numbness in his extremities nothing fazed him, least of all the likelihood that everyone aboard the plane was dead.

The pilot who'd been decapitated, body still strapped into the cockpit, was most certainly dead, he concluded. So was the co-pilot, skewered through the chest by the plane's yoke. He reconnoitered the bleak mountain terrain where fires fueled by splattered pools of diesel fuel sprouted like pagan pyres, eyes falling upon Geiger, body smoldering half-buried in snow, also quite dead, on his way to being incinerated.

What about his own condition? Mengele wondered, patting his hands over arms, legs, and upper body; checking feet, fingers, toes, and face, running his palms over forehead, cheeks, jaw, and neck, then holding them out in front of him to look for blood. There was none.

"Herr Doktor Mengele, kommen Sie schnell! There is no time!"

But these hands pulling him forward by the lapels of his SS officers' great coat were those of another man, he realized, staring dazedly into the faces of two German soldiers.

"*Kommen Sie! Sie mussen jetzt kommen!*" one of them ordered, eyes scanning the tumultuous horizon. It was tempting to scream out the simple question 'Who are you?' or 'where am I?' but the greater of Mengele's many parts prevailed, cautioning him not to expose any element of weakness, not now, not ever. So he allowed them to guide him through the wind-driven snow, now raging, to a second plane. This one still intact, propellers churning, manned by a detail of the Furher's personal security staff, such was the importance of his mission.

It was then that certain images began streaming through his mind. Clues to who he was and how he'd come to be there, spilling from subconscious to conscious, ladled like molten metal. Scalding in their importance.

Mengele . . . Mission. . .
Experiments . . . Fuhrer . . .
Breakthroughs . . .Survival . . .
He thought dazedly.

Then those images flew from out of that crucible hanging mid-air in his mind's eye emerging now like beautiful white doves. Until, with the outward thrust of a hand and clutch of his right fist, Mengele seized one, and examined it, but the dove had become a Swastika branded onto the palm of his hand still roiling with the smell of burning flesh. During that instant, everything became clear to him—his mission, his experiments—a sense of loss and panic traveling through him like a jolt of electricity.

"Nein! Nein!" he screamed, breaking loose from his rescuers. "I must go back! I must return to the plane!"

"Herr Doktor, the storm is worsening!" the officer in

charge shouted barely, audible over the whine of Condor engines. "We have not a moment to waste!"

"The case!?" he pled. "It's still there! In the wreckage! At the crash site!"

"We must leave now!" a second *SS* officer growled impatiently, seizing him from behind, dragging him forcibly toward the plane.

"You idiots! You don't understand!" Mengele bellowed into the torrents of snow and howling mountain winds. "You're leaving behind the genesis of the Fourth Reich!"

THE
BEGINNING

Chapter One

San Francisco, California
November 2016

R ingo's was a dive; was there another way to describe
it? But like Obama used say about Chicago arm
twister, Rahm Emanuel, 'yes, he's a little bastard, but
he's *my* little bastard.' So it was with Ringo's. Just off the
docks, three blocks from the Catholic church where Yankee great Joe DiMaggio was baptized, its décor consisted
of yellowed newspaper clippings of the 'Yankee Clipper'
pasted on whitewashed walls and the reproduction of Bel-
low's painting of Jack Dempsey being knocked out of the
ring by Luis Firpo circa 1923, this a favorite amongst the
sailors, drunks, drug dealers, and whores that patronized
the place. But during these past three months with my
prospects for work as a private investigator dried up as a
desert gulch, Ringo's had become *my* dive at least until I
could get back on my feet again.

So far as the job itself most days handling the dual
role of bar tending and bouncing were routine. Besides, I
preferred working days when it was slow, wanting to keep
my dance card open for cool San Francisco nights when
North Beach, Sunset, and Soma came to life and I could

hit the clubs. In that respect, Frisco had its charm with plenty of unattached ladies eager to party.

But on this particular afternoon, the tide was running rough. You could feel it prowling the room like an unanchored menace; hear its steady drone like a vibration in your ears. More crowded than usual, the regulars looked uglier, the walk-ins more aggressive, with Sergei Maslov—an enforcer for what passed as the Russian mob these days—staggering around the room more sinister today than pathetic.

"When she come home from store wit gross-ry, I smack her in mout' like you do-it dawg . . . BAM!" he demonstrated with the flip of his backhanded. "'What dis for?' she ask-it, wit nose bleed-ink an' gross-ry everywhere on floor. 'Dat my luv-ee girl is for next time you do-it some-tink wrong!'" he roared with laughter, downing his umpteenth shot of the day, washing it down with a swig of Anchor Steam.

Of course, I despised Sergei to the quick though I didn't show it, a win some-lose some smile curling the corners of my lips as I sipped Glenlivet from a coffee cup quietly watching.

That's when a sixty-something Nam vet dressed in weathered army shirt, pants, and boots blundered through the back door, plopped down onto a bar stool, and looked across the room to me.

"Jack Daniels straight up," he said.

I nodded, took a last pull from my coffee cup, eyes still locked on Maslov while taking the temperature of the alchy regulars, walk-in tourists, Outlaw gang members and biker groupies, that populated Ringo Jennings' *paradis sur terre*. Far from finding a scintilla of amusement in Sergei's tough guy act, what I was really doing as I poured the Vet his drink was sizing the Russian up since the odds of a confrontation were increasing exponentially.

"Thanks, pal," the Vet muttered taking down the first Jack, then touching the rim of his glass for another.

God how I hated guys with Maslov's physique—short, muscular, stout as a fireplug—I calculated, generous as I filled the old man's glass, taking note of the Bronze Star pinned to his shirt. Sergei had no neck so he could absorb a punch. His legs were like tree trunks, so taking him to the ground wouldn't be easy and wasted on meth and booze like he was, he'd be numbed to pain so getting him to quit would be no walk in the park, either. *'Guess you're going to have to kill the motherfucker,'* I concluded, carefully watching the Nam burn-out raise his glass in a toast while Maslov stomped up from behind.

"Airborne Ranger, where have you been?" the old man sang-out turning to the clientele while Maslov's weight shifted, front to back foot, ready to pounce. "I been around the world three times and ba-ack again!" he lustily proclaimed downing his drink, then appraising the man in front of him, laughing as he swung around to face me, the mirror, Jack Dempsey, and me.

"Fucking Rangers is not-tink but pack of cowards," Maslov taunted, staggering backward. "All-ways vuz, all-ways vill be!"

The Vet tapped the rim of his glass again. I poured. Then, swiveling around on the bar stool, he gazed straight into the Russian's face, threw the Jack down, wiped his lips dry, and smiled. "Airborne Ranger, Airborne Ranger, how did you go?" he began, belting the lyric out like a battle cry. "In a C-130 transport plane fly-in' low!" he roared, pounding the beat out, closed fist onto the bar, to the delight of everyone — bikers, derelicts, crack whores — but not Maslov.

Glowering at the old man, now laughing along with his newfound audience, the Russian launched a powerful round-house punch that knocked him stool-to-floor, then began pummeling him with bone-shattering kicks to his legs, head, and upper torso. Caught off guard and help-less, the Vet used elbows and arms to cover himself, but Maslov was savage in his attack, a twisted grin stamped across his face as he climbed onto his chest, positioning himself to inflict maximum damage.

If I possessed a sixth sense, I'd always assumed it wasn't located between my ears, but like an axe the malice in the room had fallen and strange as it may seem I'd already hopped the bar in anticipation of the assault, ripping Maslov off the old man with a level of strength surprising even to myself. And during that moment of abandon, I swear, everything around me turned red, *blood red*, and, like a man possessed, I seized Maslov by the throat with my left hand while driving rights straight into his face, not know-ing or caring whether he lived to tell about it. "I-don't-like-bullies!" I seethed, pounding his face, one head-snapping blow escalating beyond the other until, sated, the demon flew from me as suddenly as he'd arrived, my vice-like grip around Maslov's throat relaxing as he dropped uncon-scious against the bar, head lolling to one side, his face a bloody mask of flesh, bone, and cartilage.

Coming back after one of the blackouts I'd begun experiencing lately was like parachuting from a plane sev-eral thousand feet up and landing on solid ground again. Like the *petit mal* seizures I'd begun researching, it was as if my soul deserted my body during those mind-bending episodes, leaving it to perform whatever deeds it desired until I awakened with only the foggiest recollection of what had gone on.

I peered down at the Vet who lay on the floor, semi-conscious, blood gushing from a broken nose, sans front teeth. I used to be a cop, I remembered grimly, a deputy sheriff who transported federal prisoners, and carried the scars to prove it. There's the mark of a shotgun wound on my left side, a gouged-out patch of twisted flesh that I'm told could be rendered invisible by a plastic surgeon. But no surgeon could make the scars inside me disappear, I'd begun to ponder lately, for that an exorcist seemed more in order.

"You okay?" I asked, kneeling on the saw dust covered floor beside him.

He sat up, pushed his tongue through the gap where his front teeth had been, then began collecting each tooth from the floor. "Fuck you," he answered, tossing them one at a time into his mouth like Chicklets, swallowing them down.

My first reaction was to laugh, but the Ranger's ballsy reaction raised no more than a chortle, my attention diverted by two young women staring at me from across the room. They smiled. I responded likewise. Dressed in halter tops with black-studded pencil dresses and spike heels, even they couldn't compete with the wail of approaching police sirens that tore me away in time to see four cops burst through the door. Guns drawn, they were expecting a cell of Uzi-toting ISIS terrorists, I imagined, but found only me.

The first to enter was Markus Henderson, a 6'10" former Frisco State basketballer, thick in the middle these

days with large soulful eyes, head crowned with a dispro-
portionally large Afro and a mustache that resembled
some species of *Lepidoptera.*

"Second fight this week, Tough Guy," he said holster-
ing his Glock 9mm. "Keep it up and we're gonna close this
shithouse permanent."

"Can't argue that," I answered, eyes doubling back to
the girls, giggling now, sexier than ever. "I'll just tell Ringo
that Frisco's Finest shut us down for the day."

"Sergie, is it?" he asked.

I nodded.

"Cuff him," Henderson instructed his white partner as
paramedics and a gurney trundled past him on their way
to the fallen vet.

"Fuck you," the Ranger growled when they tried
to put him on a stretcher, walking unaided toward the
ambulance.

"Hey!" I called out, toting the shot of Jack Daniels to
him as cops stuffed Maslov into the back seat of a patrol car.
"No fightin' men tougher than the Airborne Rangers!"

With CLOSED sign hung in its door window,
Ringo's—so raucous just twenty minutes earlier—was
quiet as a church yard. But not the modest room above
that I called home where Scratch Perry's "Havin' A Party"
blared over Dolby speakers and the two biker chicks,
Jolene and Smuffit, swilled Cuervo from the bottle, dancing two-on-one with me, up close and personal.

> *"We're havin' a party,*
>   *A shotgun party,*
>   *We're havin' a party tonight,"* Scratch sang over the
>   sound of a saxophone wailing.

"Say, where'd ya get that?" Jolene asked grinding her privates into my crotch.

I glanced down at the silver ID bracelet dangling from my wrist. "Had it for years," I told her over the throb of bass guitar. "A gift from an old flame."

Smuffit, gyrating against my right thigh, held it between her fingertips. Its front bore the inscription 'JACK' with the words *'consfianza en su corazon'* written on its reverse side.

"What's it say?" Jolene wondered, downing a slug of tequila.

"Means 'trust in your heart', it's a Hemingway quote," I slurred, taking a drink, passing the Cuervo to Smuffit.

"Well, Christ-to-a-cross," she proclaimed, hoisting the bottle above her, "that Hemingway bitch musta been some fuck!"

> *"Drink your drink,*
> *Dink you dink,*
> *Smoke your weed,*
> *And stink your stink!"* Scratch urged, speakers
> pounding its pulsing rhythm.

So, okay, Smuffit and Jolene — trashed on booze and meth, halter tops discarded — were no literary scholars, but I never knew a guy who reached up a girl's skirt to find a library card and I proved no exception. Girl-girl-boy, boy-girl-girl, girl-boy-girl, our permutations reconfigured feverish into the night until the three of us collapsed into a heap of steaming flesh onto the stripped down mattress that passed for a bed at chez Madson.

My sleep was deep, a long dark well of dreamless night

filled with memories of my time as a Wall Street takeover artist, the theft of high-tech pharmaceutical formulations, and my flight from the Law to Mexico, all culminating in a career-ending felony arrest, until my one eye lifted to the Panasonic clock-radio: *2 a.m.* Ugh!, a groan as mournful as the wail of dinosaurs dying was the only sound my current circumstance could evoke. I staggered to my feet headed for the bathroom despairing whether I would ever return to the man I'd once been when the battering crash of an oversized fist pounding on the door stopped me dead in my tracks.

"Jolene, I know you in there! Jolene, Darlin', open up this fucking door!"

Jarred to something approaching sobriety, my eyes shifted door-to-mattress where the girls lay, bodies intertwined, sleeping. Quietly I began collecting my jeans, wallet, and gun from the armoire, then padded barefooted into the closet-sized bathroom. Locking the door behind me, I shoved the wallet into my back pocket and the Walther semi-automatic into my waistband then dialed a number on my cell phone glancing out the window to assess my prospects: five Harley Road Kings parked outside the front entrance, *not good*, I surmised.

"I asked once and I ain't askin' again," Jolene's boyfriend threatened, rattling the rafters with the force of his pounding. "I'm here with 'im, Smuffit," a second biker called out from behind the door, "and I know you in there with her. Now, we unnerstand what you done and we'se willin' to forgive 'n forgit, but if you don't open this fucking door, I'm gonna knock it down and blow your head off with this here Remington shotgun I brought along for the ride. You hear me, you thankless whore!"

Understanding these salutations harbingered nothing pleasant for me, I breathed a sigh of relief when longtime pal, Eddie Lawler, now running a marina on St. John's island, answered.

"Remember last time we talked about my plans? Well, things aren't workin' out exactly the way I wanted, Eddie," I explained, images of myself disoriented post-blackouts at Ringo's or alone in my apartment, whistling through my mind like a lancing Bay wind. "You gotta get me somethin', *anything*, I need some breathing room, Buddy!"

"You know, you're like a brilliant mathematician who loves mathematics truly but always get the answers to the problems wrong," Eddie chuckled. "New York or Jersey, sure, I still got juice there, but Frisco? Things ain't like they used to be, Jackie . . ."

"Yeah, what is?" I asked, climbing out the window onto the fire escape.

"Listen, you still got a credit card, don't ya? Catch a plane to New York, check into the Elysee hotel and five hundred cash will be waitin' at the front desk, how's that sound?"

"It sounds great, Eddie," I pledged, the sound of a shotgun blast timed perfectly to my jump—ladder to street—where jogging away, I watched four Outlaws glowering at me from the window, Jolene and Smuffit beside them waving their 'bye-byes'!

Chapter Two

Soaring eastward at 30,000 feet in the Boeing 757, my long-muscled body sprawled on a first class lounger, I popped two Ambien and an Oxycodone, washed them down with a gulp of Glenlivet. The Exec in the seat astride me — dressed like a Brooks Brothers' manikin — observed the ritual disapprovingly, then turned back to pecking out a memo on his Dell laptop thinking maybe I gave a rat's ass about what he thought, but he could not have been more mistaken.

Eyes rimmed red from the kind of exhaustion no amount of sleep could remedy, my attention turned to the glass of Scotch I held and the silver **ID BRACELET**, shimmering with the words *'confianza en su corazon'* dangling from my wrist. Like Santiago's marlin, the sharks had been taking meaty chunks out of me all along the way, I conceded, before heavy as midnight my eyes clamped shut, and I found myself freefalling like an astronaut broke loose from his tether, mind — *sense of self* — attenuated like a vast net flung out into the void until suddenly it was yanked tight, snaring — what would one call them? — visions: Far deeper than thoughts, more tangible than the most vivid nightmares dredged from the seabed of a lunatic's sub-conscious!

NOW I am in the cab of a **FERRIS WHEEL** overlook-ing Paris, arm around Amy Caulfield. She pulls away and turns to me, amber eyes large and fluid. "Always remem-ber to keep a giggle inside you," she whispers, then smiling mischievously, glittery eyes closing, leans forward and kisses me flush on the mouth. "I love you, Jack. I always will," she pledges, slipping kitten-like into my arms, smiling content-edly like it would be that way until the end of time.

Breathless, I wait, praying that it's over and knowing that it's not. My body quakes. An icy sweat rises up from my flesh as the grip of its tentacles tighten. I shiver. A thin smile curls the corners of my lips at the familiarity of the sensation, but not for long as the first stab of pain like an ice pick's jab shoots through my brain. I gather courage. Brace for the onslaught. Then, it erupts. An explosion of white light inside my head. Brilliant as the flash of one hundred atom bombs!

NOW I am in the pew of a clapboard church stand-ing amongst the congregation, "Death be not proud!" **THE PREACHER** thunders from the pulpit above, veins in his neck popped-out like snakes writhing. "One short sleep past, we wake eternally. Death, thou shalt die!" Heart pounding, I look around horrified to see the congrega-tion staring at me: the searing eyes of burly men and frail women; children with menacing stares; tough-minded farmers; old women dressed as from centuries past; infants held in mothers' arms, gazes fixed like wax figures in a museum. All those eyes burning into me white hot as a blow torch until in desperation I wrench my eyes shut, open them, and they are gone.

Back to myself for a fraction of a moment, I feel the musculature in my face, hands, and skull tighten and then, yes, perhaps drug-induced—and in the only manner of sleep that comes to me these days and nights without end—I am plunged into a park or college campus where I not only see, but feel everything about the young woman looming in front of me!

> *voices*
> *"open silent messaging"*
> *i hear*
> *static*

NOW *I am watching a student race down the stairs of her dormitory. Her body is on fire, skin oozing an acidy oil, the smell of which causes her to shudder as she bursts from the dorm like a swimmer breaking water. She drinks of the cool night air. But it does no good. It's wrong; all of it. The thoughts. The feelings. Contradictions live like snakes inside her, feeding one upon the other. And at times Mary Linda Schumann wonders just who she is because truly there seem two of her. Mary Linda, the bright, young Princeton frosh and now this, the other self, the one that causes her consummate dread.*

She glances over her shoulder to Blair Hall, its gothic towers pasted against the brooding October sky, tracing the neat rows of apertures cut deep into its stone walls and sees the roommate, Jill Peyton, staring out, face wracked with concern.

The impulse had come upon her quietly, she remembers. And at first there was resistance. Natural. But unrooted. And if it wasn't rooted. Deeply rooted. Well, They liked that. And now she was Theirs. Not totally. Because They weren't quite ready for that. But enough to make her want to participate. Freely. Openly. A cog in a wheel. Locked in a network of one million wheels. In a shiny white skeleton of machinery that now exposed would sweep like a cold wind through this graveyard called Princeton.

No need to be concerned Lil' Jilly. No one need be concerned ever again. Not about her, she vows, trudging forward as arms, legs, brain seek out the highest building on campus.

Beyond the moon-drenched canopy of magnolia blossoms blackened with autumn's poison, she stalks amongst the night-time shadows; cavorting along the edge amongst the 'Others' mocking the one she used to be. The one called Mary. For this was a mission. And she isn't afraid. Not of death. Or of anything. For tonight she'd learned what no one had ever told her. Not her parents. Not her boyfriend. Not anyone. Perhaps because they did not themselves know. Likely because they would not allow themselves to see. But this was the Truth: all of your worst nightmares; all of the tiny horrors and cataclysmic abominations that a human being could imagine were real.

She passes Prospect House, lit up like a Christmas tree. There is a party of some kind; an occasion. But that does not interest her. Rather, her eyes fall upon the Garden thick with ivy, elm, and English yew, remembering a university tour she and her parents had taken, it seemed, lifetimes ago. "I suspect the buildings and trees of a campus give messages," the guide had told them, "suggesting the kind of place it is, whether it is and has been cherished." Well, the guide was right. They send messages all right. Like a fucking broadcast tower, she is thinking, as she crosses Washington Road and the legs come to an abrupt stop.

Mary Linda's eyes like red lasers home in on Fine and Jadwin Halls which together form the university's center for mathematics and physics. Slowly, they lift from the ground floor to each of the twelve floors that comprise the tower of the ultra-modern mathematics building. She smiles, then proceeds without pause.

*She enters Fine Hall through the main entrance. The corri-
dors are deserted. She passes through the lobby, then takes the staircase up to the third floor leading to the tower.*

*Her black eyes set in red-rimmed sockets are like lead slag
poured into boring to seal away something virulent as she casts a
sullen stare into the Common Room where above the fireplace Einstein's words, "God is subtle, but he is not malicious" are etched
into the stone, then moves on, implacable.*

*She enters the elevator, pushes the button for the top floor. When
the elevator doors open, she marches toward the door marked, 'Professors' Lounge', turns the doorknob and enters. The lounge is
empty. She strides to a coffee table in the center of the room as she
reaches into the pocket of her khaki pants. Then, seizing a pen
as if it is a dagger, scrawls these words deep into the wood of the
mahogany table.*

"The World Is Filled With Small Minds"

*She stands straight up again, pen dropping onto the tabletop
from out of her limp hand. She walks across the room to the large
picture windows. She opens them as far as they will go and stares,
wind gusting through her hair, at the panoramic view of the campus and surrounding countryside. She climbs out onto the narrow
concrete ledge.*

Then, she jumps.

> *voices*
> *"close silent messaging"*
> *i hear*
> *static, static*

Once arrived at Newark Liberty, I collected my tattered
Georgetown gym bag, picked up the red Stingray convertible I'd rented with the last gasp of credit on my AmEx

then cruised through the Lincoln tunnel into Manhattan thoughts consumed by the nightmare, so stunningly real to me.

What did it all mean? I anguished, mind racing as I headed uptown. The fragged sequences leading up to it? Those, I'd gotten used to, but recounting a young woman's suicide seemed a sure sign that my condition was worsening, its intrusions into my psyche deepened, its effect on me sharper, more sustained.

Could it be that a steady diet of amphetamines by day, barbiturates by night, and alcohol along the way for the past half of one decade had finally caught up with me? I pondered, pulling up to the entrance of the Elysee Hotel. True, I'd had nightmares, these visions, before. But never like this, never so fucking in-your-face real!

I checked in at the front desk where, true to his word, Eddie had $500 cash waiting. Afterward, I treated myself to a hot shower, followed by eight hours of dead-to-the-world sleep that could have passed for coma had the phone not rung to awaken me.

"Madson," I rasped into the receiver.

"It's me, Eddie. I got you a case."

"You're kidding," I answered, voice lifting an octave.

"It ain't much, but could lead to others. Parents of a girl jumped from a building, killed herself."

"Not what I . . ."

"But it pays well," he hastened to add. "Pick up a cool twenty grand if you play 'em right. Parents think there's more to it. Like maybe she was pushed or there's some kinda conspiracy behind it."

"Police?"

"Course they investigated. Drugs, jealous boyfriend, who the fuck knows?"

"And?"

"No suspects. No motives. Kid was bright so maybe she calculated life's a crock of shit, got up one day, and offed herself. So you go there, ask a few questions, stretch it out for what it's worth, tell them the kid was depressed like everyone else in this fucked up world."

"What's her name?"

"Schumann, Mary Linda Schumann, nineteen years young."

"Where'd it happen?"

"Princeton University campus. She was a freshman. Course the media's havin' a field day. Candle light vigils, a battalion of shrinks, TV coverage 24/7, but the cops? They're done with it."

"Okay, Eddie, I appreciate the help. I was treadin' water and on my way down for the third time."

"Ain't that the truth," he concluded fatefully. "So don't fuck this up!"

Slow to set the receiver back into its cradle, I sat on the edge of my bed thinking long careful thoughts about the case, my life, and the young woman who'd leapt to her death.

This wasn't what I did. Cheating wives and husbands, child custody disputes, and suicides was territory I avoided like the Ebola virus. Clearly, I'd spiraled a long way down from my salad days on Wall Street. Even as a PI—unlicensed in perpetuity—my stock and trade was white-collar crime, embezzlement, stock fraud, the kind of villainy I'd mastered myself at NuGen.

But suicides were the worst, particularly one where the
victim was young and brilliant. What could one hope to
uncover, after all, a relationship gone south, a sensitive
soul unable to cope with the pressures of the Ivy League,
with disillusionment your steady companion every step of
the way? Yeah, this one had all the earmarks of a star-span-
gled cluster fuck: parents, inconsolable; police, exhausted
on the topic; media, hungry for a fresh spin; investigator,
well, we know about him.

So why take it? Three reasons: one, was money. I had
none. Two, was my daughter, Tiffany, from whose life I'd
been estranged, now a student at Columbia University
in New York. Three, a distant third, my ex-wife, Jennifer
Crowley-Madson, institutionalized at Greystone Sanitar-
ium since the NuGen debacle some five years ago.

I got out of bed, lumbered into the bathroom where I
opened the faucet and threw cold water on my face. Odd,
the crushing ironies of human existence, I contemplated
staring into the mirror with the prescience of a heavy-
weight contender about to engage in the fight of a lifetime.

I'd dreamt about a young co-ed leaping to her death
from a building on a university campus; now I'd taken a
case involving exactly that.

Chapter Three

Princeton Police Department
Princeton, New Jersey

I didn't know what to expect when I passed through the door marked 'Detective Bureau' at Princeton's Public Safety Building. The Borough and Township police departments had recently merged. Worse, I'd learned that Princeton University's security worked in conjunction with three separate localities based on campus geography. 'Jurisdictional disputes' was the first thought that came to mind, 'confusion' was the second. But with OPRA filings approved and a letter of introduction from the Schumann family, I knew I'd have access to the information I needed even if the cops were wary of an outsider investigating a death already classified 'SUICIDE, CASE CLOSED.'

The first to greet me was Detective Lieutenant Tommy Gifford, a bright-eyed Afro-American and former all-state Tigers' running back. "You must be Madson," he said, extending his hand to me. "This is Detective Don Donnolly."

I shook hands with each, studying them in equal proportion to their curiosity about me. Gifford was compact of build, economical in temperament, handsome and confident in the manner of an up-and-coming Wall Street broker. Donnolly, by contrast, was a lumbering 6'3" 260 pounder permanently red-faced with green eyes that looked boiled, the sinews of chronic distemper brought on, I was guessing, by decades of living in the company of criminals and other assorted low lives.

"Thanks for taking the time to see me."

"No problem," was Gifford's predictable response given the public pressure the department was still in the throes of managing, "we were both active on the Schumann case. Her suicide put this town on its heels. I can only imagine how the parents felt."

"Can't be easy," I agreed. "Guess you received my Open Act Records filing and letter of introduction?"

"We did," Donnolly, interjected, anxious to make his presence felt, "and I suppose you got some ID, maybe a Jersey PI license, you'd like to show us."

"Afraid this will have to do," I answered reaching for the California driver's license in my wallet, "but since the investigation is complete, I'm sure you know any citizen with paper from Government Records has a right to review the case file."

"An out-of-state driver's license? That's what you got to show us?" the Irishman marveled, a rumbling hack rising up from his barrel chest as he turned to Gifford. "Do you believe this fucking guy?"

"Look, I'm hoping we can cooperate and put this situation to rest, if not for me, for the girl's parents. Hell, I used to be a cop, Washington, D.C., so don't think I'm here to make a hero of myself. But you need to understand that to do that I'm going to want to see crime scene reports, photos of the victim, transcripts of interviews with persons of interest, ME review, everything about this girl, follicle to toenail."

"Let me set you straight on somethin', Madson. We don't *need* to understand anything," Donnolly bristled, gathering up his huge frame, stepping toward me, "but you do. We been takin' shit about this kid's suicide for better 'n six weeks from local media, the university, even our own people at county and state, so trust me when I tell you we're sick of bein' second-guessed by amateurs and guns for hire like you. Sure, we'll give you access to whatever the Government Records Council requires, but don't expect us to take you by the cock and walk you through it, and don't expect us to be happy about it either, you got that?" He craned his head around to Gifford. "I'd fucking bet this bastard's got a felony arrest behind him. That's why he got no license!"

"You like to make your points crystal clear, well so do I," I said glaring up at him, "so let me give you some free advice: big, fat, and stupid doesn't intimidate me. So far as the rest, I figure you're about as lazy as you look, sloppy in your work, frightened as a school girl I'll find evidence you overlooked proving Mary Linda's death wasn't suicide. Say," I remarked, face aglow at the prospect, "wouldn't it be just dandy if I got my Jersey PI license, honorary, based on information I uncovered overturning your disposition of the case?"

"Keep it up, asshole," the big man rumbled. "You just keep that up and see where it gets you."

"Jesus Christ!" Gifford intervened, stepping between us. "We're not rivals here! If there's another avenue to pursue, why wouldn't we want that?" he asked, shepherding Donnolly from me, our eyes still locked on one another's. "Come to my office, Madson. Let's get a cup of coffee and you can ask all questions you want. Afterward, I'll take you to 'Records' where the Schumann file will be waiting, complete and without redactions, fair enough?"

I offered a clipped nod of assent, eyes still riveted on Donnolly who, like a Rottweiler heeding the call of his master, eased away then followed behind us.

Once in Gifford's office, replete with mementos from his Tiger football days, the Lieutenant motioned toward one of four chairs. I took one. He poured coffee into Styrofoam cups. Donnolly closed the door behind, positioning himself in the far corner of the room, arms akimbo.

"You'd be wrong to think we take the death of a student on campus lightly," Gifford began, handing me a cup. "We're a small department, but we do our best. This is a university town. We deal mostly with kids who drink too much after a football game, a racing bike stolen by outsiders who see Princeton as an easy mark, an occasional assault, and just two times in the twelve years I've been here, a murder."

"What about suicides?" I ventured.

He sat down behind his desk. "We get our share," he said, sipping from the steaming cup, "but when anything like that happens, even a Category 2 or 3, we're not shy about contacting the county prosecutor's office for help, and that's exactly what happened with the Schumann investigation."

"What kind of help?"

"Mobile crime lab, forensics, fatal accident team, even a reconstructionist. Hey, man," he said, voice rising an octave, "I'm Princeton alum! You think I don't care about a nineteen year old kid jumping to her death from one of our buildings?"

I leaned back in my chair, "Come on, Tommy, this wasn't just any suicide."

"He means the writing on the table," Donnolly translated. "Ain't that right, Madson?"

"It qualifies," I retorted fiercely, eyes shifting to him. "Suicide victims either leave a note or they don't. If they do, it's straightforward and on paper, 'My boyfriend left me, there's no reason to go on living' or 'I embezzled $5M, got caught, and don't want to go to prison'. Most notes explain why they're doing it. But 'The world is filled with Small Minds' carved with a pen deep into the wood of a tabletop? What's that supposed to mean? The violence involved in an act like that. The words, themselves. What was she trying to tell us?"

"It's weird, I'll give you that. But finding the 'why' isn't what we get paid for. The university has psychologists for that. Our job was to determine if there was anything more to it than suicide, and in the Schumann case we did exactly that."

"Who found her?"

"Campus security," Donnolly answered, consuming the contents of his cup in a prolonged slurp. "Indian kid, Gunga Din type, making rounds at Pine Hall seconds before your girlfriend discovers she can't fly. Some mess, let me tell ya, broken neck, shattered cranium, brain tissue projected three feet-nine inches beyond point of impact."

"Maybe she was pushed," I countered, not bothering to conceal my enmity for him. "And those words scrawled onto the tabletop, who says they were hers? Maybe somebody was in the room with her?"

"There's no evidence to suggest that," Gifford objected, anxious to snuff any glint of conjecture. "The Cross pen she held had her prints on it. Same with the window frame and hasp she unlocked to climb out onto the ledge. Even the words carved into the table were a match to samples of her handwriting. No," he stated emphatically, "forensics combed that room stem to stern. There was no one else in that room with her."

"How about statements from roommates, professors, phone records. Was there anything to suggest she was agitated or engaged in a dispute with a colleague or student organization that didn't see things the way she did. Could it be that carving 'Small Minds' into that tabletop was her way of getting even with someone."

"Fuck's sake!" Donnolly erupted. "She's dead, Madson! There's nothing going to change that. She got depressed. She jumped out a window. Now she's dead. Believe it or not, it's not so uncommon with these Ivy League types. Pressure. Stress. Depression. It all goes hand-in-hand, can't you see that? The bitch jumped out a fucking window, deep-sixed herself, and that's all there is to it!"

"I see that," I answered, straining to suppress my rage, "but let me ask you something: who would know this girl better than her parents? Her thoughts? Her moods? Her innermost fears? The answer is Bob and Doris Schumann, and they're not buying your suicide theory. They're also not paying me to rubber stamp what you think you know. They want the truth, Donnolly, a rare commodity in this peculiar society during these particular times, but they're going to get the truth from me, with or without your cooperation!"

Gifford drew a long breath and let it out like a man just made land after a hard swim.

"He's right, Don. Let it go. Take a walk with me next

door to 'Records', Madson. Study her file," he said, rising slow from his chair like the arthritic he'd become. "Afterward, we'll take you to 'Evidence' and then you'll have seen it all, everything we have. If you have questions, we'll try to answer them. If there's something you need beyond that, I'll put you in touch with the Prosecutor's office, can you live with that?"

"Yeah, I can, Lieutenant, I shot back nodding, myself an aficionado of pain unmeasured.

"Oh, and the question you asked, about statements?" he recalled, accidentally on purpose. "We interviewed anyone even tangentially associated with Miss Schumann. The result," he concluded forming a zero with his thumb and forefinger, "was one dry well after another. By all accounts, Mary Linda Schumann was a vibrant young woman, model student, well-liked and well-adjusted."

Taking Gifford up on his offer, I spent the next two days scrutinizing every scintilla of information collected by local, county, state investigators: police reports, crime lab findings, video-taped interviews, medical examiner observations, Fatal Accident Team recreations, but nothing consequential emerged until day three when staring like a somnambulist at a table covered with morgue photos, Donnolly unlocked the drawer to a file cabinet and produced the charred remnants of a diary, torched in a dormitory fireplace hours before Mary Linda leapt to her death.

"Since we're supposed to be asshole buddies now, I want to show you this," he told me, dropping the polyvinyl baggy containing burnt scraps of paper onto the table in front of me.

"That's it?"

"What can I tell you? The kid knew how to burn stuff," he explained. "Fuck, yeah, that's it."

"Can I open it? I mean, can I read the words?"

"Why not?" he snickered. "There's a typewritten transcript, but if you wanna read the original knock yourself out."

Then Donnolly left, laughing. No, more than a laugh, it was for him a celebration of futility knowing that the thoughts, feelings, and emotions Mary Linda had experienced moments before her demise would remain a mystery to me forever.

I opened the baggy that contained the torn pages, crumbling like the tattered scrolls of the ancients, and held them in my hands.

". . . than merely the harmless (indecipherable) I believed them to be . . ." read one partial sentence. ". . . I can no longer associate myself . . ." was another. ". . . sharks drawn to blood . . ." was another, and ". . . must stop myself from thinking . . ." the last phrase written by her to survive the fire.

Charred scraps of paper like the random pieces of a puzzle, senseless and incomplete, begging for form, substance, meaning, I pondered. Then nothing. Fragments of scattered half-truths left behind like the detritus of a dead civilization for strangers like me to contemplate.

Convinced it was suicide, I repackaged the remnants of her diary staring down at the desktop covered with forensic photos of the girl now at rest for all eternity, just one question still eating at me.

"Mary Linda Schumann," I asked, a sense of foreboding mounting at the fringes of my consciousness, *"why are you dead?"*

Chapter Four

Greystone Psychiatric Hospital
Morris Plains, New Jersey

E xhausted by the time I made it back to the hotel, I slept like a babe sucking his Mamma's right tit that night. Or at least I imagined it so since I awoke next morning devoid of hangover and untainted by the residue of night terrors that like succubi stole away into bed along with me most nights. 'A fresh start is a terrible thing to waste', I was thinking as I threw on a pair of jeans and a Hoya sweatshirt, grabbed a cup of coffee black, then face-timed Eddie Lawler.

"If you got the money, Honey, I got the time," my elfin friend chimed by way of salutation, his words barely rising above the din of Island music and girls gone wild.

"Eddie, this is Jack."

"Jackie Boy!" he proclaimed downing a rum punch while displaying my face on his iPhone to the gaggle of bikini-clad women fawning over him.

"What time is it on St. John's?" I asked.

"You in New York?"

"Elysee Hotel."

"Same time here, same time there," he answered to the rhythm of the steel drums playing in the background.

"Same time here, same time there," he reveled breaking into his Happy Dance to the delight of his college-age companions who began shaking what they had along with him.

"Jesus, Eddie, isn't it a little early for a blow-out?"

"Shit, man!" he roared turning the iPhone for a selfie. "We're still partyin' from last night!"

"All right, look, I called to tell you the Schumann case is wrapped," I shouted, my voice all but drowned out by the clamor of his girlfriends. "The cops had it right. It was suicide. I'll pass my report along to the parents, look in on Jennifer at Greystone and a priest friend at Princeton, then I'm heading back to Frisco."

"Your call, Jack! In the meantime, let's see if I can't line you up with somethin' a little less physical than tendin' bar at Ringo's. You know neither of us is twenty-five no more."

"Tell that to Sergei Maslov. I don't think he'll be pushing Nam vets around anytime soon."

"Jackie baby," Eddie howled over the cacophony of wassailers breaking into a chorus of *"Hot Hot Hot"*, "it ain't Maslov I worry about."

There was something disquieting about Greystone Psychiatric Hospital, I speculated, taking my Vette beyond its wrought iron gates. Maybe it was the condemned Kinbridge Building looming stark as a haunted castle on the horizon. More likely, it was the knowledge that before it reopened Greystone Lunatic Asylum was shut down by state investigations charging sexual abuse, rape, and torture of incoming patients once ensconced within its stone walls.

So this is what it came down to, I ruminated, passing through the building's main entrance. If there was such thing as poetic justice, Jennifer's plunge from Manhattan socialite to welfare indigent after the loss of her father's estate to back taxes was nothing short of Homeric. Truth be told, God had never put a more fiercesome bitch on the planet than Jennifer Crowley Madson, daughter of deceased New Jersey Supreme Court Judge Barton Crowley, my ex-wife of five years. Sure, I took responsibility for deserting her after the NuGen scam blew up in my face — *that was my doing*— but deep down inside a filament of resentment glimmered with the knowledge that she and her mobbed up father had driven me to it!

Once signed in at Registration, Cephus Jackson, a muscled-bound, Afro-American orderly, introduced himself as my escort to the EOU where 'acute care' patients resided. I followed behind as he navigated the vestibule where outpatients registered for appointments and relatives waited for visitors' passes, their comings and goings monitored by Security who watched surveillance screens from behind a desk in the lobby's north-side corner.

We took the elevator up eight floors, stepped into the corridor. My eyes scanned its length. There was no registration desk, just a long hallway separated from the main wing by two heavy-gauged steel doors. We passed through the first into an open area where clusters of white-smocked patients socialized while others mopped the floor around us. At its center stood a glass-paneled security booth.

"This here's the 'open' ward," Cephus explained snapping a wad of Juicy Fruit as he craned his head around to me. "The patients here are inmate-trustees, but we call 'em riskees cause they always escapin' 'fore we bring 'em back here again." He turned as if to share a profound remark. "Now we got to register with Security 'fore they let you in the 'disturbed' ward."

Together, we approached the registration desk. The smell of ammonia stung my nostrils as I took notice of the inmates surrounding us. Some stood by dazedly while others chatted with unbound animation. A dwarfed cretin flashed a secretive grin as he mopped the floor beside me. I turned away in time to catch the furtive glance of a young girl whose eyes had risen from her covey of friends. The phrase *anorexia nervosa* passed through my mind as the eyes of the tall, emaciated girl flew back to the group. She couldn't have weighed more than seventy pounds.

The black nurse at Registration peered up from her paperwork. Her voice sounded muffled from behind the 3" thick glass that encased her.

"Can I help you?"

"This here's Mr. Madson," Cephus announced sprightly. "He here to see Miss Crowley."

She cast me an appraising stare, brown eyes lifting from the 'approved' list. "Through there," she said, pointing. "Mr. Jackson will escort you."

We walked toward the second gray door. A wave of cackles flooded the room as we passed into the next wing. My stomach turned as a waft of stale air—salient and choking—settled upon us with the subtlety of a fog bank engulfing a small coastal town. But it was the odor beyond the ammonia that I recognized. That same suffocating stench I'd experienced as a cop transporting the criminally insane from penal institutions to asylums. It was the smell of madness.

We followed the cacophony of discord down the hallway into a solarium, then stood at its outer lip watching patients playing chess and reading comic books while a gaggle of others encircled a black kid dribbling a basket-

ball to the beat of Wu-Tang Clan's *Ain't Nothin' Ta Fuck Wit*
blaring from his boom box. The solitary custodian who
supervised the group barely took notice as Cephus and
I delved beyond the third set of doors. These, hinged on
heavy re-enforced frames, marked the entrance to the 'disturbed' ward.

"You ever been inside one of these places?" Cephus
asked.

"Once or twice to spend the night," I answered ruefully.

"Maybe so, but you ain't seen nothin' like we got at
Greystone. Intrestin' for a hot shot private eye like you.
That's what you is, ain't it?" he asked looking for confir-
mation, sniggering when he didn't get it. "You ever heard
of Steven Darrell?" he asked pointing to the Patient's
Lounge.

I looked across the room to the frail high-strung man
sitting on a divan paging through the *Wall Street Journal.*

'Ol Stevie be a hot shot stock broker in the city few
years back. He an' his family lived happy enough. Lots a
money, big house in Mendham, 'fore he went through
what Doc calls a *hysterical conversion reaction.* That mean, he
come home one night totally changed—body, mind, full
package—bashes his wife and three kids' heads in with
an axe, packs up the pieces of they bodies in neat little
boxes, then ships 'em Fed Ex to kinfolk livin' all around
the state. Then," he concluded, snapping his fingers, "he
vanish into thin air."

"That's right, I remember now. I read that he disappeared in the papers, then nothing!"

"True that," Cephus said, nodding fatefully. "Nobody
know what become a Steven Darrell: not the cops, not his

family, not even his best friends 'til three years later, mail-man calls the po-lice to report someone who look like Dar-rell standin' outside his house where those murders been committed."

"I don't follow . . ."

"No one else did, neither, 'til Homicide find out he spent the past thirty-six months livin' in New England under the name of Jonathan Kruger with no memory of the murders, his chil'ren, or that he ever been married. Doc says somewhere 'tween the time he left home and come back that day, Steven Darrell, Wall Street exec with the nice family and plenty of money, turn into—I mean, actually become—Jonathan Kruger, the mass murderer, who think he born in Massachusetts!"

I cast a hard stare in the direction of the thin, jittery murderer. Darrell's blue eyes leapt over the newspaper. *They glistened.*

"You say he changed physically?" I asked breaking loose from his stare. "What changes?"

"The face he got now ain't nothin' like the one he had 'fore the murders. Hair, neither. 'Cording to Doc, this guy was bald as an eagle when he axed his wife and kids to death. Hell, look at him now, man. He like the fuckin' wolf man! Doc say even his eye color changed, used to be brown, now they is blue, 'til he be like a whole different person." Cephus shook his head in awe of the maniac sit-ting across the room from us. "Doc say the most powerful weapon on earth be the human mind, but the rest of them doctors? He say they won't never understand a genius like him."

Cephus turned. I followed in his wake, trekking deeper into the bowels of Greystone. Finally, we stopped at the entrance to a courtyard where patients mulled around in sweaters or sat in wheel chairs swathed in blankets to warm themselves against the mid-December's chill, some talking, most staring into empty space.

"Well, there she be!" Cephus announced unfurling his hand toward the center of the courtyard. "I know you ain't seen her for a long time, but that your wife, Madson. Jennifer Crowley is what she call herself now. I'm sure she look different since las' time you seen her."

My eyes followed his gesture. A doctor, flanked by two attendants, injected a middle-aged woman who stood paralyzed in a catatonic stupor. A shaggy mane of blonde hair sheathed her gaunt face as her head sagged downward with her right arm outstretched and rigid as if pointing at me. He pulled the hypodermic needle from her upper bicep. She shuddered violently and threw her head back laughing, a male nurse seizing her from behind. "Take this one to her room," the doctor ordered as the attendants lowered her into a wheelchair.

It was only then that I recognized Jennifer, two young women standing alongside her: one, a uniformed nurse, who rushed to comfort her; the other, my daughter, Tiffany.

"Daddy!" she called out, rushing to me, arms wide open.

And at that moment as I wrapped my arms around her, warmth like a roaring fire on the coldest day in winter swept over me.

"It's so good to see you, baby," I whispered, pulling her nearer to me, holding her like I'd never see her again. "It's been so long, too long, can you forgive me?"

"Yes, I know," she soothed. "I understand, really I do."

"I didn't know you'd be here . . ."

"But I am!" she affirmed. "We're together now and I'm not letting you get away ever again," she vowed, a grin as large as Gibraltar lighting up her face as she took a step back searching my eyes for answers about why I'd left her so many years before, trying to recognize the father I once was, the man I'd now become. "Oh, I'm so sorry!" Tiffany apologized, turning to the twenty-something nurse who stood alongside the wheelchair preening Jennifer's blonde hair with her fingertips. "Dad, this is Nurse Keating, Laurie Keating, the angel who's looked after Mom these past months. And she's done wonders! Tell him, Laurie," Tiffany urged, "tell him about the progress Mom's made."

But it was the doctor, not the nurse, who spoke up extending his hand with the familiarity of an old college chum. "I'm Doctor Stone, Darius Stone, so nice to meet you. I've been caring for Jennifer since she arrived."

"Pleased to meet you. I suppose I should say 'thanks'," I ventured, puzzled at his enthusiasm, yet somehow feeling we'd met before.

"Don't think twice about it! I knew Judge Crowley. Not to say we were friends, but we met occasionally and like everyone else I greatly admired him."

"Saying something nice about Barton Crowley is like saying something nice about small pox."

He gave a smile with no amusement in it, "Well, he spoke highly of you."

"Did he?" I asked, appraising the onyx eyes, bounding personality, and scrubbed face that left me wondering whether politics and not medicine had been his true calling at Harvard or Yale or whatever Ivy League school he'd attended. "If you heard Jen's dad say something nice about me, it must have been while under a psychiatrist's care here at Greystone. Fact is, if we had any relationship at all it was based on mutual disaffection."

"It doesn't take you long to get to the point, does it?" he observed, still smiling, eyes raking me over feature by feature, when Tiffany stepped between us.

"Nurse Keating was just telling my father about the progress Mom's been making," she interjected. "Isn't that right, Laurie?"

Laurie Keating smiled uncomfortably, too shy to discuss whatever minor miracles she may have performed, fingertips gently brushing Jennifer's cheek as she spoke.

"Well, I'm not a doctor," she demurred, "but we try to make her as comfortable as possible, and we do get her out here in the courtyard each day, and yesterday," she added, eyes brightening, "Miss Crowley—I mean, Mrs. Madson—played a game of checkers and carried on a real conversation with me about," she thought for a moment, "oh, yes, about breakthrough medical procedures, as yet unavailable to the public, that would make diseases like Alzheimer's, schizophrenia, even old age a thing of the past. Treatments so advanced even medical professionals like Dr. Stone don't know about them yet."

"Fascinating!" I remarked, responding as much to her pristine nature as the words she'd spoken. "I'm happy to see that Jen's so well cared for."

"I'm afraid it's not quite that simple," the doctor felt compelled to explain. "Mr. Madson, your wife suffers from paranoid schizophrenia of the ambulatory type. It's gradual, often progressive. She's lucid at times, but can experience anxiety, even hallucinations, at others."

"What causes an illness like that?" I asked.

"A lot of work has been done recently linking it to hereditary disposition, but as often it's brought to catharsis—from breakdown, to setting-in, to burn-out—by some personal catastrophe. Its onset often represents a retreat from the reality of a failure or trauma that the patient can't bring themselves to accept."

"But she wasn't like this before, Doctor Stone," Tiffany objected. "Why only a year ago she was living like a house on fire! She never seemed . . ."

"Crazy?"

Tiffany nodded.

"That's the tricky thing about it. Most chronic schizophrenics can care for themselves. They endanger no one and are in reasonable contact with reality much of the time. That makes them difficult to diagnose, even for a professional."

"The prognosis?" I asked, drawing Tiffany closer to me.

"Sadly, the condition is untreatable. Your wife will wind up like an entire ward of patients here, a physical and mental burn-out," he explained, then suppressing the lecture beginning to emerge, switched tact. "But you came here to spend time with Jennifer, not hear a treatise on schizophrenia so let me leave you to do just that. Tiffany, good to see you again," he said nodding a curt goodbye. "Mr. Madson," he beamed, "I can't tell you how pleased I am to have finally met you."

With that Stone deserted the courtyard, Cephus a half step behind, leaving what was left of the Madson family reunited for the first time in five years.

Tiffany and I approached Jennifer, her mind as devoid of life as a cratered asteroid, forcing myself to remember that once—for no matter how short a time—we had shared the same bed and produced a fine and beautiful child. Where, in what cemetery of the heavens, did the tender words of lovers rest when they loved no longer? I brooded, feeling the weight of Nurse Keating's gaze upon me.

"I could leave, if you'd like to be alone with her," she offered.

But that was not what I wanted. And at that moment I couldn't help but wonder if God really did exist, and if He marshaled justice unbounded as in the Old Testament, and if perhaps Jennifer and her Mafia-bought father were penitents, one banished here at Greystone, the other to Hell where he belonged.

"No, I don't think so," I answered. "I've got some business in Princeton then I'll be heading back West."

"I'm sorry to hear that, Jack," she lamented, then catching herself added, "what I mean is, it was nice to meet you. Have a safe trip back to San Francisco."

I thanked Laurie for her kindness. Then, Tiffany and I strolled, hand-in-hand across the courtyard.

"You realize Mom knows when people are with her. Sometimes even who they are and why they're there, don't you, Dad?"

"Couldn't prove it by me," I observed.

"Well, it's true whether it seemed like that today or not."

I didn't answer. We kept walking until we ran out of courtyard.

"So what do you think of Laurie Keating?" she asked, beginning freshly.

"Very professional, I'd say."

"Bet I know somethin' you don't," she teased.

"Yeah, what's that?"

"I think she's got the hots for you," Tiffany confided with a matchmaker's glint.

"Don't be ridiculous! I'm old enough to be her father or older brother, anyway!"

"No, I mean it," she said nuzzling her face into my shoulder. "Besides, one way or the other, you'll be seeing her again."

"Oh? And when will that be?"

"I want you to visit next Tuesday. It's Mom's birthday," Tiffany exhorted, head tilted up, pretty face alight with promise. "It would mean so much to her, and me, to have you with us, Daddy."

I reached out, took her to my chest and held her there, the warmth of her face and wetness of her tears penetrating shirt, skin, and heart.

"I'll do my best to make it, baby."

"Promise?" she asked, muffled words spoken into the fabric of my Yankees' warm up jacket.

"Yeah, sure, I promise. 'Be there or be square', isn't that what we used to say?"

"'After while crocodile'," she countered, emerging from my embrace, beaming. "Yeah, that's what we used to say."

"I love you, Tiffany."

"Me, too," she answered taking full account of the man who stood before her: externally, six feet tall, mane of black hair, killer grin and killer ego, most folks would be sure to add; internally, strung-out with drugs and booze, mind fragged, life coming apart at the seams. She saw both. "You know you're a mess, don't you, Daddy? But you're a beautiful mess and no matter what happens," she concluded, standing on tip-toe to peck me on the cheek, "I'll always love you."

I exited the elevator for the lobby at Greystone still digesting the particulars of my encounter with Stone. His prognosis exposed a raw nerve and left it throbbing, not just about Jeniffer's condition, but my own. Wasn't there something terrifying about mental illness? I asked myself. In our own idiosyncratic way weren't we all, at times, something other than 'normal'? And who to better understand those terrors than me, plagued as I was by migraines blinding in their suddenness, paralyzing in their power. Not to mention the self-fashioned 'visions' that swept through my mind along with them until I began to feel I was actually living inside them!

"Jack! Jack Madson!" I heard a man call out as I traded the lobby's stultifying environs for the December chill outside.

"A word? May I have a word with you?" a tall strapping man wearing a Stetson hat and lizard skin cowboy boots inquired, trotting alongside me. "You're Jack Madson, right?" he asked, thrusting his hand out at me.

"Who wants to know?"

"Name's Ty Rollins, local reporter, *Star Ledger*. I got a question for you, won't take a minute," he answered, hand shrinking back to his side.

"*Ledger*, huh? Funny, but you don't look like you're from Newark."

He flashed a big shit-eating grin, "Born in Plano, Texas. Come out east to work in the newspaper business five years ago. Still waitin' on that call from the *New York Times*."

"What's your question?"

"Mary Linda Schumann, suicide or murder? You

answer that question and five minutes from now we're in
the front seat of my pick-up poppin' flip tops off an ice-
cold six pack a Lone Stars."

"It was suicide. Nothing I found would indicate otherwise," I said resuming the walk back to my Vette. "Keep
the beer."

"I got three CSIs from State say the local cops fucked
up the investigation, evidence along with it."

"They're local cops, Rollins. They did the best they
could with the resources they had."

"But they fucked it up," he prodded, trying to keep up.
"Not 'cause they wanted to, but because they didn't know
no better, that's what it comes down to, don't it?"

My footsteps came to an abrupt halt, "So what, Ty, you
going to start putting words in my mouth? The Princeton
cops did a professional investigation that came to the right
conclusion. Can I be any clearer than that? Except . . ."

"Except what?"

"Except for motive," I answered haltingly. "There was
something troubling about this particular suicide, and
that's 'why did she do it?' What would lead a young woman
with so much promise to kill herself? That's what keeps
me awake at night. That's the missing piece I doubt any
investigation will ever uncover."

"Thanks much, pardner," he drawled, scribbling the
words into a notepad. "You don't mind if I quote you?"

I kept walking.

"Say, one last thing, a personal thing, 'bout your ex-
wife! I did an expose on Greystone 'bout a year ago. You
take this and read it," he urged handing me a cinch of
papers. "Complaints from relatives of patients committed

here, right off the internet. Greysone ain't no place for civilized human beings. Ain't no place for no one, Madson."

"Thanks," I said, perusing the top page as Rollins strutted, cowboy-style, back toward the main building. 'This
place is like living in Hell . . . ' it read. 'They unlawfully
detain innocent persons . . . Falsify medical diagnosis when
threatened with litigation . . . They are criminals . . . They
are kidnappers . . . DO NOT TRUST THESE PEOPLE!'

Yeah, Greystone was a shit hole, I was thinking as I
hopped into the Vette headed for a visit with my friend and
mentor, Jeremiah. And, yeah, what happened to Jennifer
was awful. All of it. For her. For Tiffany. For me. But this
was the United States of America where money talked and
everything — even an individual's freedom — came price
tag attached. Cops. Courts. Judges like Barton Crowley.

Sure, I could protest. Maybe write my congressman.
But broke as I was, and surrounded 24/7 by my own species of demons, in the end I knew there wasn't a goddamned thing I could do about it!

Chapter Five

University Chapel
Princeton Campus

The forty minute drive Morris Plains to Princeton might have taken ten minutes or ten hours, so conflicted was I between guilt over Jennifer's condition and satisfaction about my reconciliation with Tiffany. I glanced into the rearview to change lanes, eyes held steady, but the image reflected seemed the face of a stranger. The jaw was square, cheekbones high, skin taut and firm, but it was the eyes that sent a chill through me. Like two black pools at the bottom of a well glinting back at me with the rage of a man who'd just lost his arm to the gears of a machine not knowing whether to blame the engine or the finger in some upstairs office that flicked the switch to turn it all on.

Obsession, I was beginning to realize, was like a magnetic field that keeps pulling you back into a direction you have not chosen. For months, maybe longer, I'd been racing down a superhighway toward something I could no more adequately describe than the shadow of a dream. But still, I knew it was out there waiting. Whether by fate or decree I cannot say, but certainly the loss of identity, *call it soul,* that so tormented me was not a choice and that

knowledge, as much as what it was leading me to, filled me
with dread.

When my father killed himself at the age of fifty-seven,
trying to escape debt, mental illness, and his lot in life as
a truck driver, I was eight years old and home from school
because of a cold. My father had left work to come home
that day, burned his bills in the basement, told my Mom he
felt poorly, then went upstairs and closed the door.

I was watching TV on the couch downstairs, but
remember the sound of the shot ringing through the
house. My heart jumped when I heard it. I leapt from the
couch, TV still blaring, and ran up the staircase to the second floor. I knocked at the door to my parents' bedroom.
"Daddy!" I screamed, trying the doorknob and when no
one answered, pushed on it with all my might. Finally, the
door opened and in the darkened room, with all shades
drawn, there on the bed lay my father, making hoarse
breathing noises. His eyes were closed, and in that first
instant as I walked toward him nothing seemed wrong. I
put my hand beneath my father's head. My palm slipped
under easily and when I brought it out again it was wet to
the arm with blood. That's when I saw the shotgun lying
beside him, the smoke from burnt gunpowder swirling out
of its barrels. *"Daddy . . . Oh, Daddy . . . Daddy,"* I remember
standing there saying before a policeman came and pulled
me out of the room.

I stared into the Vette's rearview, lips drawn back from
my teeth. My eyes, wide and racing, were equal to those
of rabid animal. What do you do when all the screams
in hell wouldn't be as loud as you wanted to scream? I
asked myself, shocked to discover I'd already covered the
distance between Morris Plains and Princeton and was

parked not one hundred yards from University Chapel where, in semi-retirement, Father Jeremiah tended to his campus ministry.

It took the walk from my car to the chapel to get my head straight but standing at the foot of the cathedral-like structure, eyes elevating from the sandstone steps to the heavy oak doors of its entrance, concerns about Jennifer and Greystone flew from me and I was back to my old self again. Besides, I thought, spirits buoyed, I was about to see Jeremiah, friend and mentor going back to my high school days at St. Damian's, the boys' prep school that shone bright as a beacon amid the wreckage of bars, deserted high-rise buildings and burnt-out stores that was Newark's Central Ward back then.

The contrast between sight and sound couldn't have been larger than when I entered, gaze falling upon the façade of Christ seated on a golden throne, eardrums throbbing with the blare of Joey Ramone's "It's a Wonderful World" blasting over the organ master's speaker system with enough force to push me back a step.

Once acclimated I couldn't help but stand there laughing at the sight of Jeremiah, grayer than I'd remembered, animated as both Cohen brothers combined directing Harlan Haberman, who was autistic, and Julianne Johnson, his African American caregiver, as they decorated the altar in preparation for Christmas.

"Harlan!" the old priest screamed, stomping his right foot onto the chapel floor like a petulant child, "For the love of God, could you please turn that music down!"

Of less than average height and thirty pounds overweight, Harlan shrugged helplessly, an oversized potted chrysanthemum nestled in his arms.

"Do as Father says, Harlan," Julianne instructed as she watched him waddle into the sanctuary, still embracing the urn of flowers.

"Is that b-better?" he asked, poking his head out of the alcove.

"Yes, thank you," Jeremiah answered emphatically. "I guess I'm still not convinced that the Ramones qualify as 'Christmas music'," then, with palms raised added, "but let's not discuss that now."

"It's not the Ramones plural. It's J-Joey Ramone, singular," Harlan hastened to explain, "real name Jeffrey Ross Hyman, born May 19th, 1951. In 1972, he joined the g-glam punk band, Sniper, who played Max's Kansas City with the New York D-dolls . . ."

"You've told me about the Ramones a thousand times!" Jeremiah kvetched, abbreviating what promised to be a list of every song the group had ever recorded.

"Father doesn't want to hear the history of punk rock, Harlan. We've got a church to decorate!" Julianne, neat, handsome, and no doubt beautiful once upon a time, fussed marching toward him. "Now put that pot of flowers on the altar," she said, pointing, "before they wilt for all the time you've been carrying them!"

She swung around smiling a big bright grin, her gaze falling first on Jeremiah who stood massaging his temples, then to the chapel's nave where I stood watching. I clapped my hands together slow then faster until the light in Julianne's eyes turned from wary to joyful again.

"Looks like we've got an audience, Father," Harlan's companion said, brown eyes held steady with mine.

"Ja-a-ck!" Jeremiah boomed drifting toward me until his frail body was lost in grips of my massive bear hug.

"It's great to see you, Father!"

"What are you doing in Princeton? Last card I received was postmarked San Francisco," he said, stepping back to get a look at me. "How've you been? You're not in trouble, are you, son?"

"Not this time," I laughed, "though I suppose that's when a guy's got to worry, right?"

"Nonsense," he answered, "though you look like you could use a hot meal and good night's rest. Harlan! Julianne!" he reveled, turning back toward the half-decorated altar. "I want you to meet Jack Madson, former student of mine, from San Francisco," he told them. "Jack, this is Harlan Haberman and his friend, Julianne Johnson. Harlan helps out around the chapel. Julianne helps Harlan help me out."

Harlan offered his hand, "Pleased to meet you, Mr. Madson. Do you like baseball?"

Julianne, frowned, "Mr. Madson didn't come all the way from San Francisco to talk about baseball, Harlan," she chided, stepping forward with a firm handshake of her own. "Jeremiah often talks about his days at St. Damian's, mostly about you, Mr. Madson."

"That's because I was the only one to ever graduate after being expelled twice with four suspensions!"

"It was worse than that," the old priest quipped. "Suspended two times and expelled four, but the monks at St. Mary's always saw you as having great potential. The prodigal son returned stronger, wiser, ready to face the world!"

"Well, no one's going to confuse my career with Steve Jobs' . . ."

"Joe DiMaggio!" Harlan cried out, eyes dropping

like stones from the chapel ceiling. "DiMaggio was from San Francisco just like you, Mr. Madson. 'Joltin' Joe', the 'Yankee Clipper' . . . joined the Yanks in 1936, 31 home runs, 137 RBIs, 3 stolen bases, b-batting average, .323 . . ."

I studied the neat little man—belly protruding beyond his belt, hyper-focused eyes, blue shirt buttoned to the neck, gray trousers, brown penny loafers—looking to Jeremiah, who shrugged, and finally, Julianne for an explanation.

"Batting averages," she explained, the hint of a smile crossing her lips. "Harlan loves Joe DiMaggio. We don't know why exactly, but one thing sure, he knows *every thing* about the man—birth date to where he bought the last dozen roses to put on Marilyn Monroe's grave."

". . . 31 home runs, 137 RBIs, 3 stolen bases . . ." he continued, ". . . 1941, 30 home runs, 125 RBIs, 4 stolen bases . . ."

"You sure know your baseball, Harlan," I said admiringly. "So help me decide a bet comes up most every night at Ringo's where I tend bar. Who's the best all-round ever—Mays or DiMaggio? The 'Yankee Clipper' grew up in Frisco. The 'Say Hey Kid' played there. Guys at the bar can't find any light between 'em!"

The cavalcade of stats and delineations broke-off like a snapped wishbone as Harlan's mind jumped tracks and came to a halt. He seemed confused at first then smiled broadly.

"It's DiMaggio," he answered, "based on lifetime averages . . . Willie Mays career games, 2992; at bats, 10,881; runs, 2062; RBIs, 1903 . . ."

"Harlan," I said.

". . . doubles, 523; triples, 140; lifetime batting average, .302 . . ."

"Harlan!"

"Yes?"

"Know what?"

"What?"

"You're right" I said, clapping my arm around him. "Willie Mays was great, but *DiMaggio* was *DiMaggio!*"

"'None g-greater,'" he stammered, "that's what Casey Stengel said . . . 'Joltin' Joe', the 'Yankee Clipper', born North Branch, San Francisco . . . Galileo high school, 1931 . . ." he started in again, eyes screwed to the ceiling, then stopping abruptly drew back from me. "What's it like where DiMaggio g-grew up, Jack? What's it like in San Francisco?"

"No place like it," I answered. "There's the Mission district, Richmond, the Marina. All kinds of people. Every color, race, life-style you can imagine. But somehow they all get along. And it gets cold there," I warned. "Wind comes off the Bay, cuts through you like a surgeon's scalpel. But then the fog lifts. The sun shines. You look out at the Golden Gate Bridge and suddenly it's all okay. I think you'd like it there, Harlan."

"Me, too, Jack. I think a guy like me would do just fine in San Francisco!"

"Will you be joining us for dinner?" Jeremiah asked, mindful of the connection struck between us. "Once we finish here, the three of us usually grab a bite over at Winberrie's."

"Not this time, but there was something I wanted to discuss. A situation I was hoping you might offer some insight into."

"No time like the present," he said, reading my mind without effort. "We can talk in the sacristy. And you two," he added, leveling a lethal stare at Harlan and Julianne I'd not witnessed since my days at St. Damian's, "flowers potted, watered, and arranged on the altar, or no desert for either of you!"

The scent of wine laced the air of the sacristy, the old priest's gold chalice left drying on the pine wood counter, his cassock hung in an open wardrobe as we sat on two metal folding chairs, facing one another.

"Harlan is what used to be called an 'idiot savant'," he began. "He can calculate the distance earth to the planet Jupiter, but not what it costs to buy a burger at McDonald's. Julianne's his full time nurse. She watches him. He putters around the chapel trying to help. And they do, by way of inspiration, Harlan with his gentle nature and Julianne with her indefatigable patience!"

"Quite a pair," I nodded, laughing.

"So, how long will you be in Princeton, Jack? Seems you're in a hurry to leave."

"Maybe," I answered.

"Still tending bar?"

I nodded.

"Girlfriend? Any friends?"

"A friend is just an enemy you haven't made yet," I quipped, sitting back in my chair.

"Then you've got nothing there to . . ."

"I've got nothing here, Father!" I shot back, voice flaring. "Just memories, most of them bad," I added, ratcheting it back a notch. "Jennifer, who's taken up permanent residence at Greystone; Tiffany, who barely knows what I look like, and a Wall Street resume paints a picture worse than Bernie Madoff!"

"Is that what you wanted to talk about? Your resume?"

"No," I admitted, eyes searching the floor for a detour from the path our conversation was taking. "I still work as a PI when a case comes my way. Nothing big. Embezzlement. Securities fraud. The kind of scams bankrupt amateurs try to pull off as a last resort. But here in Princeton, it's different. You know about the Schumann suicide?" I asked. "Well, her parents saw it different, hired me to take a second look."

"Find anything?"

"No more than the local police, Father, though to be honest, I'm still struggling with it."

"In what way?"

"It's not what happened. That's clear. She ran across campus that night, climbed the stairs to Fine Hall, scribbled some words onto a table top, then got onto the window ledge and jumped. No question, that happened, and it happened that way."

"So?"

"But why, Father? Why did she do it? Why does a healthy, well-balanced young woman suddenly jump from the window of a building and kill herself? It makes no sense!"

"Materialism, spiritual void, post-9/11 angst," he rattled off, "often it's not one thing, Jack, it's the cumulative sum of a culture that grows silent as cancer inside these kids. I'm not sure anyone will ever know the reason Mary Linda Schumann did what she did except God and though it may seem disingenuous I can tell you, there is no true happiness for you, me, or these kids without the love of Jesus Christ in their lives."

"You're right," I grinned. "It's disingenuous! But I'm signed off now. Forwarded my report to the parents. It's 'case closed' for me at this point."

"Tell me, Jack," Jeremiah ventured, leaning forward in his chair, eyes lit with enthusiasm, "did I ever tell you about my theory of angels?"

"No," I moaned, "but I guess I'm going to hear about it, right?"

"It came to me after reading a biblical passage that suggests Christ didn't know he was the Son of God until adolescence," he continued, not missing a beat, "and maybe later than that, while on the cross. Well, it got me to thinking, if that's true, there could also be angels right here on earth among us, men and women who go through life not knowing that they're God's own emissaries: flawed, sure; acting like asses, some of the time; but on the whole, despite those missteps, put on earth as flesh and blood mortals for a purpose they're not even aware of until sometime later when their destiny reveals itself to them."

"Hope for me yet!" I declared, rising from my chair.

"Hope for us all, Jack. Christ died on the cross to offer us eternal life."

"My God, Jeremiah, you never stop trying to win the world over, do you?" I marveled, clasping his hand as I turned to leave. "I'll give you a call once I'm back in Frisco!"

"Oh, and Jack, there's something else you should know," he remembered, watching as I turned to face him again. "It's about Princeton. Maybe it's coincidence or perhaps there are things we don't know about yet—ways in which a geography, or place, or building can quite literally be malign — but the suicide rate at Princeton is higher than the next five Ivy League schools added together. There've been studies, they've even sealed the dormitory windows with locked hasps above the third floor, but still it goes on. No one knows why."

When I returned to the Vette and checked for messages there was a text from Eddie Lawler waiting on my iPhone along with a photo. The photo was of him sans swim suit, Hawaiian shirt pulled over his head passed out under a bar stool. The text read:

'Jacko, Got you a new case! Professor Cadence King, PhD. Love triangle. Pays $15K. Three days work — max. Prof will call. Up yours! Edwardo

Great news! I thought then, pressing the ignition button to the roar of the Vette's 6.2 liter engine: a new case, a quick buck, the chance to stay in Princeton to rekindle my relationship with Tiffany.

So why were the hairs on the back of my neck standing on end?

ONSLAUGHT

Chapter Six

J.B. Winberrie's
Princeton, New Jersey

J.B. Winberrie's was a popular hang-out for students in search of pub food and a cold beer and based on my phone conversation with Professor King I'd be needing the latter in large quantities. Short version, Cadence was a lesbian of the scholarly persuasion. A Harvard PhD who'd published two books—*Conjectures on a Female-Dominated World,* and a sci-fi novel *Frontier Lesbian Overlords from the Planet Muton*—having built her reputation teaching feminist studies while, apparently, sticking her nose where it didn't belong amongst the student body.

It seemed Ms. King, who was engaged in a torrid romance with Hadley Moran, captain of the Tiger's women's soccer team, was inconsolable since Hadley decided to run off with Henry Loggman, a campus worker, whose most impressive academic credential was a high-pressure boiler maintenance license awarded to him by the State of New Jersey. What did she want from me? Find her! Bring Hadley back at any cost as soon as possible!

So it was with no small degree of trepidation that I sat at a Winberrie's table, nursing a cup of coffee topped with a double shot of Jameson's waiting for Cadence King to appear.

The moment she entered, I knew it was her. Not from a faculty photo or Google "images", but because she appeared exactly as I'd envisioned: mid-sixties, raven black hair in a bun, tall and stately, bone-white complexion, stern of face with sharp features, dressed in a gray women's business suit.

"Mr. Madson, I presume," she said, extending her hand across the table.

I stole a nip from my coffee cup and accepted, "Pleased to meet you," I muttered.

"I'm not one to stand on amenities, Mr. Madson," she declared, setting herself upright in her chair, "I believe you know the fundamentals surrounding this travesty, now what are you going to do about it?"

"Coffee?" the approaching waitress asked.

"Black," Cadence snapped back. "And so, I ask you," she persisted, "what are you going to do about bringing back my Hadley? It's impossible to fathom her willfully running off with this janitor, so he must have made off with her while rendered unconscious by one of those date rape pharmaceuticals! Isn't that the very definition of kidnapping, Mr. Madson? Isn't that the essence of the male-female sexual dichotomy as it relates to violence against women in this so-called civilized society?"

I signaled a re-fill to the waitress who was pouring coffee for my newest client, praying I was magician enough to transport two additional ounces of whiskey from the bar into my cup by way of telepathy.

"There are some obvious sources we can tap into to determine what happened to your girlfriend, Ms. King.

We'll start with the registrar's office, campus police, roommates, if she had any, even her parents. Have you checked to see if Hadley withdrew from the classes she'd been taking? A sabbatical? Something along those lines?"

"Of course, that's the first place I checked once I realized she'd packed up and left," she retorted, rattling her cup in its saucer before taking a sip. "Hadley had withdrawn weeks before. Dropped out, but not by choice, you can be certain of that!"

"Roommates . . ."

"She lived with me, Mr. Madson. She drank my beer in sufficient quantities to float an armada. Ate my food with the appetite of a Clydesdale. But, my god," she said shaking her head in wonderment, "could that little vixen eat pussy! Does that shock you, Mr. Madson?" she asked plucking a photo of Hadley bedecked in Princeton jersey and white short-shorts from her wallet and waving it at me. "Perhaps you've never been in the company of a feminist lesbian anarchist before?"

The next several minutes, I must confess, were something of a blur during which Cadence pontificated on subjects ranging from a treatise proposing that Shakespeare was really a woman, to the proportions of Hadley Moran's clitoris (a large one, as I recall), to a trip she was planning to New Guinea to retrace Margret Mead's footsteps leading to the discovery of the exclusively female Arapesh tribe, "an apt model for 21st century America", she proclaimed. Why a blur? So tuned out was I that with eyes glued to the big screen TV above the bar, I sat mesmerized by an info-commercial featuring billionaire businessman, Elon Powers, touting the virtues of "feather lift" plastic surgery, the slogan '*ALATON, Better People For a Better World!*'

floating in pastel colors across the screen, when Cadence caught me watching.

"Mr. Madson!" she objected. "You haven't been listening to one word I've said!"

"No, but I've heard enough, Ms. King," I said, eyes drawn to the empty doorway I somehow knew would soon be occupied by a student named Dimitri Wilder. "Sorry, but I can't take your case."

It was happening. I could feel it. The first ice pick jabs knifing their way into my brain . . . **FERRIS WHEEL** . . . Amy Caulfield . . . No! Not now! Force yourself to keep control! Concentrate on where you are! Who you are! I try to resist, mind suddenly split like two hill kingdoms facing each other across the abyss. Clapboard church . . . **PREACHER** . . . death be not proud!

"But why, Mr. Madson?" King implored. "Can't you see that I love her? That I cannot go on living without my Hadley?"

"That's the point, Ms. King! She's not your Hadley. She's not anybody's 'Hadley'! She's a young woman who you seduced at the age of seventeen and kept locked up in a psychological dungeon you constructed to entomb her. You don't want love, Ms. King. You want a sex slave and now she's run off with the first man she could find to help her escape! Is that so impossible to conceive?"

'JACK', the **ID BRACELET** reads. Remember facts, details, any scrap of information to hold onto! "*Confianza en su corazon,*" I recited in a deep-throated whisper.

NOW I am looming over the table glaring at Cadence King, right hand wrapped so tightly around the silver bracelet that I'd ground my fingernails bloody into the flesh!

"Mr. Madson?" Cadence King asks, the proposition that I had gone stark raving mad finally dawning upon her. "Mr. Madson!"

I look to her, eyes racing, then to the still empty doorway. Fight it! Keep it off you! I exhort, willing myself to pull free! "ALATON," Elon Powers proudly proclaims, peering down at me from the TV above the bar, "*Better People for a Better World!*"

NOW Wilder becomes a kind of broadcast tower exuding communications, pulsing his every thought out at me like high intensity microwave. And I am lost. Plunged into the mind of Dimitri Wilder as he approaches, Cadence King mouthing soundless words at me, torn between Wilder's consciousness and my own!

voices emerging
"open silent messaging"
fingers clawing
at closed doors from within

He switches off the headlights to his 2016 white Porche 911 convertible. He exits the car for the swirling December air, it's very atoms infused with anticipation. Eyes transfixed, brain blazing, he stands for a thoughtful moment, savoring these sensations so new and yet so familiar to him.

His eyes, blood red from lack of sleep, home in on the string of storefronts, each tucked neatly into Tudor facades. He knows what he wants. He knows where he is going, reading the name Winberrie's emblazoned on the plate glass window. Haven for students and professors. The hypocritical scum that would dare to mitigate his presence.

Wilder smiles as he hears a voice beyond the three day old ringing in his ears; dulcet and ominous, the one that announced boxing matches in Las Vegas. "Let's get ready to ru-m-ble!" Michael Buffer bellows amidst the roar of the blood-thirsty crowd. And he can relate to that. Because now he wants to rumble. He wants to sate their hunger, he is thinking, as he crosses Witherspoon Street, a Princeton cop watching from his traffic post fifty yards away.

Dressed in faded Calvin Kleins with hi-top sneakers, he is bare-chested wearing a tattered Burberry's trench coat that hangs down from his broad shoulders giving him the other-worldly appearance of some desiccated effigy unearthed from a tomb, an 18" long machete strung from a leather sheaf dangling beneath his arm.

He brushes a lick of black, greasy hair from his brow leaching perspiration. His sunken eyes dart amongst the crowd as if the world before him had been altered, made alien by what he's witnessed in a place few knew and no one ever talked about.

The blonde waitress dressed in jeans and peasant blouse approaches. The smile on her face withers as she notices his dishev-eled appearance; more the feeling — was it anger? despair? — that shrouds him like its own atmosphere.

"Can I help you?"

He looks to her, distracted. "No," he answers, eyes relentless as he sorts through the blur of faces. Then, "I see the one I want."

Plowing forward, he senses in himself a sudden sensation of raw mental and physical power. It is a feeling he can enjoy. No, that he revels in. "Dimitri Wilder, the quiet and thoughtful math major; captain of the chess team," he remembers, a low growl of satisfaction rising up from the very soul of him. Call it a com-ing out party. Because tonight he would show Them what he was really about. What everything was really about.

He stops suddenly, looming over a table where a young man and two girls sit watching the game on a big screen TV sipping beers and espresso.

"I want to sit."

The young man looks up about to say something, but thinks better of it sensing a presence ragged with danger.

"That chair is already taken," he replies. "A friend is going to join us."

Wilder ignores him. He sits, turns his chair facing the television, crosses his legs broadly, and lights up a Camel cigarette.

"It's fourth with six yards to go for the 49ers," he hears the color commentator announce over the buzz of bar talk. "Giants ten, San Francisco seven with three minutes left in the fourth quarter!"

"Fucking aye fantastic," Wilder cheers, clapping his hands together, standing. "Bravo! Goddamned bravissimo multo!"

The people around him stare and whisper. The students at the table look to one another trying not to laugh. A full five seconds later, Wilder is still clapping, hands held high above him, until Dave Hensen, Princeton's first string quarterback, finally turns.

"You know, we all appreciate how much you must love football, bud, but I'm with my girlfriend." Hensen stares threateningly into Wilder's shiny eyes, holding it on him for emphasis. "So, you think you could watch your language?"

The twenty year old chess champion stares straight ahead like a reptile about to strike. To the back of his mind he hears the voice of Michael Buffer roaring, "Let's get ready to rum-ble!" And it makes him smile to think of what is going to happen next.

Hensen glances to the others at the table who shrug indicating they haven't a clue who he was or where he was from.

"Just watch it," the football star warns, turning again to his girlfriend and the game, with his back to him.

"Fucking scum," Dimitri Wilder mutters as the people around him talk and cheer. "Do you have any idea who I am?" he rumbles, voice gathering strength as he raves on. "The power I posess?"

.

Patrons look up from their seats staring; voices can now be heard above the TV's blare screaming, "Just get him out of here!" "Somebody call the police!"

"You ignorant pack of hyenas," he hisses. "Your minds so small. Your perspectives so backward. You make me want to puke!" he bellows and that was enough for Hensen.

The six foot two, one hundred ninety pound quarterback turns to him grabbing Wilder by the front of his trench coat, lifting him to his feet.

"I warned you before, didn't I? I told you there were ladies here and people who want to watch the game. Now, get the hell out of here before I throw you out myself!" he snarls, tossing the scrawny student to the floor like a rag doll.

But Wilder is undeterred and as the football star returns to his seat, he rises, dusts himself off and reaches inside his trench coat for the machete stomping, weapon in hand, toward Hansen. Then, with no sign of emotion, not anger, not even insanity, he takes the football player's huge right hand into his own clawing grip forcing it down onto the tabletop. He raises the machete above his head then brings it down like a butcher's cleaver, severing three of his fingers and one-quarter of the hand, itself! The horror of what is happening stuns those around him and it is, perhaps, this momentary paralysis that allows Wilder to observe where the section of fingers and hand lie, so that he can take the severed appendages and cut them once again!

It takes more than a second for Hensen to react as he falls off to his left, away from Wilder, cowering from a potential second assault, holding what remains of his right hand in his good one then doubling over it in agony before he has the presence of mind to scream.

For Wilder's part none of this seems to matter. Customers run from him. He returns the machete to its sheath, then calmly walks toward the front of Winberie's to leave. But for me it is different as Wilder's hold over me weakens and at last I break loose from it shoving Cadence King aside, rushing to confront the maniac!

static
 "close silent message"
words pierce veil
voice subsumed

Before Wilder and the door stands Office John Forsythe, a patrolman who happens upon the mayhem. "Forsythe to Dispatcher," he says into the clip microphone of his Motorola APX making his way toward the disturbance, "fight in progress, 14 Witherspoon. Need backup, over."

Within the confines of the restaurant Forsythe doesn't dare pull the Glock 9mm he's wielding, but holds a nightstick above his hip ready to swing for the fences. From behind, Rob Ryding, Henson's teammate, having gathered the courage to pursue him, creeps up on Wilder ready to take him to the floor.

I search the madman's shimmering eyes, unnerved to see no human emotion in them much less fear. My glower shoots beyond Forsythe to the Princeton jock who makes his move, lunging full-body at him. And it appears a stroke of genius. A solitary act that creates diversion enough for me to join the fray as Wilder is driven to the floor, but not before seizing the Glock from Forsythe's holster, taking the cop down with him.

Forsythe twists and turns, locked in his powerful clutches trying to crack him with his Billy club but to no effect as Wilder puts the gun to Forsythe's temple and is about to fire when I jerk it from him, a single shot shattering the mirror behind the bar. But from out of the tumult of bodies—Wilder's, Ryding's, Forsythe's and mine—it is Wilder who emerges!

Call it luck or call it brute strength, but Dimitri Wilder is on his feet walking toward the restaurant exit, machete abandoned, Glock in hand. But we would not surrender so easily for even as Wilder takes his final steps toward the door, Hensen's teammate and I leap atop him. And down to the ground the one hundred and forty pound chess player is thrown, only to get up again after having driven a section of Ryding's facial bone clear into his brain with a single blow.

Forsythe watches through the restaurant's plate glass window from the floor, encouraged by the arrival of a patrol car and sight of me still clinging to the maniac. In horror and awe, he observes that unable to use their weapons they, too, are forced to physically confront Wilder as he storms back to his car. But such was his strength that three full-sized men cannot restrain him! Dumas, who has a bad back, slips a disk early. Anderson, the second to respond, is hoisted in the air and thrown into the center of Witherspoon, me still riding Wilder's back, a choke hold firm around his jugular, until holding me above him, he sends me crashing through the window of a woman's dress shop while dozens of bystanders look on in amazement!

From my front row seat ensconced amongst mani-kins posed in high-fashion winter wear, I assess the flow of blood pouring from the gash cut on the left side of my abdomen, then turn my attention back to Wilder think-ing maybe it was time to call it a night, when beyond the battlefield moans of Dumas and Anderson, Forsythe comes crawling out into the street screaming, "Don't let him get away! He got my Glock!" And that was it for me! No, I wouldn't be waving any white flags of surrender this tonight, I vowed, suddenly realizing that with the patrol car's engine still running, and the maniac in no hurry, there was still a chance to pursue him, catch him, and beat the son of a bitch senseless!

It was with these noble notions of crime and punishment that I extricated myself from the morass of plastic women in polyester dresses and lifted my sorry ass into the street rushing toward the fallen cops' Ford Utility, burning rubber as I U-turned it in hell bent pursuit of Dimitri Wilder!

"Forsythe to Dispatcher," I heard a voice cry out, breathless, over the two-way, "We've got a star spangled melee down here at Winberrie's. Three officers down, at least that many civilians!"

"John, are you all right?"

"Put a call out on Plectron for a Mobile Intensive Care unit," he gasped, "and cross patch us with State 'cause I think we're going to need 'em. Suspect, white male, armed and dangerous, wanted for aggravated assault and possible homicide. Last seen traveling south on Witherspoon driving 2015 Porsche."

"MIC on the way, John, so you just sit tight. I've already put out a Mercer County Crime Alert on statewide!"

"Dispatch, this is Gifford," an urgent voice cut in over the garble of transmissions, "Donnolly and I in vicinity proceeding north on Spring Street, over."

Blue dome light flashing, siren screaming, by then I'd already caught up with Wilder and had a visual on him.

"Gifford, this is Jack Madson," I said ripping the APX

from its cradle. "I have a visual on suspect driving white Porsche, license D-I-M-M-I, proceeding south on 571. We're just passing Penn's Neck, anticipate he'll take Rt. 1 south headed for the Interstate, over."

"What the hell?" Gifford asked incredulously. "Who is this?"

"It's Madson, Lieutenant. Relax and I think we can nail this sucker before he hurts anyone else. He's got Forsythe's Glock, Tommy . . ."

"Glock, my ass!" Donnolly screamed back, tearing the handheld from Gifford. "You stand down and pull that car roadside or I swear I'll see you doing a ten years in Rahway for grand larceny!"

"The suspect is a Princeton student named Wilder, Dimitri Wilder," I shot back. "If he makes it Rt. 1 to the Turnpike in that Porsche he's driving he could make it out of state!"

"Okay, we'll deal with the rest later," Gifford vowed putting the brakes on Donnolly and his own sense of indignation. "You've made contact? You can see him? Over."

"Madson back. Yeah, Lieutenant, I'm behind him now and I can tell you this guy's crazy all right. He's blown through every red light we've come across doin', has to be, seventy miles an hour!"

I hit a pothole, the Interceptor bucked like a wild stallion, speedometer now clocking a hundred!

"Gifford back. We're not far behind," he hollered trying to penetrate the veil of radio traffic and blaring sirens. "And take care at those red lights. If this kid wants to get waffled, that's his business, over."

"Madson back," I said, flying by a caravan of tractor trailers. "Suspect just turned 571 onto Rt. 1 South, over."

"You're breaking up . . . Didn't get you . . ." Gifford pled. "Did he turn onto Rt.1?"

I started to respond but thought better of it listening to the three-way patch between Princeton Police, Dispatch, and State.

"State Police officer Barry Redd to Madson," he drawled sounding more West Virginia than Jersey. "We got your boy headed south down Rt. 1, over."

"Madson back. Then you must see me 'cause I'm on his ass now," I answered, trying to maintain a visual as the Porsche ploughed through a bank of low-hanging fog. "Are your flashers on?"

"Yes, sir."

"Well, I don't see you in my rearview."

"Redd to Lieutenant Gifford," the trooper retorted. "Looks like he's on his way out of state. If you have your boy back off lead car position, we can handle it from here."

"Madson to Redd. What are you a comedian? I'm a car length behind suspect. Any closer and they'd call it a bromance! I got a full tank of gas and as the car that actuated this chase, I'll maintain lead car position, over."

"Gifford to Madson, you've got a set of balls on you, you know that, Madson? But you're right, if Wilder makes it to the Turnpike he'll be clocking one-fifty straight through to Pennsylvania. Maintain position. Keep him in sight while we actuate Emergency Containment Procedures in case he tries to lose us on the ancillaries."

"Madson back. Hey, that's a Porsche 911 with twin-turbo engine out there, Lieutenant," I said blowing past a spate of civilian cars like they were lampposts. "This is a Ford Utility with 365 HP under the hood, not a Ferrari."

"Donnolly back. He didn't say drag race him! Just

maintain a goddamned visual, you think you can do that, asshole?"

"Fuck it!" I muttered stomping down on the gas pedal and keeping it floored, doing one thirty or better, for the next thirty miles!

Then, as the caravan of cars—Wilder's, mine, Redd's and now Gifford's—ripped through the late night fog nearing Rt. 68, an amazing thing happened. Instead of turning onto the Interstate, Dimitri Wilder opted to stay on Rt. 1 headed for Trenton.

"That's it, Dimitri, you sick bastard!" I shouted into the APX, astounded. "You just bought the farm!"

"Gifford back. What? What happened?"

"He missed the Interstate. Wilder's staying on Rt. 1. Ten miles south he's going to find a nest of highways leading into and out of Trenton where you can shut down all the exits you like, no problem!"

I reached for the Motorola to request permission to talk car-to-car, but stopped before my hand touched the transmitter. What the hell? I wondered as did every one of the scores of cops involved in the chase.

All watched or listened on police monitors in stunned amazement as Dimitri Wilder veered his 2016 white Porsche into the right lane, then rammed it headlong into the back of a twenty ton Grief Brothers tractor trailer at one hundred and fifty miles per hour!

The outcome should have been obvious to anyone given what happened, but the reality was something altogether different because the Porsche, while wedged inexorably beneath the huge truck was not immediately crushed. Nor did it immediately burst into flames. Rather, it was dragged beneath the carriage of the trailer for a hundred yards and only after the driver realized what had happened did he panic, hitting the brakes so hard he nearly jackknifed, shaking the Porsche loose, then tossing it like a toy into an overpass where it burst into a vaulting ball of fire!

Seconds later, I stood watching what was left of the Porsche burn, black smoke billowing up from it like lava spewing from the mouth of a volcano. When Gifford, Redd, and the Mercer County cops arrived on the scene they, too, were shocked to silence by Wilder's irrational act of self-immolation. But not Donnolly who charged out at me from his unmarked Dodge Charger, handcuffs in hand, bloodshot eyes bulging, 260 pound frame quaking like a battleship in turbulent seas.

"Hands behind your back, asshole," he shouted. "Now!"

"Fuck your mother," I answered, returning the sentiment.

Then as Donnolly stepped forward to cuff me, I caught sight of the white shirt I was wearing.

It was red, *blood red.*

That is the last thought that passed through my mind before collapsing face down onto the asphalt.

Chapter Seven

When I awoke at University Medical Center, a morphine IV taped to my wrist, I was just groggy enough to think I'd died and God sent me to Hell for my transgressions because the first person visible to me was Tommy Gifford, Princeton police.

"Oh, Christ," I murmured.

"Guess it's true what they say, 'only the good die young,'" he chuckled, an aficionado of his own humor.

"Yeah I'm ecstatic to see you, too, Lieutenant. Where's your partner Donnolly? He must have stayed awake all night worrying about me."

"Two nights," he corrected. "You've been out since Sunday, Madson."

"Did you bring a little something along to cheer me up? A bottle of Scotch, maybe?"

"Nah," he said approaching my bed, "no Scotch. Not even a Band-Aid for that slash in your side. Lucky it didn't sever your spleen, that's what the doctors say. But, no, it's just me. Came by to see how you're doing, thank you for helping my officers the other day."

"Funny, I thought you were here to arrest me."

83

"Matter of fact, you've become something of a hero here in Princeton," he said, smiling ruefully. "At least that's the way Forsythe tells it. 'Course Donnolly wants to hang you by your balls in the public square, but the Higher Ups at State thought it was inspiring, figured they'd overlook the details. You know, *'Hero Saves Cop From Gun-Toting Maniac!'*, *'Civilian Pursues Mad Dog Killer to Fiery Demise!'* people love that crap, cub scouts, girl scouts, the home-bound elderly."

"Was there anything else you wanted to tell me, Lieutenant? Like how Hensen's doing?"

"Career's over," he replied, not overly saddened, "surgeons couldn't re-attach fingers 'cause Wilder cut'em twice; once, then in half again. We believe he did it intentionally for just that reason. Imagine a sick bastard like that."

"Dave Hensen was one of Princeton's best. Shame to have his career end that way."

"But Wilder," Gifford said, returning to the real subject of his visit, "were you close enough to hear the things he said leading to the attack, the words he may have used."

"He said Hensen and his pals were 'a pack of hyenas,' 'narrow thinkers' with 'small minds', things like that," I answered waiting for him to connect Wilder's ravings with the Schuman suicide. But he didn't, or at least didn't want me to know, if he had.

"Crazy, huh?" he asked, shaking his head with the myopic wonder of a tourist contemplating the Sphinx. "Well, I'm off to see a family whose Labradoodle went missing, fourth dog this week!"

"Lieutenant, I have a question, if you don't mind."

"What is it?" he asked, turning.

"I saw a story in the *Register* claimed Hensen was shoe-in to break your 'most yards gained' record this year. Does it bother an ex super stud like you? Henson leaving your records behind in the dust like that?"

Gifford studied me. His smile died; his eyes narrowed, "You've got a serious attitude problem, know that, Madson? But I'm going to answer anyway. See, it's all about the team. That's something you learn early in the game of football. Now why don't you just get yourself well again," he advised, "and let me worry about records and motives and murders."

My conversation with Gifford left a vibration in the air that was still resonating when Josie Kowalski, a big bosomed nurse who looked like she'd just exited a time machine circa 1960 entered.

"Good morning, Mr. Madson . . ." she greeted cheerily.

"Jack," I said.

"Good morning, Jack," she began again shambling toward the IV unit, "you might like to know that you're at University Medical Center and that it's Tuesday, December 10th."

"Thanks, I was afraid I was in Newark," I groaned, a stab of pain accompanying the remark. "Any visitors come to see me aside from Clouseau?"

"Yeah," she replied, adjusting my supply of morphine sulfate, "a man named Harlan and a woman named Julianne came by this morning. Now, ain't they a pair," she laughed, pausing, "but there was something else might interest you."

I turned painfully to look up at the stout blonde with the beehive hairdo, "What's that?"

"Coco Channing, the Hollywood actress, was admitted Sunday morning. *Drug rehab*," she added confidentially.

"Coco Channing here?" I chuckled. "Sorry, but I didn't notice."

"Well, she noticed you," she said, flicking her fingertip at the IV line. "You told her three-hundred pound body guard to 'go fuck himself', but probably don't remember. This here," she explained, eyes raising to the infusion bag, "not to mention the blood you lost."

"Okay, now let me tell you something," I slurred, teasing. "She may be Coco Channing to you, but to me she's Amy Caulfield. We were an item once upon a time . . ." I said nodding off as the morphine sulfate took effect, ". . . before she went Hollywood . . . and left me flat in Paris," I began, eyes drawing down like the shields of a fortress, smile turning to a tight-lipped grimace as sleep, when it came, brought harried dreams.

NOW my bed is a raft floating on gentle ripples, swaying and tilting pleasantly, Amy Caulfield's body pulled up warm against me.

"Feel," she says guiding my hand to her breast. "Do you feel it, Jack? That's my heart. Aren't we truly one, Jack? We share the same heart, and hands, and legs with no boundaries between us."

"Yes," I pledge. "I feel it. I am you and you are me, and all of one is the other."

NOW, I am running in the rain, hand-in-hand with Amy through Paris streets to the shelter of a café with red, white and blue trimmed veranda where friendly strangers await us. I know that I'm dreaming and I know that I don't want it to stop, but soon Eddie Lawler's face squeezes into our world large enough to fill the screen of a movie theater, until Amy has all but disappeared and Eddie, no longer Eddie, turns into Adolf Hitler screaming from off the huge white screen, *"Der Tod ist nicht stolz!"* he is shouting. *"Tod sollst du sterben!"* Then, calmly, dressed in an operating gown with mask obscuring his face, I look up to see a surgeon peering down at me, "Yes, it's all real," he confides, a conspirator's gleam winked from his deep-socketed eyes. "Cock-sucking Jew bastards! I cut off their teats, take their ova, and sometimes, *das Augen*, their eyes. This I do to fulfill the Aryan destiny!"

I turn away in horror, and now I am watching Pope Francis sitting on a yacht locked in deep discussion with Elvis Presley dressed in black leather, looking better than ever. "I'm certain they've already done it with humans in China, perhaps even Switzerland," the Pope casually mentions, eyes riveted upon me. "Think of the savings in health care costs, and education!" he continues, addressing his remarks to Elvis, until both look up to the bridge where Eddie Lawler, regaled in a Captain's uniform, stands amid weather forecasting equipment shouting, "Typhoon!"

"What'd he say?" Presley asks.

"Typhoon!" Eddie continues screaming, clouds darkening, giant waves pounding the yacht, flashes of lightning ripping the sky open. "It killed six hundred in Bali and it's headed our way!"

And I know that Eddie's right. And I know that I must warn the Pope. But with the waves overwhelming and wind blowing deadly, the raft is sinking and I am caught in its vortex slipping down into the depths!

"Jesus!" I am shouting. "Jesus Christ! Save me!"

And in the blink of an eye, there is silence. Total. Complete. All else disappears and I am alone. Standing at the foot of the wooden cross where Christ is hanging, nails driven through hands and feet, blood streaming down the sides of his torn and battered countenance, dying!

Then, from beyond the landscape of dreams, I hear a sound that wakes me. I shudder, my hospital gown drenched in sweat. It is the phone ringing. I pick it up.

"Mr. Madson," the voice spills from out of the receiver, "this is Marjorie Kurtz. I work as a geneticist-virologist for the university and the defense contractor, ALATON."

"Yes?"

"I spoke with your friend, Mr. Lawler, who recommended you," she urgently whispers. "He said you were the only one who could stop it. Put an end to what's going on here at Princeton! I can't talk now, but please take down this information . . ."

"Yes, of course, absolutely," I say, fumbling for a pen and notepad. "What is it? What information? *It's important that I know!*"

I fell back to sleep afterward, or perhaps I'd never really awakened, but when a knock sounded at the door to my room, I didn't know whether to expect a doctor, nurse, or Custer's Seventh Calvary. Still, I wasn't complaining when I saw Coco Channing's perky face and contagious smile peering beyond the crack in the door.

"Amy?"

"Yes, it's me," she giggled, dressed in nothing but a Giant's jersey with the words 'Coco Channing Breakfast of Champions' on its front and a pair of spike heels that click-clacked with every mincing step forward. "My god, Jackie, it's me, not Rosie O'Donnell! You look like you've just seen a ghost!"

"Or a goddamned angel!" I sighed so delighted to see

her I thought I might still be bouncing off billowy clouds in Morphine Land.

"Figured you could use some company," she said, sidling up beside me. "You were so whacked out last night! I never saw Rampage Johnson back down like that before. He usually breaks guys in half and eats them before they get that far!"

She studied my face, drawn and haggard, brushing a lick of stray black hair back from my forehead. "You look like a bottle of Iodine you know that, don't you, mister?"

"Won't somebody be missing you, Amy?"

"No one's called me Amy since I left Jersey," she observed with a coquettish wriggle of her nose. "Name's Coco now, baby. I've changed!"

"Okay, Coco," I amended still grinning ear-to-ear, "won't someone be missing you at this late hour?"

"Just my bitch publicist, Bianca," she pouted, "and that cowboy reporter, Ty Rollins, from the *Inquirer,* following me around with all this hub-bub about drug addiction."

"Is it true?"

"No!" she snapped back, eyes aflutter, then hesitated, a churlish grin dancing across her cherry lips, "and, yes, I suppose."

I chortled at the existential nature of her remark and the persona of Coco Channing generally.

"What's so funny?"

"I see now why you're such a fine actress.

You possess the rare ability to put your soul in your eyes. I've only met one other woman who could do that. Her name was Havana Spice."

"And that's a good thing?"

"For you!" I laughed. "For you, it's a good thing!"

"Oh, come on, Jackie, why you say it like that?" she asked slipping her arms around me, nuzzling, while she lapped cat-like at my ear lobe.

"You're the one left me flat in a Paris hotel to pursue your 'cah-ree-er' in Hollywood," I reminded with a thespian's penache. "Can't say that did much for my ego. I was destroyed. Couldn't get a hard on, must have been, two days!"

Disheveled and beautiful, she looked into my eyes, a lock of stray blonde hair flounced over her right brow, and the dozen years that separated us might never have existed.

"You dissolve me, baby, you know that? Even laid up like now, you're still the sexist man I ever laid eyes on. Touch the point of my chin with your fingertip and I'm wet enough to need diapers."

"Magic touch, huh?"

"Midas touch," she bested.

"The things I've touched lately?" I said, eyes diverting. "Well, it's not exactly gold they've turned into."

"Broke? Is that your problem? I been broke and a lot worse than that! Done a lot of things I'm not proud of, but what's that got to do with us now? I got enough money for you, me, and the French Foreign Legion, so don't worry about where you been or what you've done. Look!" she said pulling the Giant's jersey over her head, putting a forefinger to the nipple of the breast nearest me. "See my nipples, Jack? They're dark and erect like a five star General just walked in the room, know why?"

"You ate your Wheaties this morning?"

"No, silly, it's because you turn me on! You always did, Jack, now more than ever because, tell the truth, I been chastened! I never found another lover like you and I been lonely," she whispered, pulling me close enough to feel the wetness of her tears on my cheek. "All these Hollywood types? For the birds! Phonies and not really friends at all. Not like you. Not like when we were together! And when I saw you Sunday morning, all those feelings came back," she confessed, searching my eyes for a connection, "and I realized what a terrible mistake I made leaving you in the first place! Do you forgive me, baby?"

"I was in a bad way after you left. Married Jennifer on the rebound, and for her father's money, I suppose, got hooked up with a Wall Street firm crooked as a Brit's front teeth. That was my big mistake, my downfall I guess you'd call it, but what the hell? 'Forgive and forget', that's what I say!"

"Hey," she asked then, eyes sparkling, "you wanna dance? I brought my 'party kit'," she explained, opening an ermine purse she'd brought along for the occasion. "I got my iPhone for tunes, a flask of Southern Comfort for lubrication, and an eight ball to get the party started!" she declared, showing them off, proud as the winner of the eighth grade science fair.

"Maybe a taste of that Comfort," I suggested taking a pull while Coco dispensed two white lines on the surface of a pocket mirror. "So is snorting blow part of your rehab regimen?" I asked, voice more stern than intended. "Guess, you'd call it non-traditional treatment?"

Coco's head bobbed up from the mirror dropping the rolled hundred she'd been using atop it. "Say, mister," she asked with a loopy grin and dollop of white powder on the tip of her nose, "how 'bout that dance you promised?"

I glanced forlornly to my abdomen and the forty stitches holding my left side together.

"Oh, I get it," she said eager to oblige. "You're one of those guys wants the girl doin' all the work! Sure, I'll dance for you, Jackie," she said, opening up My Music to John Mellancamp's "I Want You to Dance Naked", strutting her stuff for me with nothing on save a pair of spike heels and the sexist smile I'd ever seen!

Soulful. Hypnotic. I was transfixed as she gyrated a body ancients would have gone to war over, starting slow then guiding my face between her ample breasts while grinding her privates into the bedpost like a woman born to indulge all things carnal.

Afterwards, we slow danced to Madeleine Peyroux's "Dance Me to the End of Love" and we did just that, swaying to the music, until all that mattered was the two of us, alone in a room, bodies locked like two pieces of a puzzle joined together body, mind, soul.

"Can you make love to me, Jack?" she sighed, ardent as a schoolgirl, then hearing no reply, assuaged, "Not to worry, baby," touching the tips of her long delicate fingers to my lips, "I got a plan."

And so like the designer of some exotic architectural configuration, Amy lay me face up on the bed then twisting atop me, head-to-toe, brought her full red lips down onto the head of my cock, and began caressing it while lowering her pussy, sweet as honey, down — then down harder — onto my uncoiled tongue.

Whatever pain I may have been feeling ebbed like a receding tide as cock, standing hard and straight, discomfort thrust forward like a bullet train to first stop, *anticipation*; second stop, *pleasure*; third stop, *ecstasy*, Amy transporting me to archipelagos of delight I never knew existed with angel licks to crown, deep throat plunges, then mouth—warm and delicate—all building like the tremors of a tectonic shift that sent us hurdling into the sky-splitting fireworks of ecstasy, her screaming "oh-my-fucking-lord!", body arcing atop me like a woman possessed, me grabbing hold of the bed sheets as would a drowning man clinging to debris in the midst of a hurricane at sea, both frenzied to madness with the sheer power of our orgasms until, sated, we collapsed in a smoldering heap, flesh melding one into the other's, locked in a final embrace.

"You're a genius," Amy uttered, breathless, licking the last pearl of semen from the corner of her lips, "and tasty, too!" she enthused, delivering a final kiss before laying her head down and dropping off into blissful slumber.

It's hard to say how long I slept, but Amy was still nuzzled into my chest asleep while I tried to reconstruct the dreams I'd experienced prior to her coming, forced to wonder about the validity of my conversation with Marjorie Kurtz, and even the phone call, itself, *did any of it really happen?*

It was with these thoughts tumbling around in my head like bolts in a mixer that I felt Amy stir, then awaken bright as a spring leaf, "What time is it?" she asked, sitting up to check her iPhone. "6 A.M.", she worried. "Bianca's going to kill me!" Then, her eyes dipped to the space between the bed and the night stand, "Say, what's this?" she wondered aloud, retrieving a scrap of paper with numbers and words scrawled across it. "Looks like a cell number, but I can't make out the words," she said handing it to me.

The handwriting was mine. The cell number Marjorie Kurtz', the phrase *'viral receptive mapping'* running off beyond the paper's edges.

But there wasn't time to comment because it was then that we heard a commotion in the hallway, Amy hopping out of bed, nurse Kowalski rushing in, stanchioning the door against an army of paparazzi led by 6′4″ Tyson Rolling snapping photos of Coco Channing hovering over her mystery lover wearing nothing but a G-string.

"I don't know why you boys get so excited about girls in G-strings," Coco cooed, wide-eyed sexy, while reporters were moved to frenzy and nurse Kowalski tried to force the door shut on them. *"Take off the G-string and what have you got?"*

With locked door now guarded by Josie Kowalski and Amy arguing with Bianca, I took the scrap of paper into both of my hands. I studied the cell number and odd phrase scrawled across it, then stopped, shocked to realize.

My hands, they were shaking.

Chapter Eight

Lake Carnegie
Princeton University Campus

After all I'd witnessed at Princeton, it didn't matter to me where Marjorie Kurtz and I met, we *were* going to meet. But it mattered to her. Rather than rendezvous at Forrestal campus, where she worked, or Starbuck's center town, she opted for Lake Carnegie, a place as close to deserted as any, with boathouse shut down for the next three months.

Together we walked north on a path that ran along the water's edge, winter's wind rattling the barren tree branches that spiked the hillside leading to main campus.

"Quiet place this time of year," I commented, casting a lonely stare at the lake and the Washington Bridge cutting across the horizon a mile beyond us.

"Peaceful," she replied without guile. "That's why I come here, especially now that I've come to terms with my work at ALATON."

I took a moment to appraise the middle-aged scientist walking alongside me. Wrapped in a winter coat with hair pinned back by a pink ballerina brooch and a complexion pale enough to suggest she hadn't seen the sun in twelve months, there was something in the banality of her appearance that seemed un-centered. Perhaps it was her demeanor, fatalistic, like the die had been cast and she was awaiting an inevitable outcome.

"Exactly what is going on at Princeton that so disturbs you, Dr. Kurtz?" I asked. "You talked about 'viral receptive mapping'. According to articles I've read, that has to do with 'gene therapy'. If I've got it right, certain viruses put their genes into our own by inserting DNA fragments. Afterwards, when those cells divide during *mitosis* that information sticks around in the daughter cells so that all the cells that divide from the infected ones have the transcribed gene. Bottom line, if you choose the right virus and use it to deliver predetermined genetic material, you've in effect 'mapped' the results and altered the genetic makeup going forward."

"There are multiple methods to introduce chromosomal changes that affect genomics. Of course, viral receptors are the one most appealing to me, but you don't need to work in a Tactical Technology laboratory to see the feasibility of gene-altering performance. Take the Olympics where officials constantly worry about gene-doping among athletes. Surely, your research has led you to reports in *Scientific American* and *Time* magazine."

"But we're not talking about Olympic athletes, Dr. Kurtz, are we?"

She cast a long stare out onto the lake, dark and icy, visualizing like me, I suspect, a bright spring day bristling with the sights and sounds of Princeton's rowing team sculling across the water.

"Human-directed evolution has the potential to change the way humans interact with their environment forever. If I believed it to be anything less, I would not have devoted my life to it," she said, Polish accent prominent. "You see, Mr. Madson, I was raised in Birkenau. You may know it as Auschwitz, the extermination camp operated by the Nazis during the Second World War. After I graduated from Poznan University, I continued my studies at Stanford based on a paper I'd published in the British medical journal, *Lancet*, on the subject of viral receptors. It was rudimentary work, but the professors were impressed enough to let me complete my studies and fund my research through federal grants. Of course, like they say, *nie ma nic za darmo*, nothing is for nothing, and before the ink had dried on my diploma, your Department of Defense made me an offer I could not refuse," she explained, dark eyes lifting to meet mine. "Somehow I'd misunderstood their initial offer, they told me, and the grants were really loans. Still, I didn't complain when they replaced my debt with a six-figure salary to work in the genetic research laboratories here at Princeton."

"So you relocated?"

"Of course."

"And the projects?"

"Like I said, "highly classified" experiments performed in TT laboratories constructed beneath the Plasma Fusion Reactor. Hiding in plain sight, as they say!" She stopped to strike a match, shielding it from the wind, as she lit up a Marlboro. "So why am I talking to you about it?" she asked, the question riding a stream of cigarette smoke before starting down the path again. "For me, it's academic. You see, Mr. Madson, human-directed evolution means different things to different people. Take Josef Mengele. It wasn't better athletes he wanted to create, it was super soldiers, *schlach maschines*, translated literally, 'slaughter machines'."

"Mengele? He was executed after the Nuremberg trials back in the 1940s, wasn't he?"

"I see your ignorance concerning genetics is rivalled only by your grasp of 20th century history," she observed, bluntly. "No, Mengele was not executed. He escaped Germany, along with other *SS* officers through the 'ratline' operated by your country's *OSS*. Josef Mengele died of natural causes, a free man in Brazil, thirty years after the war ended."

"Thanks for the news flash," I said, not bothering to hide my annoyance, "but now may be a good time to tell me why I should give a damn about any of this."

Kurtz stopped dead in her tracks, then shot a stare at me so withering I had to catch my breath for the force of it.

"Because still it goes on!" she shrieked through gritted teeth. "That's why they recruited me: genetics at Paznan, virology at Stanford! Don't you see, they're experimenting on human subjects, Mr. Madson, unsuspecting soldiers, federal prisoners, students here on campus! They call it MAYHEM but in reality it's an extension of Mengele's early work in radical evolution. Imagine Hitler's armies stalled at the gates of Stalingrad for three years just one generation ago. Troops exhausted, freezing to death in sub-zero temperatures. It cost him the war and what the Nazis believed was their destiny! Now imagine a battalion of *schlach maschines*, slaughter machines, dropped behind enemy lines created to kill every living thing in their path without fear or remorse, lethal for weeks at a time with no need for sleep, or food, even water, until they simply stop, existence eradicated by a termination gene supplanted in their DNA months, even years, before! That's what we're discussing now, Mr. Madson, not the three minute mile or a female athlete genetically altered to produce enhanced levels of testosterone. This isn't about the Olympics, it's about a non-nuclear strategy for a land war with China!"

"And the suicides? Schuman? Wilder?"

"'Casualties of war', 'collateral damage', 'you can't make an omelet without breaking eggs!' " She rattled off the cliches. "It's called GRIN—genetics, robotics, intelligence, nano technologies. MAYHEM is based on it as are the other classified projects. We've been keeping the brains of freshly killed combat troops harvested in Afghanistan alive in our testing labs for more than a decade for surgical procedures to develop ALATON'S "three-legged stool" of *Wunderwaffen*: genetically engineered soldiers, silent messaging, cloning. These programs carried out by ALATON and funded by DARPA, the Defense Advanced Research Projects Agency, are worth hundreds of millions to universities like Stanford, Harvard, and Princeton. So long as it's stamped "National Security" they know they're shielded by the very agencies that should be prosecuting them for violations of the most basic scientific codes of conduct!"

My eyes darted from Kurtz to the Washington Bridge where cars looking like toys traversed the Delaware River, a quiet storm of indignation mounting at the sheer chutzpah it took for her to believe I'd be sucked so easily into the world of paranoia and delusion she'd created for herself.

"I'm not sure what you want me to do about any of this, Dr. Kurtz. I'm a private investigator, not a reporter for the *Washington Post*, but assuming I believed even a modicum of what you've told me, what makes you think I'd want to get involved?"

"I have twenty-thousand dollars, cash," she answered without blinking. "I'll pay you ten in advance if you'll agree to investigate. Prove me wrong and the remaining ten will be in your hands, no questions asked."

Then, sensing my lack of enthusiasm, she gathered herself up, looking suddenly dignified, even courageous. "I know now that I was a fool to get involved in this, Mr. Madson, but like the other scientists I was blinded by the power one feels working on projects of this magnitude. They appealed to our patriotism, convinced us that we were exceptional minds with unique skills that could help safeguard future generations from terrorists and emerging military threats from Russia and China. I know I was naïve but that's what I believed, or wanted to believe! Mr. Lawler told me . . ."

"Eddie Lawler?" I laughed out loud. " 'Mister Lawler told me', did you really just say that? Eddie is a friend but even he'd tell you the extent of his interest in bio-engineering starts with a copy of *Hustler* magazine and ends in a sauna with two hits of Ecstasy and a twenty-year old coed!"

"He told me you were a good man, dogged and resourceful," she scoffed, "that once you understood the magnitude of the situation you wouldn't stop until you uncovered the truth about ALATON and everything else that's been going on here at Princeton!"

I heaved an exasperated sigh, shaking my head, empathetic if not receptive to her situation, real or imagined.

"Look, Dr. Kurtz, I believe that you believe what you've told me is true. So, how about this," I offered, if only to get those tortured eyes off me, "I go back to my hotel, do some research on DARPA, Mengele, and the rest, and we'll meet again to discuss your situation. Like I told you, I'm not the guy for this, but maybe I can point you in the direction of someone more qualified and, frankly, more interested in government conspiracies than me. Is that fair enough, for now?"

On that happy note, I left Kurtz standing at the edge of Lake Carnegie, smoking a cigarette as she pondered science, government agencies, and slaughter machines, I supposed, glad to be free from the gravity of her obsessions, able to breathe again!

Still, I wondered, headed up the graded landing leading to campus: if all that she'd told me was the product of an unhinged mind, who was the man standing on the roof of Cameron Hall with binoculars? Why was he spying on Marjorie Kurtz?

Chapter Nine

Elysee Hotel
Manhattan, NYC

Once returned to the Elysee, I poured a half-glass of Glenlivet and sat down at the desk in front of my Dell laptop searching the topics 'DARPA', 'Mengele', 'ALATON', curiosity piqued.

I started with Mengele because the Nazi scientist's name had been raised during my discussion with Kurtz. But it was more than that because even today, I realized, the mention of the name 'Mengele' evoked horrifying images that gave one a feeling not unlike being thrown into a dark room with the Devil, himself. To think that his work provided the basis for DARPA and ALATON research seemed beyond the pale, even for me!

I opened *Wikipedia* scanning the results for 'Mengele Biography': "Josef Mengele (German: 16 March 1911-February 1979) German *Schutzstaffel* (*SS*) . . . officer and physician Auschwitz concentration camp. . .called 'Angel of Death' by inmates . . . notorious for performing deadly human experiments . . . second son of Bavarian industrialist . . . joined right wing *Stahlhelm* (steel helmets) 1931 . . ." Then, scrolling down the screen to *history.com*: ". . . matriculated from universities in Munich, Vienna, Frankfurt . . .

concentration on physical anthropology, the genetics of his time . . . studied under Otmar Verschner at Institute of Hereditary Biology and Racial Hygiene . . . quest for "biologized" society based on individual genetic character-istics . . ." From there I went to *prnewswire*. ". . . Mengele performed lethal experiments on 1500 sets of twins at Aus-chwitz in search of ways to artificially manipulate character-istics of human beings . . . twins kept in barracks between experiments which ranged from injections of various dyes into eyes in attempt to change color to surgically connect-ing their organs while still alive in effort to create Siamese twins . . ." I came upon a series of articles published in German scientific journals, 1940-42, some translated, others not, finally settling on "Theories on the Creation of an Aryan World" by Dr. Werner Von Hyde describing Mengele's early experiments in genetic engineering and mind control.

> Truly, Mengele is a genius! The goal of Der Docktor's work is to unlock the secrets of racial morphology and use it to devise methods for eradicating inferior genetic strains from the human population as a means to create a Ger-man super-race. Mengele believes that only by testing subjects for whom "life and death is at stake" can he achieve reliable results. He calls each real-life experiment 'terminal' in that the tests do not end when the subject's life is threat-ened. Indeed, because their minds have been "conditioned" to accept treatment, very often the subjects have no idea they are part of an experiment!

Next, I moved on to 'DARPA' at *www.darpa.com* greeted
by the banner headline: "Defense Advanced Research Projects Agency . . . arm of U.S. Department of Defense . . .
created by President Eisenhower for purpose of executing
research projects to expand frontiers of military technology far beyond immediate requirements." Then, scrolling
through a plethora of articles like "Converging Technologies for Superior Battlefield Performance" by Joel Gott-
lieb, Deputy Director, US Defense Science Office, interviews with scientists such as Jean-Louis "Dutch" DeGay,
Chief Officer Warrior Technology Programs, I stopped at
a YouTube speech delivered by Elon Powers, Chairman
of ALATON at a *DarpaTech* conference, titled "Studies in
Radical Evolution, A Path toward Military Domination in
The 21st Century". I took a pull from my glass of Glenlivet,
eyes narrowing:

> "There are few organizations in the world that
> look as far forward as DARPA which regu-
> larly thinks thirty to forty years out," a tanned
> and trim Powers confidently asserted. "Today,
> DARPA and ALATON are in the business of cre-
> ating better humans. Soldiers having no physi-
> cal, physiological or cognitive limitations will be
> key to operational dominance in the future,"
> Powers declared. "Imagine soldiers that com-
> municate by thoughts alone. Contemplate, for
> a moment, a world in which learning is as easy
> as eating, and the replacements of damaged
> body parts as convenient as a fast-food drive-
> through. These bold visions have the potential
> to profoundly alter our world forever. And while

these achievements may be out of reach to technology competitors such as China, Russia and ISIS, when ALATON talks about "high risk, high reward" experimentation, we're talking about science fact, not science fiction!"

I sat back savoring the last of my drink, images of Mengele, Powers, and Kurtz swarming through the dungeons of my mind. Clearly, Mengele had been obsessing over Hitler's theories of German genetic superiority even before joining the Nazi party as witnessed by papers he'd written on "racial morphology" and "artificial transference of intelligence" while a student in Munich. But throughout the bits and pieces of biography, three observations came to the fore.

First, there seemed two Mengeles: one, the avuncular, near angelic, figure smiling benevolently as he dispensed sweets to child inmates. The other, a detached monster capable of surgically dissecting those same children, organ by organ, in the blink of an eye. Hence, the moniker "Angel of Death". The second observation had to do with Mengele's obsession for perfection. A painting hung slightly askew was something he could not abide, a scuff mark on one of his black riding boots could rocket him to apoplexy, a birth defect observed in an incoming prisoner a death sentence administered personally at point blank range.

But it was the third observation affirming Kurtz' claims about the MAYHEM-OPERATION REBIRTH connection that proved most compelling. According to those closest to him, Der Docktor was always rushing "to beat a deadline", obsessed with providing "the final result" for the Fuhrer causing me to wonder: could it be that the *schlautang maschines* Mengele so feverishly worked to perfect was the "wonder weapon" Hitler spoke about—often and publicly—during the final days of World War II?

I poured myself a second glass of the gold stuff, side wound howling as I reached for a handful of MS Contins taking them down in a single gulp. If one had imagination enough to see Mengele's 'final result' and Hitler's 'wonder weapon' as one and the same, and conceded Mengele's Auschwitz experiments were an attempt to create so-called 'slaughter machines', the divide between the Nazis' OPERATION REBIRTH and DARPA's MAYHEM was as good as bridged!

I sat back mulling over the possibility, then pen in hand hunched over the desktop to draw a schematic that might describe the progression.

> *1935:* HITLER GERMAN SUPER RACE THEO-
> RIES > *1935–9:* MENGELE GENETIC ENGIN-
> ERING RESEARCH > *1940–41:* HITLER
> 'WONDER WEAPON' CONCEPT > *1940:* NAZIS
> THWARTED MOSCOW > *1941:* MENGELE'S
> GENETIC EXPERIMENTS HUMANS AUSH-
> WITZ > *1942:* NAZIS THWARTED STALIN-
> GRAD > *1942–45:* MENGELE PURSUES *'DAS
> SCHLAUTANG MASCHINES'*

But that's where the logic of my theory came to a screeching halt! In February 1945, Mengele supposedly fled Auschwitz disguised as a member of the German infantry. Three months later, he turned up at Matthausen where he re-united with death camp colleague Aribert

Heim. Finally, in the fall of 1948, three years later, historians tell us Mengele relocated to Argentina where he lived
until February 1979, his death confirmed by DNA testing
two decades later!

I stared blurry-eyed at the diagram I'd configured,
morphine sulfate taking effect as I recollected Ockham's
Razor, a theory of logic the CIA often used when presented with speculative problems. In it, Ockham proposed
that the explanation that corresponded most closely to the
known facts was usually the correct one. And so it was with
Ockham's cold eye that I examined Kurtz' claim that DAR-
PA'S MAYHEM was spawned by REBIRTH, the applied
technology undertaken by Mengele seventy years earlier!

Could MAYHEM actually be REBIRTH carried forward
in time? I dared to wonder. Was it possible that the 'highly
classified' experiments being carried out five stories
beneath Princeton's campus were a continuation of the
Nazis' attempt to create an army of 'slaughter machines'?
The notion seemed more science fiction than detective
work! Still, I had only to recall the invention of radar by
the British, the atomic bomb by the Americans, the Sputnik by the Soviets, or laser-guided drones to understand
the history of cooperation between advanced technology
and modern military warfare. So, why wouldn't DARPA
research the possibility of super-soldiers? I asked myself.
Beyond that, why wouldn't they outsource so-called GRIN
research like 'accelerated healing of wounds' or 'replace-
ment of body parts for soldier-amputees' to mega corpora-
tions with a track record like ALATON's?

I re-opened my timed-out laptop, the image of Josef
Mengele, bedecked in Nazi officers' uniform filling the
screen as I scrolled to *holocaustsurvivors.com* interested

now, not in the mass murderer, but in the millions of lives he'd destroyed.

Eyes riveted, I scrolled down Mengele's seemingly endless list of victims, finally stopping at one of the hundreds of survivor accounts, Nuremberg Trial 1945-46, and began reading.

> Isabella Leitner, Age: 20 Born: Budapest, Hungary, 1924, "I packed for my journey to Auschwitz on May 28, 1944—my 20th birthday . . . As we alighted from the cattle car—my mother, my brother, and my foursisters—there was Mengele looking magnificent with his dog, his pistol, his riding crop. He sent my mother, my brother, and my four sisters to the crematorium immediately, but sent me to the work camp . . . Mengele was as elegant as you could imagine, good-looking even. You would never suspect the evil. He was the genius of Death."

Fascinated and repulsed in equal measure, my eyes fell upon the next account, Evil Incarnate dancing off the screen to greet me.

> Moshe Offer, Age: 7 Born: Warsaw, Poland, 1936, "Dr. Mengele had always been more interested in Tibi. I am not sure why—perhaps because he was the older twin. He made several operations on Tibi. One surgery left my brother paralyzed. He could not walk anymore. Then they took out his sexual organs. After the fourth operation, I did not see Tibi anymore. It is impossible to put

into words how I felt. They had taken my father, my mother, my two older brothers—and now my twin."

I raised my glass, the morphine sulfate coursing through me like an electrical current as I sucked a scotch-tinged ice cube, and continued reading.

> Mark Berkowitz, Age: 12 Born: Prague, Czecho-slovakia, 1930, "Before the experiments began, Mengele came and tattooed my number personally. They put us in freezing baths, smeared chemicals on our skin, but it was the needles the children were most afraid of. After the first 150 injections we stopped counting . . . One morning I spotted my mother among a long-line of women moving toward the gas chamber. Mengele called me in and gave me an errand to the crematorium. He knew I would see my mother go to her death . . . A couple of days later he asked me if I still believed in God."

Then I stopped; simply could not go on reading! Ockham's Razor? Glacial eye of logic? I asked myself, still struggling to comprehend how horrors of this magnitude could happen in so-called civilized societies, a skein of sweat mapping my forehead as I anguished, *could it happen again?*

Absolutely not, the Ockham part of me reasoned, these atrocities occurred during a particular moment in history (Hitler's Germany) under a particular set of circumstances (World War II) in a particular place (Auschwitz death camp) totally unlike 21st century America, let alone, on the campus of one of our most prestigious universities! No, whatever research DARPA and ALATON were conducting at Princeton could not be related to Josef Mengele, Nazi 'wonder weapons', 'slaughter machines', or anything like it, I concluded.

For me it was over, I would have nothing more to do with the Kurtz case!

Chapter Ten

Elysee Hotel
Manhattan, New York

Satisfied with my decision to abandon the case, I unclasped the silver **ID BRACELET** I wore from my wrist, placed it on the night table, and fell into bed staring at the ceiling, second guesses filtering through my certitude like water leeching through a membrane.

I remembered remarks made by holocaust survivors stunned when they confronted their tormentors face-to-face in courtrooms at Nuremberg: 'he looks so normal,' they marveled, 'so unlike the monster I remember!' I recalled Nazi hunter Ellie Wiesel's remark about the 'banality of evil', Churchill's warning that 'those who do not study history are doomed to repeated it', and the surprising result of a DNA test presented to me by ex-wife, Jennifer, confirming her suspicion that upbringing notwithstanding I was 'really Jewish' and 'not Catholic at all', each a prelude to the seminal questions that weighed upon me like the rising water behind a dam: What if Kurtz was right? What if America wasn't the paragon of virtue we believed it to be? What if there was a direct link between Mengele's 'slaughter machine' experiments and the 'high risk, high reward' research being carried out at Princeton University?

I bucketed up in my bed, mind feverish as it navigated the backwater reaches leading from Auschwitz to Argentina to Princeton feeling a fatigue not unlike that of a wounded animal that pauses, blood dripping, gathering itself to climb one more hill. Daylight spilled in from my bedroom window. Its rays caught the polished surface of the ID bracelet on the night table beside me. I watched it glimmer, diamond-like, recalling my tryst in Paris with Amy, our love making, and how we were back together again.

Yes, I resolved then, easing my head back onto the pillow studying the random play of city lights across the ceiling, Paris, is what I wanted to think about: the **FERRIS WHEEL** where Amy first swore her love to me, our sprint through the rain to that sidewalk cafe with the red, white and blue portico, the **PREACHER** thundering down from his pulpit in that clapboard church! Yes, I needed to think about those things, I suddenly understood, body lifting above the bed and into the clouds as I sailed weightless on the good ship Morphine.

NOW I am traversing the epochs of time. My eyes raise to meet the half-formed specter of Mafia chieftain, Bill Bonanno, long dead, standing at my bedside staring at me from out of the cosmic darkness.

"Bill?"

"Yeah, it's me."

"What do you want?"

"I seen all kinds a guys, Jack," he tells me, voice crackling as with a defective satellite connection. "Guys who kill and like killing. But not like this. Never like him."

I search the empty space in front of me.

"What are you trying to tell me, Bill?"

"A warning to you, Jackie, for the friendship and prayers," he cautions. "Stay the fuck away from this one!"

Taken aback, I watch Bonnano vanish, rarify into thin air, as if he never existed in this world or any other. But it's not answers I need, I realize then, *it's prayers* because now I am standing face-to-face with the killer, more 'thing' than person, more 'monster' than serial murderer!

> *voices*
> *seeping into my head*
> *"open silent messaging"*
> *i am there!*

The washtub's chrome faucet resembles the snow-white neck of a swan rising up from out of the basic plumbing then curving delicately over the tub itself where his victim sits short, stubby legs hanging over the outer edge.

Her eyes are bugged, hysterical, as she stares at the predator confronting her as few ever have, face-to-face, as he glares down at her, amused.

Paralyzed by precise injections of succinylcholine chloride except for involuntary behaviors such as breathing and heartbeat, the geneticist-virologist can only watch, her body incapable of voluntary motion, as he sets about his work like the master surgeon he is, unpacking instruments; offering his own hellish version of bedside manner while music of the Lost Generation plays lavishly in the background.

She cannot speak, but her mind has risen to a level of horror that allows communication without words through eye contact (the eyes were bulging) and skin color (it was raging pink) and smell (was there an adjective to describe the odor of saturate terror?). But these are all elements of the program, the killer savors,

tapping his foot to the mellifluous crooning of a teenaged Sina-
tra as he singing "Love of my Life", the Big Band sound of the
Tommy Dorsey big-sound orchestra booming behind him.

"'You are the love of my life!' isn't that what they all say? Isn't
that what you Americans sing about so much of the time 'love'? Or is
it modern rap music from Nigger ghettoes you prefer? 'Street music',
isn't that what you call it?" he asks unfurling an egg-shaped circle
of thin, catheter tubing, a number 10 lumen hanging from the end
of it like the wide-open fangs of a cobra. "To me, these words have a
different meaning entirely. 'I love to see you suffer. I love to see you
anguish in pain', oh-so-interested, over what I am going to do to
you next. It gives me great pleasure, you see," he patiently explains,
pushing his face forward. "Well, let me give you a hint," he taunts,
his hot, rank breath tumbling down onto her like a blast of air from
the bowels of Hell, "I despise ballerinas."

He takes a half step back, then smiling reaches for a pair of
surgical bone scissors and cuts loose the pink brooch along with a
lock of hair.

"Now, that wasn't so bad, was it?" he asks, watching them
tumble as in slow motion from head-to-shoulder down onto the
floor. But then adds menacingly, "This time, it was the ballerina,"
as he unravels the remainder of tubing, lining up a series of half-
pint glass bottles on the floor beneath her dangling legs.

He taps his right foot with bravado, turning awkwardly in a
circle to the beat of the music, right arm hoisted above him in some
bizarre imitation of a Spanish flamenco dancer.

> *'You are my love,*
> *The dream I've been waiting for,*
> *The kiss I've been longing for,*
> *You are my love,*
> *The l-love of my life!'*

The predator stops, then stares bold-faced at her as Gene Kru-pa's "Sing, Sing, Sing," blares, drums beating tribal, from out of Sennheiser speakers.

"You don't like the romantic numbers, do you?" he dares to wonder. "Figures," he rumbles disgustedly, rolling up the left sleeve of her white Kohl's blouse, finding the radial artery above the thumb, then shoving the sharp, knife-like lumen into it.

Her eyes widen in panic.

"Scared?" he asks, watching the steady stream of red blood fill the tube then track down through the open lip of a half-pint specimen bottle. "Not to worry," he says in mock-comfort. "The fun is just beginning because I've got lots of surprises in store for you." He bends slightly drawing hands over mouth then, unable to contain himself, roars confirmation with a madman's glee, "Yes-sah! We gonna have fun tonight. Yes! We gonna play with your innards. Yes! Tonight we gonna suspend all the rules; all the conventions of those small-minded idiots who tell everyone what to do and how to do it!"

Again, he thrusts his face forward staring deep into her eyes, bulged and racing, then feigning disappointment, says, "You know, I don't think you're having a very good time so far, am I right?"

He frowns, reaches for the surgical bone scissors once more. He holds, fondles her left hand and snips off her pinky like a twig from a bush that needs pruning.

The pasty-white digit spins to the floor now simply a 'thing'; an anatomical curiosity, separate and apart from the body as it was, and a 'finger' no longer. As anticipated, the bleeding, with five bottles already filled, is negligible. A fact not wasted on her surgeon.

He holds the pale, white stub of his victim's left hand up so that he can examine the extent of hemorrhage watching as it

diminishes with each heartbeat, every surge of blood flowing out
through the catheter.

"Very nice," he observes, gently placing the hand down onto
her leg, taking a step toward a black duffle bag from out of which
he produces a battery operated Blount and Davis orthopedic cir-
cular saw.

He flicks off the safety lock and depresses the trigger starting
the circular blade buzzing with a strident whine. He turns to the
geneticist-virologist and starts it again watching as her eyes, set
like sparkling gems amid her catatonic deadpan, shimmer ever
deeper with the hollow emptiness of consummate horror.

His face brightens as he edges the blazing circular saw closer
toward his subject's left humerus.

"Und now it ist show time, Dr. Kurtz!" he announces, his
razor-sharp, stainless steel teeth now extended beyond his jawline,
uncaring of his German accent any longer, "WELCOME TO
HELL!"

> **static static**
> **man's voice**
> **static static**
> **"close silent message"**

To say I awoke in a cold sweat as if jolted by the third
rail of a subway would not capture the degree of horror
that gripped me at that moment. Truly, I did not know
where I was, not even who I was, eyes darting madly around
the room in search of an anchor, any familiar thing, to
ground me!

Panting like a runner come off a marathon, I deserted
my bed—was it my coffin?—and padded into the adjoin-
ing room where a bottle of Jameson's beckoned. I tore the

cork from the bottle, luxuriated in a long desperate gulp. *Nightmare* was the first word that came to mind as I lowered the bottle from my lips, filling my lungs deep with the smoky amalgam of oxygen and booze, blowing it out like a blacksmith's bellows. Christ Almighty! What I'd seen was sacrilegious, a massacre beyond human comprehension! I was thinking as I plucked my iPhone from the counter.

Body quaking, I dialed Amy's cell.

"Jack?"

"Yeah, where are you?"

"I'm in my trailer between takes, honey. Is something wrong?"

Maybe it was the question, so straight forward, or her tone of voice, so grounded, but it caused me to take stock of myself. A dream? A fucking nightmare? This is your problem?

"No, nothing," I lied. "I had a nightmare," I said, ruefully. "Are you filming?"

"Yes! It's called "Twisted", Jack! And guess who's my leading man?"

"Lon Chaney, Jr.?"

"No, silly! It's Josh Brolin. He's been in back-to-back hits and I'm playing opposite him. See, he's a Brooklyn cop chasing down a terrorist cell that's infiltrated Wall Street," she enthused blonde hair tussled, I imagined, amber eyes wide with excitement. "They say this could be my breakout role! My chance, you know, for an award . . ."

I listened as best I could, still fixated on the abomination I'd witnessed, driven like a steel spike into my brain.

"Want to hear a Hollywood story?" I asked.

"Sure, Jackie, but I got to go back to work, you know . . ."

"It's about a director I knew who after his film was

wrapped couldn't stop living with the camera and crew and actors," I explained. "Everyone had left for their respective lives, but he'd awaken every night with fresh commands. 'Lawrence, we have to reshoot the chase sequence today. Tell Production it's a hundred extras at least!' He would be out of bed and shaving before he'd say to himself, 'The movie is over. You have gone mad. You can't shoot anymore.' But, as he explained to me, he'd stepped through the looking glass. The film was more real than his life. Sometimes I think I'm like that director," I confessed. "Sometimes I feel like I'm losing it, Amy, like I'm on a runaway train headed for some cold, dark place where I'll be banished forever, and it scares the shit out of me."

"You know, I worry about you, Jackie, about your," she struggled for the word, "stability. Yeah, sure, I may be a little crazy, but you?"

"You mean the nightmares?"

"I mean you, Jack! Everything about you! If we're going to get serious, there are things we need to know about each other," she said, her voice trailing off to a hollow whisper. "A long time ago I had an abortion. I knew about the baby in Paris . . ."

"Jesus, Amy, why didn't you tell me!"

"Because you weren't ready," she answered more calm than I'd ever heard her speak. "It was my fault, not yours. You didn't want a baby. You probably never really wanted me. Not the way I wanted you. So I had an abortion."

"My God . . ."

"Then I got depressed. In that order: I got pregnant, I left you, I got an abortion, I got depressed. But somewhere between stages three and four, I prayed for forgiveness and pledged my life to God. Now I talk to Him all the time, unlimited minutes," she joked sadly. "Fact is, I'm a junky, Jack, have been for a long time."

"Yeah, I know," I told her. "It was China White, not coke, you were doing at the hospital that night, wasn't it?"

"God knows my heart!" she countered. "He knows I do the best I can! But I do love you, Jack. I did back in Paris and I still do now." There was a drawn pause during which I imagined her leaning over a table in her trailer snorting a white line, head bobbing up, bright and hopeful. "Oh, Jack, let's just go on like this forever and not worry, wouldn't that just be Heaven? To make love and do exactly what we want and not be afraid anymore?"

"Yeah, it would," I answered trying my best to replicate her enthusiasm. "Look, it sounds like you're on a roll with Brolin. How 'bout you come over to the Elysee tonight? I promise a good steak, a bottle of wine, and pair of open arms will be waiting, no questions asked."

Amy agreed, but what she'd confided made me afraid, and it was tangible fear, as if the moment I left my hotel room the buried corpses of half the world would be laying outside my door. And during that moment of reflection, I couldn't think of Amy or of myself or anything but flesh, and flesh came into my mind, bursting flesh, rotting flesh, flesh hung on spikes in butcher stalls, flesh burning, flesh gone to blood.

Chapter Eleven

Forrestal Campus
Princeton, New Jersey

With one eye open, I peeked at the digital clock on the night stand. *3 a.m.*, I groaned, after four hours of roiling slumber. Marjorie Kurtz had chosen an odd time to meet, rivaled only by the location: Forrestal campus where five stories below Princeton's Tokamak fusion reactor she claimed radical experiments were being carried out on human subjects under the aegis of DARPA.

Outside a winter storm had swept in from the Atlantic bringing with it massive peals of thunder and pitiless fits of lightning that shook the Elysee's foundation and lit my suite filling it with an odor not unlike burning ozone. I drifted dazedly from out of bed, threw on a pair of jeans and *NY Yankee* jersey, a sense of foreboding mounting at the outer fringes of my consciousness. Was it possible Kurtz had chosen this dark and lonely hour to visit the Tactical Technology laboratories so I could see the result of ALATON's applied research with my own eyes? If so, given the far-flung objectives of their GRIN experiments there was much to consider, I speculated, drifting like a sleepwalker into my Vette and taking it through the Lincoln Tunnel.

First, it would be more than foolish for her to invite me inside a top secret military facility under false pretenses, it was a federal crime. Second, for a man purporting a lack of interest in her case, it seemed goddamned crazy to find myself on the Jersey Turnpike cruising into a juggernaut my gut was telling me could only end in disaster.

So why do it? I asked myself arriving at a simple conclusion that despite misgivings I did care. Maybe it was reading the testimony of Auschwitz survivors, or the irresistible allure of danger this strange and arcane case presented, but like a terrier my instincts told me I was pursuing something much larger than two random suicides at an upscale university town in Jersey. What that was, I dared not imagine, but believed to my soul it was somehow important to me, Kurtz, and the thousands of victims murdered, and worse, by the geneticist-monster Josef Mengele.

I slowed the Vette as the Plasma Physics Laboratory came into view feeling every ounce of the weight of my decision. Turning off Rt. 1, I pulled the car into the visitors' lot remembering the history of James Forrestal for whom the 825 acre campus had been named. After graduating from Princeton, he served along with classmate Allen Dulles in the Army Intelligence Corps and was instrumental in organizing the CIA. In 1947, he was appointed Secretary of State, but never finished his term because on a bleak winter's night in 1949, James Forrestal ended his career and his life leaping from the fourteenth floor window of a Washington, D.C. hospital.

I left the Vette for the PPL wondering if there was something in the soul of Princeton University responsible for these tragedies; something predatory beneath its veneer that could do irreparable damage to a person before they ever knew it happened: sometimes I wondered if it wasn't happening to me.

The Princeton Plasma Laboratory was constructed in the style of the Pentagon in Washington, D.C., square and stolid, like six huge slabs of concrete, steel, and two-inch thick plate glass pancaked atop one another. The reason, I suspected after being buzzed into the lobby, had as much to do with secrecy as security. With nearly 500,000 square feet of space and 850 permanent employees it seemed more futuristic city than university R&D center; a city crowned by the 219,000 square foot Tokamak nuclear fusion reactor that once perfected would generate millions of megawatts of electricity to the Tri-State area.

I approached the Security desk. Its back wall was a bank of closed-circuit monitors with camera hook-ups that peered into every entrance, hallway, and elevator going up six floors but down only three, stopping five short of Level 8 where Kurtz claimed ALATON carried out its high-risk, high-reward experiments.

"My name's Jack Madson," I told the guard, who looked ex-military.

"Okay, Mr. Madson. Smile for the camera," he sang-out snapping my photo. "Now press your palm down onto the glass pad and sign in," he said motioning toward a VERIFI scanner, "and I'll have someone take you to Dr. Kurtz' laboratory. She's expecting you."

After I finished, an Intel type in a blue blazer escorted me to a bank of elevators. He slipped his security card into the UNIX recognition device and down we descended, Levels 1, 2, 3, exiting into a wide corridor overlooking the ITER reactor. Standing five stories high with sprawling nests of stainless steel transfer coils and giant electro-magnets, I knew now what Kurtz meant when she talked about "hiding in plain sight" as I was escorted to a second bank of elevators, the detached eye of surveillance cameras glaring down at us from every imaginable angle.

The government's work on Tokamak had been declassified years earlier allowing an open exchange of technology between the U.S. and other countries. What the DOD left out of their media spin was that, shielded by Tokamak, "black project" research went on 24/7 in laboratories five stories below while grammar school science classes toured the facility five days a week!

Again, we descended — this time to Levels 4, 5, 6, 7, 8 — which judging by the length of the ride were embedded significantly deeper than the first three.

"Come with me," the man in the blue blazer said. "We're going to Level 8 Security where Hallary will take you to the TT labs."

I nodded then followed him to a stop-and-search station where a white-haired guard with an overspill of paunch and hint of a Irish brogue waited.

"Mr. Madson," he said greeting me like a man unused to new faces, "you've been cleared. Dr. Kurtz is waiting down the hall, Lab 3, on the right."

So this was Level 8, the nerve center for MAYHEM, I was thinking as I stalked down the deserted corridor arriving at a heavy-gauge steel door marked 'Tactical Technology, LAB 3'. I rapped on it and stood waiting for a response. When none came, I pulled the door open and stepped into the dimly lit chamber, staggered, as if struck by a physical blow!

I clamped my eyes shut then opened them a second time unable to comprehend what I'd first seen and now had no choice but to accept. My feet slid forward as if shod with iron. The steel door slammed shut behind me and at that moment I felt like I was standing at the edge of the universe, vertiginous, as I contemplated the carnage that confronted me: floors, walls, even the laboratory ceiling, splattered with blood, bone, and human brain tissue, my mind sent reeling into a kaleidoscope of possibilities, what man, *what thing*, was capable of such an abomination?

My eyes dropped to the floor where Marjorie Kurtz' body lay in ruins, arms, legs, head detached, bone-white torso—once parts of a human being—now shriveled things completely drained of blood. I heard a rustling sound and turned instinctively catching sight of an indistinguishable figure lurking in the darkened tunnel leading to Lab 4 and Lab 5. Our eyes searched one another's, the killer's chilling gaze drilled deadly, grim, and unblinking into my own. Then, before I could give chase, or even call out after him, he vanished with the stealth of a feral animal into the shadows!

As a guy who'd seen his share of savagery—axe murders, child killers, shotgun suicides—I can tell you, the experience of confronting what I saw that night rattled me to the core, my surroundings a virtual slaughter house raised from the depths of Hell, I began to realize, as my eyes raked over the contents of Kurtz' laboratory and shock gave way to disbelief: brains floating in oversized beakers, electrodes attached to temporal lobes with wires leading refrigerator-sized CDC Cyber computers monitoring the thoughts of still living human beings; long, tube-shaped vessels containing multiple iterations of humanoid specimens suspended in clear liquid some dead, others still breathing, wintry blue eyes coated in yellowish membrane seeing — watching me — some with no eyes at all!

"Motherfuckers!" my screams rang-out through the empty corridors. "Cock sucking bastards!" I bellowed at the top of my lungs as I absorbed all that was real and surreal around me, a mounting desire to tear that man, the killer I'd encountered, apart with my bare hands in a righteous battle for all that was sacred. I staggered backward and it was like standing at the intersection of competing universes, emotions sweeping past me like bullet trains: revulsion, fear, anger, relief.

Why was I still alive? I wondered, staring balefully at what was left of Marjorie Kurtz. Armed with the element of surprise and — I had to believe — an arsenal of weapons, the madman chose to flee. Why? The question kept repeating like the lyric from a defective recording until a flashing icon on the screen of Kurtz' computer, not ten feet from her, caught my eye.

Warily, I gravitated forward, my footsteps coming to a halt as I studied the icon of a hooded executioner — cyber identity 'DARK ANGEL' — flashing on the screen daring me to engage whoever, or whatever, was responsible for the desecration that lay at my feet.

With feelings of shock and fear subsumed by an overwhelming sense of outrage, I shoved my finger hard down onto the icon, astounded to hear the sound of Nat King Cole's "Paper Moon" swirling large and eerily upbeat through the concrete and steel labyrinth, a video of Kurtz' slaughter playing out on the computer screen, exactly as it happened in the 'vision' I'd experienced twenty-four hours before!

I jerked my head away, turning from the moment-to-moment dissection of a living breathing human being, eyes catching sight of a white envelope atop Kurtz' work bench. Feverish with anticipation–video still visible on the monitor, music sweeping through the corridors—I tore the envelope open. In it was a stack of twenty dollar bills, one hundred to be exact, totaling twenty thousand dollars, along with a typewritten note. "If you don't stop him, he will go on forever," it read, the fleeting image of bodies piled high in Nazi death camps passing like a dark shadow through my mind as my sodden gaze diverted back to Kurtz.

Pulse racing, brain throbbing at levels of concentration that could only be described as manic I edged toward the scattered remnants of flayed flesh and mangled bone kneeling beside it. Then, with an intensity so focused as to be reverent, I took Kurtz' head into my hands. Carved with meticulous precision, raw and deep into her forehead, were just two words. "SMALL MIND", I uttered, aware now of a trail of bloody footsteps leading away from the laboratory to a gray steel door marked 'maintenance'.

Drawing from a reservoir of strength beyond my 6' 1", 190 pound body, I took hold of a metal stool and snapped off one of its legs trudging with murderous intent toward the maintenance room. Right hand raised shoulder-high with makeshift weapon clasped tight in my grip, I turned the door knob and flicked on the light.

Dangling from a wire in the center of the ceiling, a naked light bulb cast an eerie saffron glow upon equipment hung from hooks on the walls around me—hammers, wrenches, a hand saw—their outlines incandescent like detritus broke loose from another dimension as ghost-like I drifted toward a rack clung to the far wall feeling suddenly lightheaded, the air sucked from out of my lungs the instant I saw it. Stacked in neat configurations on the painted metal shelf were thirty half-pint bottles.

They contained Marjorie Kurtz' entire blood supply.

Chapter Twelve

Elysee Hotel
Manhattan, New York

The ride back into the city was fractured and dream-like, *bad dream-like,* and I swear if someone adminis-tered a lie detector test to determine what I'd seen along the way the word 'nothing' would stand up to expert scrutiny. I remembered doubling back to retrieve Kurtz' UNIX card and downloading the video of her murder onto a thumb drive, shocked that when I emerged not a living soul awaited me: not Hallary, not even the gaggle of Security who huddled like vultures over the closed-circuit monitors. Then, bursting from the building like a trapped miner escaped into daylight, I left the barbarity of the PPL behind running breathless to the sanctuary of my car!

Standing outside the door to my suite at the Elysee ninety minutes later, hands shaking as I fumbled with the key to enter, I had to stop and catch my breath at the sight of Amy sitting, *soo* sexy-casual, on the divan wearing horn-rimmed glasses, and a black negligee, perusing a loose-leaf notebook.

"Christ, you look good enough to eat," I marveled, as relieved to be back in my suite as I was happy to see her curled up on the futon, long legs tucked beneath her, a shock of stray blonde hair swept down over her forehead. Then, recognizing my diary, I lurched forward, "Hey! That's mine!"

Amy reared back, taking the book to her breasts. "It's just your notes. The ones you already told me about! They're like pieces to a puzzle about . . . your dreams . . . your feelings. Oh, my poor Jack," she gasped, "why would you think these thoughts!"

"All right, I'm fucked-up, okay?" I seethed, snatching the diary back from her. "But those are *my* thoughts, *my* feelings, not yours!"

"I'm sorry!" Amy pouted. "It's just that I care about you. Is there something wrong with caring about someone in this crazy world? To give a damn whether they live or die or if they're even happy?"

I trundled to the bar, poured myself a drink then took the thumb drive from my pocket rolling it in my palm.

"There's more to it than just that diary," I confessed, turning back to her. "You see, I live with those thoughts, Amy, or maybe they live with me. Honestly, I can't tell anymore, but they're always there, inside my head, and they never go away! Nightmares, entire scenarios, that creep into my mind like assassins in the night, so visual, so fucking real, most too horrible to put into words. And the headaches that come along for the ride?" I laughed sardonically, "Like the Fourth of July fireworks celebrated in my head every night! I thought it might help to commit them to paper, allow me to remember more detail, possibly find out what it is that's brought them on with such ferocity."

"Does the way you're feeling have anything to do with

that?" she asked, eyes shifting to the thumb drive. "Is it that thig-a-majiggy got you so upset?"

"All part of the same nightmare," I snickered.

"I want to see it!"

"No you don't," I said holding the thumb drive up like a shaman brandishing a satanic totem. "It's a video of the murder. I've seen it twice now. Once in a vision like the ones I told you about; the second on this video recorded by the killer."

"If it's what you dreamed, I want to see it, too, Jackie. I love you!"

I didn't answer but walked to the laptop and slapped the thumb drive in. Then, grim as a midwife presenting a mongoloid monster to its mother, I carried the computer to her, Nat Cole's "Paper Moon" bounding from out of its miniature speakers while, flesh crawling, Amy watched the surgical dismemberment of Marjorie Kurtz' body, limb-by-limb, the victim's eyes popped from their sockets, speechless, still alive, and feeling.

"Why didn't he kill me when he had the chance?" I brooded, still tormented by my encounter with the killer, the depravity of all that Amy was seeing sweeping through the room like an icy wind.

"Stop it," Amy said.

"He had me dead to rights and let me fucking walk! Why would he do that?"

"Stop it . . ." she repeated. *"Stop the fucking video now, Jack!"* she shrieked, amber eyes darting up at me like arrows shot from a crossbow.

"I'm sorry," I blustered, finger plunging down onto the 'power' button. "I don't know what I was thinking, didn't realize I was even talking, for Christ's sake. Are you okay?"

But Amy didn't answer. Instead, I watched as her eyes dropped from the screen to the spot where I was standing.

"What's that, Jackie?"

"What?"

"The shiny thingy stuck to the bottom of your shoe. It looks like a claw," she said, plucking it from the sole of my Adidas', "or a tooth from the mouth of some kinda animal."

"No, wait! It might be something I carried with me from out of Kurtz' laboratory! Here," I said, pointing to a box of Kleenex. "Use a tissue, there may be prints or DNA evidence on it."

She plucked the stainless steel talon from out of my shoe then examining it with the wide-eyed wonder of an archeologist come upon an artifact from an alien civilization, meticulously crafted, skillfully honed to razor sharpness.

"There's no living creature—no human, no animal, not even a predator from the wild—that has a tooth like that. This was manufactured. Curved back and serrated. Designed to cut and tear and rip apart . . ." I marveled, stopping mid-sentence to listen to the muffled sound of footsteps outside the door.

Amy cast me a quizzical stare, our eyes met then like worlds colliding everything seemed to happen at once as a team of FBI and Homeland Security agents—four wielding shotguns and semi-automatics, the fifth with search warrant held high in the air—burst into my hotel suite, Tommy Gifford, Princeton Police, trailing a half-step behind.

"Mr. John Madson, I'm Special-Agent-in-Charge Coscarelli, Federal Bureau of Investigations," he announced as his team branched-out into every room turning over mattresses, ripping drawers from their sockets, tearing through the clothes in my closets. "This warrant, issued by the 3rd District Court, gives us authority to search these premises for evidence removed from a crime scene at the Plasma Physics Laboratory, Princeton, New Jersey earlier today."

"There's nothing here!" I fumed, allowing Amy time to shove the tissue-covered object inside her panties. "No drugs! No stolen merchandise! So exactly what evidence are you looking for, Coscarelli?"

"Mr. Madson, I suggest you take a deep breath and sit down," he advised, handing the warrant over. "If everything is like you say, we can all be watching the Giants-Dallas game this afternoon like none of this ever happened."

With that he stalked away to join his subordinates as they savaged the place, leaving Gifford to keep us company.

"I thought a crime had to be interstate to drag the Feds into it," I called-out after him, "or is storming the private residence of an American citizen like a Nazis Wolf Pack now allowed by the Patriot Act?"

"That's right, Madson," Gifford chuckled, "and the NSA don't tap Americans' phones or e-mails, neither. Now why don't you just sit in the corner with your movie star girlfriend and shut up!" Then looking to Amy, he added, "No offense, Miss Channing, but what were you thinking when you decided to share a toothbrush with this guy?"

After what seemed like half a day, the Feds departed having found nothing more than the doctor prescribed meds I took daily to keep me afloat leaving Gifford behind

looking marooned as a beached whale in the raid's aftermath.

"Want a drink?" I asked.

He glanced at his watch, "Yeah, what the hell. I'm off
the clock."

I poured three-fingers of scotch, no soda-no ice.
"Thirsty, Baby?" I asked Amy.

"What'd ring my bell is a line of blow," she giggled, suddenly serious again at the sight of Gifford's vexed expression, "or maybe a teeny-tiny whiskey," she measured with
her thumb and forefinger.

Gifford must have had a rough day judging by the way
he slugged down his first whiskey.

"You know, I pulled your rap sheet from NCIC, Madson. It's all there," he said wiping his mouth dry with the
side of his hand, "how you married into money, parlayed it
into a Wall Street job in your father-in-law's company," he
went on, trying to contain his amusement, "stole a shitload
of high-tech pharmaceutical formulas, sold them to the
Chinese, faked your death in a boat accident, then took
off for Mexico."

"Yeah?"

"Then, the Triad rips you off, beats you to a pulp in
a back alley, leave you for dead, and what does Jack Madson do?" he asked, a roll of laughter erupting. "He goes
back to Manhattan with his black whore girlfriend, breaks
into NuGen headquarters and kills a guard while downloading even more valuable high-tech info so he can sell
it to another Chinese gang!" Gifford shook his head, still
laughing. "I swear, Madson, you kill me, really, you do!"

"I'm glad you find my life so amusing, Lieutenant," I
observed taking a sip from my glass. "I was sure Coscarelli

would be taking me downtown after they finished search-ing the place."

"The Feds came snooping around headquarters ask-ing questions about Mary Linda and a phone call the NSA supposedly intercepted between you and Kurtz. Next thing I know we're off to the races, me along with them. I knew it was a fool's errand, but like they say, nobody ever lost a bet underestimating the FBI."

"They knew I was at the PPL this morning and didn't arrest me?"

"Sorry to disappoint you, Madson. Kurtz was dead long before you set foot in that laboratory, but I guess you're not much on the internet. The killer posted a video — Deep Web — minutes after the murder using the cyber identity 'Dark Angel.'"

"Do they know what he looks like?" Amy asked hope-fully.

"Killer must have known his way around the building, Miss Channing. He disabled security cameras and sub-stituted his own! Even knew the evacuation procedures in case one day that 'cold fusion' reactor they got over there gets 'hot'. Called in a 'Code 3' alert that cleared the place which is why your ass is still here and not downtown in an FBI interrogation room," he added, eyes lifting to meet mine. "All they know about you, Madson, is that you went to see her at the PPL this morning. Everything else, very *hush-hush*," he mocked with the ghost of a smile. "They don't want publicity even from you! So far as I can tell, CIA's taken the case over. From there, who knows? 'Spooks', isn't that what they call them? Guess that's because once they're finished, it's like none of what went on ever happened!"

"Another whiskey, Lieutenant?" Amy asked making her way slow and sexy across the room, bottle in hand.

"Hell, yeah, why not?" Gifford answered, holding his glass out to her. "You know, I shouldn't be tellin' you this, Madson, but if I didn't know better, I'd swear Dr. Kurtz was killed by some kind of animal, a wolf, or pack of wild dogs." He sucked down the contents of his glass in a swallow. "Her flesh was eaten, man! If you can believe it that thing, whatever it is, opened up her abdomen, removed the organs, and made a meal of her goddamned intestines! Now, you used to be a cop, transported federal prisoners — tough guys, maniacs. You ever heard of somethin' like that in Princeton or any other goddamned place?"

But I didn't need Gifford to give me details about what went on in Lab 3 that night, nor did Amy. We'd both watched the killer's gruesome ritual; me, in the vision I'd had twenty-four hours earlier; Amy, on the video he'd posted on the Deep Web, untraceable, under the pseudonym, "DARK ANGEL".

Later that night, asleep with Amy held tight in my arms, the phone rang less welcome than a second cousin at one's doorstep. It was Eddie Lawler calling from his seaside retreat in St. John's.

"What the fuck's goin' on out there, Jackie?" Eddie shouted. "This Dark Angel video's goin' viral!"

"So I hear," I said, glancing to Amy as she turned to the opposite side of the bed.

"How could this happen? It was a suicide, Jack. That's the gig I got you. You look over reports, you nod your head in the affirmative, you shake the Chief Detective's hand, and you get your ass home!"

"So why'd you sic Kurtz on me? Why get me involved in that nightmare if you wanted me in-and-out so bad?"

"She's a 'crazy', man! Met her at a party in Georgetown two years ago and she hasn't stopped calling me since. I figured you'd see through her paranoid bullshit wearin' a fucking blindfold! I never thought you'd take her on as a client!"

"Yeah, well, I didn't, Eddie. I turned her down then a day later find her dead, blood drained, body cut to pieces and, fuck's sake, I don't think I know the depth of the shit I've gotten myself into yet!"

"Okay, okay, no need to get excited," the little man cajoled. "Let me talk to some people who know some people, see what I come up with and get back to you, you good with that?"

"Yeah, Ed, I'm good with it," I retorted, a sense of resolve rising like a violent storm within me. "But one way or the other, you know I'm not leaving Princeton until I get the motherfucker who snuffed her!"

Chapter Thirteen

Forrestal Campus
PPL Complex, Level 5
Princeton, New Jersey

My night was long and restless despite hours of the most passionate lovemaking Amy and I had ever shared. Frenzied at first like our bodies were locked in mortal combat battling to see which would devour the other, lips, tongues, arms, hair. Then, once sated, it was different with bodies, minds, souls subsumed one into the other until there seemed no distinction between us; only the feeling like a vibration passing flesh to flesh until we lay on the bed in a tangle of white sheets knowing that as the vibration between us subsided it had not gone away but become part of us forever.

These were the thoughts shambling through my brain that morning as Hollywood bad girl Amy Caulfield *aka* Coco Channing, ambitious starlet, drug-addicted love goddess to millions, lay sleeping beside me until like a haunting, reality's phantoms returned to possess me. "Do you know what it feels like to be a kid who's unwanted?" Amy once asked me, I remembered, gazing as moonstruck as any fan upon her eyes, nose, mouth so beautifully proportioned, skin white as marble, and lips so inviting. "I think I might," I answered with the unattended sorrow of one amputee confiding his loss to another, "but tell me, I want to know." "It feels like you drowned and are dead," she told me, "and that you've been floating underwater in a dark cold ocean for a long, long time and the sea has washed-out all the feelings that other kids have inside but you don't. Only you're still walking around smiling and playing and looking like the others, but you know you're not like them and never will be again because the ocean has left you forsaken, as abandoned and alone as Jesus on that hillside nailed to a cross."

Now it was true that Amy was an actress, I contemplated, extricating myself from our bed, quietly dressing. Still, it was also a fact that her mother, a failed singer, and father, a convicted drug dealer, had unceremoniously handed her off to a Sisters of Charity orphanage in St. Louis after which she'd passed through no fewer than four foster homes. True also, I believed, was the vacuum that remained in the hearts of abused children, beaten and worse, by alcoholic or drug-addicted parents. And, certainly, Amy was a victim of that, finding succor both fierce and sublime in the false security of three marriages in the arms of scumbags not unlike her dad, eager to sexually gratify men, and sometimes women if the *Inquirer* was to be believed, in order to fill that void. The question for me was not who between us needed a psychiatrist, I ventured, chuckling to myself as I exited the hotel for the cobalt light of dawn, but who needed one more desperately, Amy or me?

Once arrived at Forrestal, I approached the PPL complex, pace growing slower with every step. When I reached its doors, I looked up at the drizzling sky searching for the dawn that had somehow been misplaced and the crime scene I expected to find. But the flashing red lights of squad cars were missing, so were the crime scene demarcations, mobile forensic units, technicians, cameras and reporters, stridencies blended into the predictable chaos I'd witnessed so many times before. But, no, there were none of those just the building stark and intimidating, its droves of employees rushing to beat the clock and the wet slick of the pavement beneath my feet.

I entered the lobby feeling like I was walking in a dream. And I must have looked exactly that way, stunned by the absence of activity or recognition that one of their own, a globally recognized, PhD geneticist who'd worked amongst them had been slaughtered in this very building.

"Mr. Madson!" I heard a man's voice call out.

I looked across the lobby to the security desk where a nervous-looking man dressed in a white lab coat stood clipboard in hand.

"My name is John Fetters. I work for ALATON as Managing Director, Tactical Technology," he said extending his hand.

Reluctantly, I accepted, "Does ALATON even exist here? Is there such thing as a Tactical Technology department?"

Fetters brought a hand to his mouth conscious of his bad teeth as he laughed, "It's like that here, but you get used to it," he explained. "Dr. Lindstrom, our Senior VP-Technology suggested you might be stopping by. I just finished arranging clearance for our VIP tour, normally reserved for top military brass. You should be flattered."

"That's a joke, right? You know what happened yesterday, don't you? Besides, what would make anyone think I'd be coming here this morning?"

"Dr. Lindstrom's specialty is behavioral predictability. Fact is, he pioneered its functional application years before B.F. Skinner ever considered writing *Beyond Human Freedom and Dignity.*"

"I'm guessing that title won't be on the shelves at Newark Airport?" I asked just to fuck with him.

Fetters digested the remark, a glint of recognition in his eyes before they reverted, deadly and calculating, "I can see that you're a jokester, Mr. Madson, but I'd wager when the chips are down, you're a serious man."

"Is that your professional opinion?"

"Strictly personal," he answered, turning as I followed. "I'm a bio-engineer, not a shrink. Freud, Pavlov, Skinner, all the same to me. Even Dr. Lindstrom prefers hard science. That's where his true genius lies. *Functionality*, putting divergent disciplines together — genetics, robotics, intelligence, nano technology — to achieve practical application."

"Military application?" I suggested, entering the elevator.

"Sometimes, no mostly," he admitted entering his UNIX card, pressing the number 5. "I'll be taking you to Level 5 where you can see the work that goes on here."

"What about Level 8? Will I get to see Marjorie Kurtz' body parts packed neatly into a sandwich bag inside some refrigerator for storage?"

"Dr. Kurtz had been acting strangely. Stress, I suppose," he said, shrugging, "but yesterday she left on sabbatical for a walkabout in the Australian bush. Six months of viewing Aboriginal cave paintings in Pilbara would probably do any of us a lot of good. As for the other," he chided looking up from his clipboard, eyes sly and jittery, "maybe you know this or maybe it was just another of your jokes, but there is no Level 8 in this building. Despite the phony video tapes DARPA conspiracy theorists have been pandering on the internet, Level 8 does not exist."

"Look, I didn't come here to debate. Truth be told, I'm not sure why I'm here except to scratch an itch I can't get at, but like Hemingway wrote 'No hay remedio!' Maybe there is no cure for the questions that have been eating away at me, so let's take your tour, see if it gives me some *functional* relief."

Again, that trill of a laugh as Fetters tucked his clipboard under his arm turning to a saucer-shaped platform that seemed like something out of a Philip K. Dick novel. Standing atop it, frozen mid-gesture, was ALATON's Chairman and Founder, Elon Jacobus Powers, dressed in a Chanel business suit looking so life-like I had to stop myself from taking a step forward to introduce myself. On a monorail behind the entrepreneur-genius stood a train of cars, immobile now, with robotic tour guide smiling invitingly, hand raised in salutation as he stood rigid, locked in time until reactivated.

"The display in front of us is where our tour begins with Elon welcoming his guests. Of course it's a hologram but most start believing he's real sixty seconds into his presentation. Behind Mr. Powers is the monorail that takes visitors through a series of exhibits, a kind of Disneyland on steroids that features the DOD work we're engaged in: demonstrations of special forces confronting the enemy with rapid deployment warships, robotics ranging from call girl interrogators to super-soldiers capable of repairing their wounds while in the midst of combat, even *transhuman* assassins, affectionately known as 'trannies', all here for you to see, openly, without restriction, but maybe you've already seen more than you'd like," he sniggered. "A question of being in the wrong place, at the wrong time?" he insinuated, whirling his body around to the platform, "Mr. Powers, I'd like you to meet Jack Madson!"

"Jack!" greeted Powers, extending his hand beyond the platform into 'real' space, "welcome to Level 5, ALATON's tactical technology floor where the world's most creative minds build the world's most innovative technologies." He frowned as I stood, arms akimbo, shaking my head from side-to-side in amazement. "So, you're one of those, are you?" he asked, switching on his five-thousand kilowatt charm. "Well, military technology isn't for everyone and, to be frank, wouldn't life be monotonous if everybody thought the same way! No," he concluded as if locked into a frequency that rendered my thoughts visible to him, "this is the United States of America where diversity of ideas is emblematic of the freedom we must safeguard from our nation's enemies. But now see what you've done!" he beamed, stabbing an index finger out at me in the manner of a gameshow host. "You've got me riding my high horse, lecturing a guy with an IQ of, let me guess, 157," he correctly estimated, "about technology and patriotism! So, okay, warfare isn't your bailiwick, but as intelligent men interested in the world around us, let me tell you about something wildly exciting that happened right here, Level 5, just five years ago. Will you indulge me, Jack, just for a moment?"

Then, he stared down at me, silent and expectant, until with a chilling guffaw I uttered, "Sure, Elon, go ahead."

"In May 2012, the scientists at ALATON created a previously non-existent life form, Jack. We started with DNA

and constructed a novel genetic sequence of more than
one million coded bits of information known as *nucleo-
tides*," he explained, interacting with visuals that popped
up mid-air beside him. "Seven years earlier, ALATON was
the first in history to make a living, functioning entity
spawned from similar data, so looking at the string of letters representing the DNA for a virus called *phi X174*, we
wondered, 'Can we assemble real DNA based on that same
computer model?' And so we did! Creating a virus extrap-
olated from the *phi X174* genomic code, we figured out
how to construct an artificial bacterial cell then inserted
that DNA genome inside and watched with bated breath
as the entity we synthesized moved, ate, breathed, and rep-
licated itself," he proclaimed, the pulsing lifeform appear-
ing on the palm of his outstretched hand.

"Today, thanks to the efforts of those scientists, a new
breed of biologist is taking over the frontiers of technology—a breed that views lifeforms and DNA much the
way the computer wizards who spawned IBM and Apple
once looked at basic electronics, transistors, and circuits.
Now these two fields, each with spectacular private-sector
and academic engagement, are merging to transform one
another, as computer scientists speak of "DNA-based com-
putation" and synthetic biologists talk about "life circuit
boards". The biologist, then, has become an engineer
directing evolution by coding new life forms and enhanc-
ing existing ones with prospects nothing short of awesome for science and a new America beyond our wildest
dreams!" he declared, the ALATON jingle playing while
the corporation's banner was proudly hoisted by a troupe
of frolicking bears drawn in pastels, '*ALATON Better People
for a Better World!*' it read.

Once the tour ended, I met Fetters in his office; him, behind a cluttered desk re-arranging framed photos of his wife and two good-looking kids; me, squeezed uncomfortably into a folding chair feeling disrespected and deceived.

"Care for a cigarette?" he asked reaching into the desk drawer for a pack of Salem's.

"They let you do that here?" I said, declining.

"They let *me* do it," he corrected, lighting up then tossing the match into an ashtray overflowing with cigarette butts. "See those diplomas?" he asked motioning toward the wall. "MIT, age fifteen; Georgetown, Master Degree, age seventeen; Stanford, PhD, virology, bio-engineering and genetics, age twenty. It's true," he observed as if making peace with some secret sharer inside him, "I was a prodigy back then. Still am, that's why they let me smoke to my heart's content!"

"Impressive," I replied, rising slow and menacing, "but now you're going to tell me what happened at Lab 3 yesterday because I can tell you, if Marjorie Kurtz is on a walkabout in Pilbara it's as a red stain on the bottom of her killer's shoe. She's dead, Fetters, body mutilated beyond recognition and you know it!" I threatened, lifting him by the lapels, slamming him hard against the wall. "This has all been a charade, maybe for my benefit, maybe for some other interested party," I swore driving my clenched fists deep into his trachea, "but now I want answers!"

"Okay, Kurtz is dead!" he squealed, choking as the pressure of my fists against his windpipe increased. "The sabbatical was something they told us to say to reporters and local police who'd already been told it involved national security!"

"Why was she murdered, Fetters, and by who? A

name," I demanded, fist driven deeper still, my jaw tight, teeth clenched, as his wan face turned pink, then red, and finally purple, "you know who did this and why or you wouldn't have brought me here in the first place!"

"The bitch was talking," he wheezed, gasping for air as I loosened my grip just enough to stop him from going unconscious, "giving our secrets away to the Chinese, or so they claimed. Talking to you, for Christ's sake! I'm a weak man," he groveled, "can't you see that? A coward they've been using for their own purposes!" he bawled, my fists unclenching, his shoes dangling above the bare wood floor dropped down again as he collapsed at my feet.

"Why did you bring me here? Was it because you needed to know what I knew? What I'd seen?"

"I swear it wasn't me!" he cried out, sobbing. "It was . . ."

"That would be me," I heard a commanding voice intercede, "Paul Lindstrom, Senior VP-Technology for ALATON. And you must be Jack Madson," he continued as I craned my head around to get a look at him. "Can I be of some assistance?"

Tall, strapping, exuding self-assurance, with pierced ears and equally piercing blue eyes, I assessed Princeton University's famed Nobel Laureate, not knowing whether to laugh out loud at the awkwardness of our introduction or thank him for not calling the cops on me.

"Thank you, Paul, for saving me from this madman," Fetters wimpered, getting up from the floor. "I thought he was going to kill me!"

"I doubt that," Lindstrom speculated with no small degree of sarcasm. "Mr. Madson, I suspect, keeps his methods in check along with his temper, a rather violent one it seems. Now compose yourself, John, and for God's sake *put that fucking cigarette out!* Mr. Madson," he said turning with the bearing of a military commander, "come with me."

Once in the corridor, I joined Lindstrom who strode, steps long and purposeful, not bothering to ask where he was headed.

"The research we do here is easily misunderstood by outsiders which is why we're forced to maintain secrecy. If you dare to imagine, the key technologies—our three-legged stool as I call it—involves everything from genetic engineering, to silent messaging, as it's commonly known, to the military applications of replicant cloning. In short, quantum leaps in the GRIN basics that will fast-forward evolution entire generations with the potential to transform humans into a radically new species immune to cancer, Alzheimer's, even old age!"

"What was it Einstein wrote?" I asked. " 'Giving technology to the Generals is like putting an axe into the hands of a psychopath'. What's behind all of this, Lindstrom? What's really going on here at Princeton?"

He stopped and stared down at me. In his mid-eighties, silver-haired, blue eyes colder than the interior of chasms cleaved deep into Artic glaciers, his long wolfish face exuded a glimmer of amused tolerance.

"What's going on at Forrestal Campus is science that will lead to multi-trillion dollar emerging industries. Now come along, there's something I want to show you," he said as we continued our trek into the west wing, decidedly futuristic by contrast to anything I'd seen within the complex before.

We arrived at a brightly painted door flanged on either side with plate glass. The room beyond resembled a classroom with a massive atrium through which artificial sunlight poured down so that one's eyes were drawn immediately skyward rather than to the twenty or so students, ages five to fifteen.

Most peculiar, however, were not the children—Caucasian, Black, Asian—but the fact that half of them wore headgear, *transcranial magnetic stimulators*, I later learned, hovering over powerful Cray X-MP computers while their "think pack" classmates roamed the room locked in telepathic discussions with their "connectivity" partners, some ensconced within the PPL, others as far away as California, Montana, even Hawaii.

"No!" Lindstom admonished taking hold of my wrist as I reached for the door handle, "you can't disturb them!"

"Beg pardon?"

"These 'Exceptionals', as we call them, are connected 24/7 sharing thoughts and ideas as we speak, no matter how far apart. Think of them as Siamese Twins conjoined, not by flesh and blood, but by brain functionality. You can't interrupt their work, it isn't allowed!"

"Why do the ones walking around by themselves have their heads turned to the side? Is that normal?"

"Normal isn't a word we use much around here, but the 'Exceptionals' do have this habit of cocking their heads in a certain way when they want to access information they don't yet have as if waiting for a delivery to arrive. We call it 'silent messaging', just one of the technologies we're working on that will revolutionize the world as we know it. Without Elon Powers and ALATON these children would be freaks, not the geniuses they are today, prone to estrangement, depression, even suicide."

Roiling beneath the surface of my thoughts and

Lindstrom's pitch, tugging at my cuff like a corpse come to life beneath the black water of all that I was feeling was Marjorie Kurtz: Kurtz at Lake Carnegie the day we first met; Kurtz unrecognizable, organs devoured, brain tissue, bone, and flesh painting the floors, ceilings, and walls of Lab 3, *Kurtz, Kurtz, Kurtz!*

Lindstrom must have intuited this because without uttering a syllable more about the 'Exceptionals', he took hold of my arm, "There's more," he intoned, leading me down a hallway so lavishly illuminated I felt drenched in white light. "Stimulates brain activity", I remember him commenting as we entered a gymnasium where male and female athletes engaged in amazing feats of strength and agility.

"Consider the possibility of 'metabolically dominant soldiers'," he challenged as comfortable as a professor in his lecture hall, "DARPA has. In fact, the construction of genetically engineered "super soldiers" lies at the heart of our high risk, high reward programs. As combat systems become more sophisticated, the major limiting factor for operational dominance is the war fighter. Eliminating the need for food and sleep during combat while maintaining a high level of cognitive and physical performance will create a fundamental change in the way wars are fought in the 21st century! Did you know that whales and dolphins never sleep? No, I didn't think so, and therein lies the problem, *ignorance*," he sniffed. "There is nothing nefarious about ALATON, whether at the PPL or in classified projects unknown to the public. This is our future, yours and mine," he proclaimed extending his hand across the room bustling with *trans-humans* running at unheard of speeds, matching skills in *shan shou*, boxing, and *jiu jitsu*, firing M4A1 carbines with 100% accuracy, "evolution fast-forwarded not by years but generations in less than one lifetime!"

"Impressive, Doctor, but all the parlor tricks in the world won't change the fact that people are dying on Princeton campus in horrific ways and I don't believe for a minute that you're unaware of it. Marjorie Kurtz was murdered, Fetters told me as much. What I want to know is how ALATON plays into the equation because sooner or later I'm going to find out and when I do I'm going to come after you, Lindstrom. You and Fetters and your boss, Elon Powers, if it turns out he's involved," I vowed, body rising up to meet his chest-to-chest. "Now go ahead and put that into your goddamn predictability model!"

"You're an interesting man, Madson," Lindstrom observed with the clinical curiosity of an entomologist driving a pin into the wings of an insect, "but the truth is you don't have to believe what I'm telling you. You simply need to understand your situation. You want information, but there's a price to pay for it. If you want specific kinds of information, the price gets higher, and you've got to consider whether you can afford it. If Kurtz was murdered and for reasons of national security DARPA deems it unwise to risk turning the investigation into a media circus, you need to understand that if you keep pressing, you may get the answers you're looking for, but the price will be higher than a man like you could possibly imagine. Back off, Mr. Madson. Take the $20,000 Kurtz gave you. Go back to San Francisco."

Chapter Fourteen

Private Room, Babbo
Manhattan, New York

I slipped my Vette into a space on College Road opposite the Victorian house that served as Center for Campus Ministries adamant that any plans I had to leave Jersey were history now that I'd met Lindstrom. Of course, I wanted to tell Jeremiah I'd be staying, but more important was the warning I carried about the emergence of a potential serial killer stalking Princeton campus.

I crossed College Road then took the short flight of wooden stairs leading to the entrance. It was another sunless morning and wearing just a jersey and *NY Knicks* warm up jacket shuddered as I rang the bell and waited until a tall angular man, dressed in jeans and work shirt, answered.

"Catholic ministries?" I inquired as the door opened.

He smiled good-naturedly, "Right house. Wrong religion," he said extending his hand. "I'm Bill Marshall. It's easy to get your Catholics and Presbyterians mixed-up these days. *And Benedictine's?*" he shook his head just thinking about it.

"Jack Madson, private investigator," I said clasping his hand. "Jeremiah does live here?"

155

"We share the residence," he said, stepping aside as I entered. "The good Father hasn't been robbing banks, I hope?"

"No, nothing like that," I laughed. "I'm a former student from his St. Damien days."

"I see," the minister nodded, wriggling into a ski jacket. "Now if you'll excuse me, I'm late for service. You'll find Jeremiah upstairs in the Meditation Room conducting a seminar."

I followed the familiar sound of the priest's voice to a covey of lay people arranged in a circle discussing their topic for the week "Angels in Scripture", then gravitated to the back of the room where Harlan and Julianne welcomed me in hushed tones.

"The word angel derives from the Greek word *aggelos* which means messenger," he was saying, a smile crossing his lips as he looked up from his Bible. "The Hebrew word *mal'ak* has the identical meaning, but interestingly scripture often uses those same words for particular human beings. Lucky for us, since angels are referenced nearly three hundred times in Holy Scripture there's ample information to build an understanding of who these angelic beings are and what God's mission is for them."

"Father," a middle-aged man asked, "what do angels look like? If I run into one in the supermarket, I'd like to at least say 'hello'!"

"Okay, Kevin," Jeremiah laughed, "first off, angels are essentially 'ministering spirits' without physical bodies like humans. Jesus declared that 'a spirit hath not flesh and bones as ye see we have,' *Luke 24: 37-39*. However, angels can take on the appearance of men. How else to explain men and women written about in the Bible who 'entertain angels unaware'," he quoted, "as referenced, *Hebrews 13:2?*"

"So they're not chubby infants with wings after all!" a woman across from him lamented.

"Sorry," the old priest apologized turning the pages in his Bible, "but they usually appear as full grown men or women 'radiating dazzling light' like the angel that rolled back the stone from Christ's tomb, so—and you have to trust me on this, Marian—when people in the Bible saw an angel their typical reaction was to fall to their knees in awe not reach out and tickle their tummy!"

"Father," a young student spoke up, "one last question, if you were posting a job description for an angel on *monster.com*, what duties would it include?"

"God doesn't like students who try to stump old priests, you know that, don't you, Brian?" he quipped. "But, okay, here goes, the individual applying for this position will be required to perform the following: MESSENGER, to communicate God's will as in the case of Moses when he received the Commandments, *Acts 7: 52-53;* GUIDE, it was angels who gave instructions to Joseph about the birth of Jesus, *Matthew 1-2*; PROTECTOR, Daniel was protected from lions when thrown into a den of them, *Daniel 3 and 6*; MOTIVATOR, angels fortified and encouraged Jesus during His temptation on the mount, *Matthew 4:11*; and finally, EXECUTIONER," he stated, glancing across the room to me. "God used angels to destroy the Assyrians 'behold they were all dead corpses', *Kings 19: 20-34*; the angel of death appeared to Moses during the Exodus vowing to kill the Egyptian firstborn, *Exodus 11: 4-6*; then there's St. Michael, archangel warrior, brandishing his mighty sword, commissioned by God, Himself, to decimate Satan's soldiers in Heaven and on earth, *Revelations 12: 7-9*. At the end of time," Jeremiah concluded, slapping his Bible closed for emphasis, "Scripture tells us the Anti-Christ will come to wage war with Christ and slaughter good people. But Michael and his army will defeat him. That is why we pray after Mass, 'St. Michael, defend us in the day of battle.'" He paused, studying the faces of each member of the group then stood on unsteady legs, "Okay, folks, next week our topic will be meditation, and a special prayer for the Tigers during playoff week!"

Moments later, with the group disseminating, Jeremiah made a bee-line for the back of the room where I stood, catching up, with Harlan and Julianne.

"Jack! I was afraid you'd left for San Francisco!" he called out, walking past my outstretched hand to embrace me.

"And leave my buddy Harlan at the mercy of you two? No way!" I told him as Harlan waddled over to join us.

"Now Harlan," Julianne scolded, "why can't you leave them in peace and don't be hangin' all over everybody!"

"Maybe you should come over here, too, Darlin'. You look like a first-rate hugger. What do you think, Harlan?"

"You should see her at church on Sundays hugging everyone! But wait, Jack, I have s-something for you," he stammered rocketing out of the room as the three of us looked to one another, bewildered.

"A man on a mission," I remarked.

"Don't ask me what he's up to," Julianne pled, raising her hands in surrender. "If that young man comes back holdin' a newborn puppy dog or rollin' out a movie theater popcorn machine, I had nothing to do with it!"

"Are you hungry, son?" Jeremiah asked. "Would you like something to eat?"

"Sorry, Father, I just wanted to stop by to let you know I'll be here in Jersey a while longer and to tell you about a disturbing twist in that case we discussed last week."

"The Schumann girl?"

"Yes, and Dimitri Wilder, the other Princeton student who killed himself in a car crash on Route 1 a couple days back. I'm sure you heard about it."

"Who didn't?" Julianne interjected. "It was all over campus, not to mention the news!"

"Yeah, well, something happened two days ago. A murder at the Plasma Physics Lab: grisly, horrific. I was there to see its aftermath and wanted to warn you that the killer, a man calling himself 'Dark Angel', is still at large. You're not going to hear about this on TV or in the papers because it's all classified; something to do with experiments performed by Josef Mengele, a Nazi doctor at Auschwitz death that may tie these tragedies together. It's a theory I'm still working on," I rambled awash in images of Kurtz ravaged remains. "Anyway, I came here to ask that you take special care: keep your doors locked at night, avoid interacting with strangers, or anyone suspicious, at least until they catch this maniac."

"That's awful!" Jeremiah gasped. "I can't imagine coming upon something gruesome as that!"

"Her name was Marjorie Kurtz. She worked as a scientist at the PPL. She was my client, Father . . ."

"I got the newspaper! Front page, Jack!" Harlan clamored, bursting into the room, a copy of the *Inquirer* held out in front of him. "You're famous now just like DiMaggio!"

I scanned the banner headline along with Jeremiah and Julianne, "OO-LA-LA! COCO'S PARIS ROMANCE" it read. *Yep,* I surmised, *famous.* Then, just when I thought it couldn't get worse, it did, as my eyes homed in on the photo that accompanied it. It was Amy posing butt naked alongside me in my hospital room, byline Ty Rollins, cowboy, journalist, scumbag extraordinaire!

"Thanks, Harlan," I said, snaring the paper, folding it over, "but I don't read the *Inquirer.*"

And if I imagined that within the confines of the Center for Campus Ministries—charity being a virtue—that I'd be its beneficiary from Jeremiah, who shook his head muttering "son, son, son", or Julianne, who put her hand to her mouth unable to contain her laughter, I could not have been more mistaken!

"Want to know something else?" Harlan inquired, filling a silence that threatened to swallow us whole.

"What?"

"I heard you talking about Nazis and the Kurtz' m-murder. But not to worry! Julianne and I are going to be on this case like Sherlock Holmes and Dr. Watson!"

"Uh-huh," I asked, humoring him, "and which of you is Holmes?"

"Can't you guess? It's me that's Sherlock," he concluded, handing me a computer print-out labelled 'Molter.' "I'm the one with the b-brains around here!"

"What's this?"

"It's the contact info for Ernst Molter, an expert on the Third Reich. He lives in Germany, near Wewlesburg castle, where Mengele hid before he escaped to South America. Ernst is my 'Third Reich' chat room pal. He'll h-help us!"

"Us?" I asked, and we were off to the races!

"Wewlesburg Castle was constructed 1123 by Count Friedrich Von Arnberg," Harlan began, eyes drawn up to the ceiling. "Burned to g-ground by rioting peasants after his death . . . reconstructed as triangular complex spread out over twenty acres . . . north tower destroyed by lightning 1815 . . ."

"Nazis," Julianne woefully observed, "Harlan knows everything about them; stays awake to all hours of the night tapping on his computer keyboard talkin' with his chat room buddies on skype!"

"Selected by Commander Heinrich Himmler for *SS* Headquarters 1934 . . . Niederhager death camp located 600 m-meters from castle's north tower. Thirty-nine hundred slave workers engaged in construction," he enumerated. "Called 'Center of the World' with tor-torture and Satanic cult rituals carried out in castle's 'Sacred Crypt' . . ."

"Harlan," she said trying to derail the runaway train he was riding. "*Harlan!*"

Then, like one curtain dropping as another lifted, he was himself again.

"Harlan loves Julianne," he said simply as Julianne reached out to stroke the side of his face.

"I'll make a deal with you, Harlan," I offered, zipping up my *N.Y. Knicks* jacket to leave. "You keep this copy of the *Inquirer* and I'll take the print out," I said, exchanging one for the other, "because if what you say about Mengele checks out, I'll be paying Herr Molter a visit—and it won't be on skype!"

My ass was dragging by the time I emerged from the Lincoln Tunnel back into Manhattan. Amy was filming late that night and the prospect of a hot shower seemed a half step from paradise as I entered the lobby astonished to find Elon Powers' chauffeur, Dieter Hoche—tall, impeccably dressed, and oh-so-German—waiting for me.

"Mr. Powers requests the pleasure of your company for dinner," he announced with all formality save a heel-click.

"Tonight?" I asked incredulously.

"Mr. Powers doesn't like to be kept waiting," he informed me in case I'd forgotten it was Elon asking.

"All right," I answered, mind passing through a matrix of possibilities, a logic emerging that held 'the evidence will take you there anyway'. So I agreed, accompanying Dieter on the short limo ride to Babbo, an upscale restaurant owned by celebrity chef Emeril, on Waverly Place in Greenwich Village.

When I entered, I was surprised to see the ground floor had been cleared by Security except for a long rectangular table where Powers held court with ALATON's Board of Directors, his team of flunkies calling out the latest stock prices gleaned from iPhone updates.

"Mr. Madson, welcome!" he sang out merrily puffing a Cohiba. "I told them even on short notice you'd be here. Bet a thousand dollars on it!" he laughed, catching the eye of the sycophants around him as their heads bobbed vertical, cigars planted firmly between sets of bleached teeth, thin lips curling upward into hyena grins. "Please! Take a seat across from me and get yourself something to eat!"

"Thanks," I said assessing the thirty-three year old billionaire and an atmosphere that had an effect on me equivalent to breathing pure oxygen: Harvard Medical School, MIT Bio-Engineering, Stanford MBA, Powers didn't graduate with degrees, he learned what he needed and moved on, such was his grasp of the future and his place in it. 'ALATON isn't about ushering in the future, it's about creating it', went the much-quoted trope the media scribbled next to photos of him being interviewed by FOX Business News or walking out of *Santos Party House* arm-in-arm with his latest cover girl companion.

Powers wasn't born in the United States I recalled taking a moment to study him: 5'10" tall standing straight as a pencil in Italian-made shoes with effusive smile and short-cropped black hair cut in the manner of a collegiate athlete or military man. Still, it was his ruddy, high-cheek boned face contrasted by thin straight-line lips and sparkling eyes glistening with something more distinctive than charm (call it the shimmer of madness) that made Elon freakish, yet incontestably powerful, leaving women vaguely uneasy and men thinking "fuck, maybe this guy really is all he's made out to be!" No, it wasn't the U.S., but South Africa, where Elon was born before emigrating as a seven year old from Johannesburg where his father was a successful banker and mother an apartheid-era socialite.

Aside from his resume and net worth in the multi-billions, according to *Forbes* magazine, Powers had a penchant for his own safety, I observed, taking note of his security staff dressed in tailored black blazers, skulls crowned with transmitter-receiver headsets to facilitate communications between them. The table, too, was positioned mid-floor and strategic with no one but board members nearby and white noise flooding the place to eliminate the possibility of electronic surveillance. All in keeping with rumors of basement tunnels that sprawled labyrinthine beneath city streets and heliports atop his Upper East Side penthouse to facilitate escape in the event of robbery or attempted kidnap.

"So, where was I?" Elon asked his team.

"It was money. Money is what you were titillating our fertile imaginations with," a young Exec called out to him.

"You were talking about Obama and the sacrifices ALA-TON employees make to help defend this great nation each day!"

"Right, it was about my meeting with the President last week at the White House," he confirmed leaning forward, elbows pyramided onto the tabletop, "when he puts that boney brown hand of his on my shoulder and says, 'Elon, I don't mind you bein' rich. This is America and I want everyone to be rich, but the technology your people develop and the guidance you give the Joint Chiefs, well fuck's sake, can anyone put a price on national security?' Yes, that is exactly what the President said and, Jesus on the cross, I felt like kissing that nappy-haired bastard right there in the Oval Office! I felt like saying, 'Man, I love this fucking country and I love you! I love you for the faith you have in ALATON and the freedom you give us to do what we want, when we want, and make billions doing it!'"

A waiter put a bloody rare steak in front of me as I sat listening. I cut a piece of meat and took it to my mouth. "That's a pretty cynical view for a man came here as a child from South Africa, wouldn't you say?" I asked, still chewing.

"No, I would not say that. More like factual, I would say. This country was founded on money, Mr. Madson, constructed on the principle that capital is equivalent to freedom. The only difference between George Washington and Chairman Mao is the story they tell! Washington was no revolutionary. He was a rich man who didn't want to pay taxes, who does? But, unlike you or me, he and his money-grabbing pals go out and take it, rip off an entire continent, then have the audacity to tell the world 'we did it because we want to be "free"! 'Our country tis of money,

Sweet land of money, Of money I sing!' " he recited with stony precision, transforming before my eyes from capitalist to nihilist to soulless thing afloat in the nadir. "So, what about Mao, you're probably wondering?" Powers asked, looking up and down the table. "Well, Mao was an asshole *and I don't really feel like talking about it!*" he declared burying a smile into his snifter then drawing a long gulp, sycophants around him roaring with laughter.

"But wasn't it America that took your family in after apartheid when Mandela's men threw them out of the country?" I persisted, depositing another forkful of steak into my mouth. "You show up here with millions your father stole from South Africa, get educated at our finest universities, make billions selling the government killer robots, or whatever it is you're conjuring up at ALATON's Princeton laboratories, and it makes me wonder, 'what's the plan now, Elon? Wait for the U.S. to throw you and your family out, too?' "

The blood drained from Powers' face. Suddenly his distinctive features began to look aristocratic, inbred, and vaguely unhealthy. "My plan, Mr. Madson, is to contiunue making billions. It's a simple plan, but to answer your question, no one is throwing me or anyone here tonight out of the United States of America. Not now. Not ever. We are patriots, you see. Not only are we active in DARPA research that protects U.S. citizens from ISIS, the Chinese, the Russians or whoever else lurks in dark corners of the world seeking to destroy us, we translate that science into evolutionary enhancements that will advance the human species to levels never before imagined. In short, we create the future by re-designing the present," he argued, face alight with conviction as he hoisted his snifter, draining it dry. "It's a new reality you're confronted with, Madson. One that will leave small minds like you rolling around in the dirt wondering what became of the backwater superstitions that went into their vision of what America is and will be. Look at you! The way you talk, the way you dress, the way you chew your meat. Neanderthal! Is there another way to describe a man like you?"

"Are you finished? Christ, I hope so because I've developed a fucking wicked case of indigestion," I feigned, reaching for my stomach and standing, "must be listening to all the bullshit you pass off as philosophy to these stooges you pay to agree with you, but I've had my fill of hypocrisy for today. So, gentlemen, if you don't mind, many thanks, but it's time for me to get the fuck out of here."

"'You can run, but you can't hide', isn't that what Joe Louis, the Negro boxer, said back in the 1940s. That applies to you, Madson. Dr. Lindstrom told me about your investigation into the Kurtz murder so I thought I'd invite you here to get a look at you. Now that we've met, I see it was a mistake. We have very little to discuss, you and me. Just meat, blood-red and barely cooked, I suppose."

"You're forgetting Mary Linda Schumann."

"Who?"

"The Princeton student who committed suicide; and Dimitri Wilder, the sophomore who walked into *Winberrie's*, severed a student's hand with a machete, then ran his Porsche into a concrete embankment. I'm investigating both of those deaths, too."

Powers studied me like I was some kind of strange beast escaped from a traveling circus. "You're a freak, Jack," he said at last. "You know that about yourself, don't you? In another society they'd have crushed your skull at birth and set you adrift in the nearest river, but not here in the U S of A. Dangerous to a society like ours, so many freaks prowling about, wouldn't you agree?"

I lurched forward, palms planted firmly on the table-top as I leered over the table, confronting him, "It's eugenics we're really talking about, isn't it, Elon?" I asked, two bodyguards pulling in alongside me. "You don't want to 'improve the species', men like you never do because beneath the façade what you're really all about is getting rid of anyone unlike you. Isn't that where all of this leads? Mengele's dream of a super race, or didn't you think I knew about that?"

"There are two kind of men who are brave; those who are brave by the grace of nature, and those who are brave by an act of will. Which kind are you, Jack, or are you just a fool on a suicide mission?"

"Want me to escort him from the building, Mr. Powers?" one of the security guards asked taking hold of my arm.

"No, he might get hurt," Powers answered, shaking his head, laughing, "and in some perverse way I'm actually starting to like him."

I shook myself loose from the security guard's grip, glaring.

"I made $49 million during the past twenty-four hours," Powers called out after me as I stalked out of the restaurant. "*How much money did you make today, Mister Madson?*"

Chapter Fifteen

Elysee Hotel
Manhattan, New York

O nce back in the city, I entered the hotel, never more determined to get to the bottom of the Kurtz murder, student suicides, and ALATON-Nazi connection. I scanned the lobby, in search of what, *assassins?* Who knew anymore? I wondered, coming to a halt at the sight of the big man squared up on a cushioned chair, Stetson hat in hand.

"Jack Madson!" he called out in a voice loud enough to turn heads, crossing the room as I waited for an elevator.

"You're a lying piece of shit, Rollins," I growled, hands folded so as not to smash a fist into his oversized, white-capped teeth.

His smile withered, "You don't understand! There's something you need to know . . . about you . . . about Coco!"

"Fuck off, Cowboy," I suggested, grinning happily as the elevator door closed in his face. "You show up here again and I'll put my foot so far up your ass you'll need a surgeon to remove it!"

The temperature in my suite was more like Louisiana swamp than Manhattan winter when I entered, opening

169

a window and downing a stiff drink even before checking
on Amy. It was one in the morning and after a day of filming she lay on the bed fitfully sleeping which was a shame,
I lamented, returning to the kitchen where I popped two
Ambien with a Glenlivet chaser, feeling restless and in
need of her body.

Afterward — equation back in balance as the sedative
took effect — I sat at the desk in front of my laptop to confirm Harlan's information about Wewlesburg. Unsurpris-
ingly, it was accurate. Molter, a fabled Third Reich historian,
lived in Buren, a few kilometers from the castle; Mengele
had, in fact, worked in laboratories using prisoners from
Neiderhager Death Camp as subjects for his experiments;
and even the castle, itself, a sprawling three-towered Hell
on earth where the Nazi hierarchy performed blood rituals in the so-called 'sacred crypt', the stone ceiling above
it sculpted with pagan gods, all pointing to the skull and
dagger *SS* insignia erupting from out of its center. Then,
with photos of the castle perched on a mountain above
the village, the *SS* monsters it housed, and bulldozed bodies piled up at Neiderhager spinning like pin wheels in
front of me, I booked my flight: LaGuardia to Frankfurt,
Germany.

I'm not sure what time I fell into bed but remember
Amy asking, "Are you all right, Jackie?" "Yeah, Baby, I'm
fine," I answered, but this was a gross miscalculation, I
came to realize at 3 a.m. when, locked in a night terror
amid a tangle of sweat-drenched sheets, I bucketed up in
bed and let loose a blood curdling scream, "Stop! Jesus
Christ, get them the fuck away from me!"

When I came to myself, I felt as lost as an abductee
dropped onto the ground from a UFO, heart galloping

so hard I thought it would burst, the fearsome resonance of my screams escaped, but not the terror that accompanied it. It was only then that I noticed Amy sitting beside me, eyes large and fearful, as she fumbled her way into my arms weeping piteously, perhaps at the sight of me, perhaps at the futility of the lives we were leading.

The inside of Amy's heart must look like a club fighter's face, I thought then, realizing for the first time that I might have been comforting a child, her tears soaking into my shirt, close to the flesh, as I held and rocked her. "It's always the same," I explained, stripped bare of anything resembling pride or pretense, "hands reaching out at me; hands with gloves, not white like surgeons', but charred black hands like those of demons whose hands and bodies and faces had been left that way after burning in Hell!"

I deserted our bed for the kitchen, trying to bring myself back to the moment before, the way forensic experts examine the crater at a bomb sight, sifting through debris for a fragment of the device that created it; searching for clues that might lead them to its origin.

I poured myself a drink. Amy joined me, bare body draped in a terry cloth robe.

"It begins with you," I said. "No, not bad. Beautiful, in fact. The two of us on that Ferris wheel in Paris," I recalled with a laugh thin as paper. "We get off and it's raining so we run through the streets to a café with a red, white, and blue colored awning . . ."

"Yes, I remember, Jack! How could I forget?" Amy asked, encouragingly. "It was the first time you said you loved me!"

"That's right, and the people there welcome us because they see how deeply in love we are, but after that 'vision' comes another. This one of a minister—a kind of crazy preacher—shouting down from the pulpit at his congregation, and I'm there," I said, eyes lifting to her, "listening while he preaches, no, screams, a poem," I uttered, his words drifting up from my subconscious like smoke through a key hole. "Wait a minute! The preacher is shouting 'Death be not proud!' " I remembered. "It's a sonnet written by John Donne! 'Death, be not proud, though some have called thee, Mighty and dreadful, for thou art not so; For those whom thou think'st thou dost overthrow, Die not, poor Death, nor yet canst thou kill me!' " I recited. "Donne was a 17ᵗʰ century poet who wrote that verse as part of his *Divine Meditations*. I know because we memorized it when I was a freshman St. Damien's! Now, what the hell could that mean?" I whispered, still pondering the words, 'Death be not proud,' as I took Amy into my arms, eyes wide and racing with fear.

I awakened late the next morning to find a note from Amy, who'd already departed for Chelsea where the crew for the movie *Twisted* had set up camp for the day.

> *"Enjoy yur trip—but not to much!*
> *Always horny for Baby cause*
> *I luv him sooo much an will mis him*
> *teribly! Luv Ferever,*
> *Coco'*

I couldn't help but grin at Amy or Coco, or whichever of her alter egos was responsible for the note, both amused and warmed at the heart because in truth I could not place her in any world I knew. Like a cork bobbing on the ocean, Amy could have begun her voyage on the other side of the

world or a hundred yards down the beach at the Jersey
Shore, but there was no denying, she had worked her way
into my heart and had taken up residence there.

* * *

That night I boarded a Lufthansa flight bound for
Frankfurt, Germany never doubting my decision to meet
Molter. Though most of what I knew about him was from
Harlan and the internet, there was virtually no information concerning Mengele's detour during the final
months of the war, Auschwitz to Wewlesburg. The reason,
I suspected, had to be the clandestine nature of the projects he'd undertaken on orders from Hitler, himself. Why
else the elaborate cover story? Why else travel from Poland
back into the heart of Germany and not directly to the
sanctuary that awaited him in Brazil?

I arrived at Frankfurt airport early the next morning.
I washed up in the lavatory, rented a S65 Mercedes, then
took the three hour drive, north on the Autobahn, finally
arriving at the castle—a stark and foreboding presence
even today—where Molter waited in a kitschy tourist shop
that featured *SS* memorabilia.

Ernst Molter was a barrel-chested man with dispropor-
tionally small hands and feet who enjoyed his beer and
sausage judging from the size of him, with white hair,
booming voice, and avuncular smile. We shook hands,
exchanged formalities, and talked about our friend, Harlan.

"I say he's a genius!" the German proclaimed as we left
the shop for the outdoors. "I've studied the history of the
Third Reich for fifty years, and he still surprises me with
facts he's uncovered!"

My eyes lifted to the castle walls that loomed like tall gray shields sprung up from the netherworld.

"Yeah," I answered, peering beyond the rolling berm east of us to Neiderhager death camp, "Harlan's a pit bull when it comes to research."

The silence hung heavy as we walked, bracing ourselves against a lancing wind that cut through to the bone.

"No getting used to Wewlesburg," Molter commiserated, his ruddy mask of a face inverted to a frown. "I don't come here often. Too damned depressing!" Then, catching himself, added, "But if you'd like to take a tour of the castle . . ."

"I don't need to see it," I said, rejecting the idea out of hand. "I suppose it's like Jeremiah, a priest friend of mine," I called out over the howl of gusting wind. "I'd just returned from a tour of religious sites in Jerusalem and was telling him about it, but stopped when I noticed he didn't seem interested. 'Wouldn't you like to go to Bethlehem where Jesus was born, or Calvary where He was crucified, or the tomb where He rose from the dead?' I insisted. 'No, son,' " he told me. " 'I don't need to see any of those places because I know Him. The rest is just geography. It's Jesus I want to see, Jack, and I do that every day, every place I go.' "

"So now you're a philosopher!" Molter roared, clapping his tiny hand onto my shoulder, the twinkle in his eye returning.

"No, nothing as lofty as that, but like Jeremiah, who truly believes Jesus is the Son of God, I don't need to see the Devil, the evil he does, or the places he did it. That castle there," I said, pointing, "that castle is an evil place where Satan presided, still might, and I don't need to see it."

"I didn't want to take that damned tour again, anyway!"
Molter groused. "Besides, Haberman told me it's Mengele
you want to discuss, and he spent less than a year there!"

"But escaped to South America from Wewlesburg, isn't
that right?"

"Just so," he agreed, serious again, "all part of what
the Americans called Operation Paperclip, an accom-
modation worthy of Goethe! The U.S. needed weapons
to use against the Soviets, and the Nazis had them. V2
rocket technology, spies embedded into the highest ech-
elons of Soviet government, research that promised to
create genetically-enhanced soldiers, the likes of which
no army on earth had ever contemplated! And so a Faustian deal was struck. The Nazis would turn over control of
their spies and access to their scientists. In return, the U.S.
would guarantee safe passage of the world's most notorious criminals to South American countries sympathetic to
the Reich."

"There were others?" I asked, gloomily.

"Many," he retorted. "All given sanctuary, put back on
West German payrolls within weeks of the Nazis' surrender: *Karl Adolf Eichmann*, self-proclaimed 'Jewish Special-
ist', responsible for the extermination of four million Jews
in sixteen countries," Molter recounted with glacial precision. "After fleeing to Argentina, Eichmann lived under
the name Ricardo Klement,m working for U.S. counter-
intelligence, until he was abducted, tried, and hanged,
Ramleh Prison, May 1962. *Klaus Barbi*, 'The Butcher of
Lyon', who tortured and killed thousands of men, women,
and children, breaking extremities, using electroshock,
calmly observing—snifter of wine in hand—as prisoners were eaten alive by starved dogs. Recruited by U.S.

Intelligence, Barbi was relocated to Bolivia where he attained the rank of Lt. Colonel within their armed forces before finally being extradited to stand trial in France, died July 1977. *Franz Paul Stangl, SS* Commandant responsible for the extermination of 900,000 Jews, who designed gas chambers capable of killing 2,000 victims per hour while violinists performed Viennese waltzes to calm them as they marched to their slaughter. Aided by CIA operative Bishop Alois Hudal, he was relocated to Sao Paulo, Brazil where he was tracked down by Nazi hunters. Stangl was convicted by a Dusseldorf court for crimes against humanity, died June 1971."

"And Mengele?" I persisted.

"Yes, Dr. Josef Mengele, Chief Physician at Auschwitz death camp, self-proclaimed medical genius, some would say madman," he answered gravely, tiny feet coming to a halt as like a battleship he turned his broad frame to me. "Known to prisoners as the 'Angel of Death', Mengele became famous for his experiments in 'human directed evolution' using healthy prisoners for what scientists now call 'genetic engineering'. Accounts of the results he achieved are the subject of whimsy, but evidence that he actually performed them abound. Here's a document that may be of interest to you," he said, pulling a sheaf of papers from out of his winter coat. "It surfaced during the Nuremberg trials where Theresa Eckhart, one of Mengele's medical assistants at Auschwitz, gave testimony."

I perused the first sentence of the typewritten document, marked T. ECKART TESTIMONY, WAR CRIMES TRIAL, NUREMBERG, GERMANY, NOVEMBER 24, 1947, looked up to him for affirmation and began reading in a low, deliberate voice.

"'Partly because of my orientation and based on the radical nature of Mengele's experiments, I made a shocking discovery one day at the camp,'" Eckhart's testimony began. "'Asked by Mengele to supervise the transport of a refrigerated box to Wewlesburg, I felt a strong impulse to open it and see what was inside, only to discover that it contained glass jars filled with human eyes. Dozens of them, all the clearest blue, I remember thinking. Then later, with curiosity piqued, I sneaked two levels below the main building into the doctor's 'secret' laboratory where he often worked late into the night. What I found there was even more disturbing! Human bodies, or at least partly human, some of them children, twins mostly, others fully grown, but all of them in some way—how can I say it?—disfigured. Foreheads much larger than normal, and teeth, they didn't have real teeth, but artificial ones made of steel or platinum. It was then that I realized Mengele was killing healthy people in order to obtain some sort of genetic breakthrough, and that like a god he was trying to redesign humans for a specific purpose. '*Das schlautang maschines*,' I heard a scientist at the camp call them once, 'the slaughter machines.'"

I handed the document back to Molter, struck dumb from its impact.

"Of course, we have no way of knowing whether Eckhart's testimony is true since both U.S. and Soviet Intelligence confirm that whatever research Mengele left behind at Auschwitz was destroyed by the *SS* prior to the invasion. Equally unfortunate, with the Allies closing in on Wewlesburg, Der Docktor's records were supposedly relocated to Buenos Aires where historians tell us he lived the life of a recluse until his death in 1979. Still, there are rumors, persistent rumors," Molter added with vehemence, "that Mengele was on the brink of a breakthrough based on what he called the 'three-legged stool' of radical evolution—mind control, genetic engineering, human cloning—weeks before the collapse of the Third Reich and that his research continued in the jungles outside of São Paulo, Brazil. It's also believed that prototypes from those early experiments, lost in a plane crash over the Alps while he was making his escape, were recovered by your Central Intelligence Agency."

"The plane that carried him crashed?"

"There were two planes, Mr. Madson, to cover that eventuality!" the German boomed, drawing a miniature fist to his mouth as his laugh turned to a fit of coughing, "Ironic, isn't it? Mengele devoted a lifetime to the creation of Hitler's 'super weapon' only to leave it in the Alps for the Americans to discover, all because of a goddamned snow storm!"

Chapter Sixteen

I returned to Frankfurt late that afternoon, still digesting the dimensions Molter had added to my perspective of what Nazi influence might be underlying the Kurtz murder as I sailed along the Autobahn at 180 klics per hour. Skeptical at first about Kurtz's claims of linkage between Mengele's experiments and something so macabre as 'slaughter machines', 'silent messaging' and the rest, I believed I had proven that connection. Sure, Kurtz may not have been the most reliable source, but hadn't Molter, himself, confirmed it that very day?

Lindstrom made reference to ALATON's "three-legged stool" of radical technologies, but in the case of Molter it wasn't about contemporary research being carried out at Princeton University. No, Molter's reference was to human experiments carried out at Auschwitz and Wewlesburg seventy years earlier!

What did it all mean? Given the fact that a cross-generational bridge existed, what connection, if any, was there between ALATON's applied science, Kurtz' murder, and the suicides at Princeton? How did the pieces of

179

the puzzle fit together? I wondered, finally realizing that
Molter had informed my investigation along those lines as
well. Not unlike the CIA 'ratline' that relocated war criminals extending their reach from the 1940s into the 1970s,
Molter believed U.S. Intelligence had retrieved prototypes
created from Mengele's radical evolution experiments,
recognized their value, and was actively engaged in per-
fecting their military application to this very day.

Hadn't Kurtz compared the Nazi's stalemate at Stalingrad to the conundrum the U.S. military might face in a
confrontation with China? If Hitler's best trained forces
were thwarted by superior numbers once engaged on Russian soil, wouldn't China's population numbering in the
billions versus America's population, one-fifth that size,
send a trickle of cold sweat running down the spines of
every Pentagon official faced with the prospect of an all-
out war between the two super-powers?

Sure, the U.S. could go nuclear, but likely neither
China nor the Joint Chiefs were willing to absorb casualties in the hundreds of millions. No, like the Nazis at
Stalingrad, and every city, and village in rural Russia,
Hitler needed technology that would make each of his
troops the killing equivalent to ten of theirs, just as the
U.S. would need to exact that same equation in anything
short of a nuclear war with China! And what would that
great equalizer be if not something akin to an army of
highly effective, expendable 'super-soldiers' — *trans-
human* killing machines—whose emergence derived
from a uniquely crystalized series of historical events: *Der
Docktor's* plane is downed during a storm in the Swiss Alps,
February, 1945. Amid the wreckage U.S. Intelligence discovers the prototype for Hitler's *"Superwaffe"*. The genet-

ically-enhanced embryos evolved by Mengele in Wewles-
burg make their way to the Pentagon where — parallel to
China's emergence as a military super-power — DARPA
funds the development of *trans-human* killers in ALA-
TON's TT laboratories eight stories below Princeton
University's Forrestal Campus.

High on the list of 21st century business clichés like "at
the end of the day", "bottom line is", or "we need team play-
ers", is the phrase "that's above my pay grade". The latter is
the wellspring of most, meaning, "I am a corporate stooge.
I have no balls and will do anything, no matter how destruc-
tive, to preserve my middle class life style." All of it nauseat-
ingly hackneyed, but even clichés can accurately describe
a particular moment in time and this was one of them, I
was thinking, as I turned over the keys to the Mercedes to
the valet at the Frankfurt Hilton. Whatever shit storm I'd
encountered at Princeton was levels above my pay grade
involving U.S. Intelligence, rogue science, and murder.
Nevertheless, I was no corporate stooge, had a set of brass
balls, and didn't give a tinker's damn about any middle class
lifestyle. That much I'd decided a half decade ago, when I
left my wife, daughter, and career at NuGen because these
days balls and brains was all I did have!

Later that night, after polishing off a steak and bottle of Bordeaux, I threw on a pair of Georgetown sweats
ready to call it a day when a knock sounded at the door
to my hotel room. Its cadence told me it wasn't a man's
knock and I was right, delighted to spy two beauties, one
a tanned Asian, the other a blonde, each cradling a mag-
num of Don Perignon , smiles broad and inviting, wearing cut-at-the-thigh Alex McQueen dresses that sparkled
as bright as the light in their eyes.

I opened the door, intrigued.

"Are you Jack Madson? The Asian girl inquired.

"I used to think that," I answered, killer grin intact, "who wants to know?"

"Maybe a better start is to get us out of this hallway and into your room," the Russian blonde suggested in near-perfect English.

I stepped aside as each passed, making a point of brushing their hips against my privates.

The Asian girl, slim and sexy, was the first to speak as she undid the zipper that ran down the back of her skin-tight dress.

"You friend of Ernst Molter, right?"

"I know him," I answered.

"Well, that good, or we have to put our clothes back on," she joked turning to the blonde, who smiled, wriggling out of her dress as it fell to her ankles. "My name Pussy Wan, could call me Wan Pussy," she joked again. "My friend name Kati, short for Katrina. No need to know last name since Molter send us here to suck you dick all night, let you fuck my tight pussy."

"Hence the name," I dared to speculate, "but, Pussy and Kati, I'm sorry, I've got an early morning flight tomorrow . . ."

"Mr. Molter said you'd say that," Katrina said, now standing naked as she popped the cork of the Dom Perignon. "He also said you like to drink, but like to fuck beautiful women even more than that," she commented, pouring the champagne into a glass and walking it to me. "So, I guess you're some kind of tough guy, huh?"

"I'm nice to be nice to, and not nice not to be nice to," I warned, taking the glass from her.

A foxy glitter rose at the back of her eyes. "Sure," she said, dropping to her knees.

I thought then that perhaps Molter was clairvoyant when he said, "So now you're a philosopher!" because with cock throbbing and Kati taking that carnal beast into her mouth, I might have been Socrates, Voltaire, and Ben Franklin wrapped into one as Pussy crawled across the floor on her knees behind me, ferocious, as she gobbled what Kati could not assay from the front.

During that instant passion met ecstasy like nitro meets glycerin as I took each of them, one at a time, then together—me doing them, them doing me—in a slugfest of flesh so explosive in its climax that I knew then why orgasms of this magnitude were called "the little death" because truly I was forced to contemplate the notion of fucking myself to oblivion!

Then amid the welter of sensations, my seed still blossoming from Pussy and Kati's every orifice, we started again, the two of them insatiable as we swarmed one another, locked in a frenzy of tongues, genitals, and thighs, our mouths working every stitch of flesh until a feeling not unlike a riptide, silent and unseen, began tugging then dragging me into what seemed at first a dark undersea grotto but soon became a bottomless chasm.

"Wait a minute," I remember saying, or at least believed I was saying.

Then, with the girls still rapacious, beautiful faces smiling up at me, I asked, *"Is this really happening?"* but they just smiled, their eyes diverting along with mine to Ernst Molter as he entered the room wearing a long black leather coat.

* * *

My skull felt like it would explode, my eyes like over-
inflated balloons, pressure building behind them to the
point of popping. I threw my head back running my fingers through my mop of black hair staring up at the fluo-
rescent lights that lined the ceiling of the Frankfurt Am
Main police interrogation room.

"That's the last thing I remember, then nothing, just
black for some time, maybe hours. Except," I said looking back at the Detective Lieutenant again, "there were
dreams."

"Go on."

"Horrible dreams, ugly: a surgeon performing surgeries on a boy and girl, twins, strapped to an operating table
with eyeballs removed; a killer, more animal than man
splaying someone open with the single swipe of a claw,
then pouncing on him, devouring him like a predator
ravaging its prey; the wholesale murder of an entire family—father, mother, children—blood everywhere, body
parts strewn through every room of the house!"

"Charming people, these Americans, eh Sven?" Lt.
Koehler asked, turning to his young partner who stared
at him, clueless. The detective frowned, *"Liebenswerten
Menschen, diese Amerikaner?"* he repeated, waiting until his
understudy nodded before turning back to me. "Then,
what? Try to remember," he encouraged, "it's important."

"Later, as the drug's effect wore off, I realized I
couldn't move, not a muscle, but struggled to open my
eyes anyway. Pussy and Kati were in the back of a room
that looked like part of an abandoned factory. They were
talking, but the words had no meaning. But there were
other voices," I strained to remember, "asking questions
and I must have been answering because when I looked

directly above me, I was panicked to see Molter staring down expectantly waiting for an answer. To his left and right were three men outfitted like doctors with surgeons' masks so only their eyes were visible. 'He's coming to,' Molter said, getting the attention of the others. The lead surgeon seemed annoyed, 'Another 10 ccs,' he ordered, then glared down at me or, more accurately, glared down *into* me. His eyes were deep, far too deep, like there was nothing behind them, eyes that could watch lions tear a child to pieces and not change; that could watch a man impaled and screaming in the hot sun eyelids cut off.

'That should do it,' the assistant told him. Then they were gone. Everything was gone, the room, the surgeons, Molter, the women. Vanished like mist in the light of day."

"You said they were asking questions, what kind of questions?"

"The words weren't connected," I struggled to articulate, head pounding so powerfully I thought my brains might ooze from out of my ears, nose, and mouth, "at least not sentences."

"Then tell us the words, just the words, if that's all you remember," Koehler prodded.

My head, hung down over the tabletop, jolted up, temper flaring. "I told you, I can't remember!" I screamed back at him. "Words, okay? More like sounds without rhyme or reason, haven't you heard anything I've told you? My mind is a blank, is that so fucking hard to understand?"

"It doesn't surprise me," he said with the dismissive wave of a hand as his partner left the room to take a call on his cell phone. "They did everything but embalm you. A cop on the beat found you face down in an alley across from the train station."

"Drugs?"

He nodded, lifting the toxicology report from off the tabletop.

"Which?"

"Heroin, for one."

"The others?"

"Just one," he said, appraising the report as his partner returned, holding the cell phone out to him, "a massive dose of *sodium thiopental.* It's a psychoactive drug used by BND, German counter-intelligence, to interrogate terrorists. It seems, you have information somebody wants badly," he concluded, taking hold of the phone. "*Was ist los?*" he asked his partner, then listening, handed it to me. "Call from the States. It's that cop you had vouch for you last night." He shrugged, "Says it's important."

I put the phone to my ear.

"Madson, this is Gifford," the Lieutenant rasped urgently. "There've been more killings here at Princeton. It's John Fetters. His entire family murdered in their Mercer Street home, bodies mutilated, just like Kurtz. You need to get your ass back here next flight out."

"But I hardly knew him!"

"That doesn't matter," he said in a voice luminous with horror. "Trust me for once, Madson. Get back here *now.*"

Chapter Seventeen

34 Mercer Street
Princeton, New Jersey

I arrived at Fetters' Mercer Street home happy to be back in the States from bleak and dour Germany. Fetters' house, a modest Cape elaborated upon over the decades, seemed swallowed by the carnival of police cars, mobile crime scene units, forensic technicians and media. A search helicopter veered away as I approached throbbing low over Princeton campus, its lights blinking red and green amidst the first rays of early morning sunlight.

Gifford rushed beyond the yellow ribbon marked CRIME SCENE. He took hold of my arm guiding me past the gaggle of reporters: FOX News videotaping, CNN "live" on the air, and their competitors—come to life at the sight of me—already inquiring who the fuck I might be.

"Whaddya have for us, Tommy?" a stringer from the *Star Ledger* called out.

"Yeah, come on," a black anchor from ABC reached out from over the tape, pleading, "I'm your brother, man!"

But Gifford, already a veteran of the chaos, just held his hands up like a boxer acknowledging the crowd during pre-fight introductions, never breaking stride.

"You believe those vultures already have a media handle for this place?" he asked bug-eyed as we burst into the foyer. "They're calling it the 'Princeton Death House'," he said, door slamming behind. "Well, they got that right!"

I was about to ask Gifford why he wanted me Stateside so badly but realized immediately the question could not survive an atmosphere so frenzied as this. The first floor of the Cape looked more like a laboratory than the home where a father, mother, and their seven-year old boy and girl twins, resided. The outside perimeter had been cordoned-off to protect the integrity of the crime scene. The inside was a beehive of activity where Mercer County, State, and FBI investigators, covered head-to-toe in Tyvex body suits, scoured every inch of every room for fingerprints, DNA, or other physical evidence, preliminary findings already on their way to AFIS and CODIS at the Bureau's Biometric Center in Clarkburg.

"You're gonna need to go balls up for this one, it's not good," Gifford warned as a tall, gangly man, bald with tortoise-shell glasses, approached.

"This is going to take the CSU another full day to process," the man complained, an edge of anxiety creeping into his voice. "Pathology took what was left of the bodies last night, but don't you know Liras, from Trenton, snaps his photos then spills a cup of Starbuck's across the Sirchmark outlines? Leave it to State!"

"This is Jack Madson, Doc," Gifford stated forthrightly, brown eyes lifting to the taller man. Then, turning to me, "Jack, this is Joel Shapiro," he announced, "Medical Examiner from County."

The ME nodded his oversized head appraisingly, the

glare of a forensic photographer's camera flash reflecting off the lens of his glasses.

"Good to meet you, Madson," he said, not bothering to raise his gloved hand. "There's something the Lieutenant and I need to show you, but first put these on," he instructed, handing me a set of Tyvex shoe protectors. Then three of us trudged forward, deeper into the 'Princeton Death House.'

"We're thinking the initial murder, Mrs. Fetters, happened in the kitchen," Shapiro explained taking on the manner of a lecturer. "First we secure the crime scene, then we photograph it. Next, we try to reconstruct the murder, killer-to-victim POV, then victim-to-killer. Bottom line, there's always a transfer of evidence when two people come in contact. The more violence, the better the chances of picking up samples of hair, blood smears, skin cells, semen, if he's the kinky type."

Shapiro stopped at the edge of the kitchen's linoleum floor. He smiled wanly as though to flag an advance warning.

"Jesus Christ!" I muttered staring into the room, a shiver passing through my bloodstream like jagged particles of ice.

"Fucked-up, all right," Gifford rumbled incredulously.

"The wife's body parts were taken to the morgue along with the other victims' where a forensic re-constructionist will try to put Humpty Dumpty together again," Shapiro quipped mirthlessly. "They'll also study bite marks since the killer consumed her flesh, leg up to femur, sucking the bone marrow out, eating the genitals; hers, her husband's, even the kids'."

Neither Gifford nor I could find the words to say, a

question to ask, and I felt as if I'd just been struck by a hard blow to the head, Shapiro's lecturer's voice beginning to sound suddenly distant and removed.

"The Sirchmark outlines show where she was found when the responding officers first arrived. The position of the torso is important because it suggests how she may have been murdered, front, back, taken from the side, even from above. Believe me, you see it all in my line of work."

"But there must be," I hesitated, "seven outlines here, and the sink, it's filled with blood, for Christ's sake!"

"I lied," Shapiro confessed, head cocked to one side as he peered down at me. "I haven't seen it all because, truth is, I've never seen anything so incomprehensibly brutal as this and what happened to these kids and their father up on the second floor. We believe the killer entered through the front door since there's no sign of forced entry. From there, he must have been facing her," he continued, motioning to the center of the kitchen where *cyanoacrylate* lifters had produced a shoeprint, "maybe even talking to her while she was sitting in that chair, bound hand and foot," he explained, pointing to it. "Her death wasn't quick. Nor was it painless."

"Like Kurtz," I suggested.

"Exactly like Kurtz. Tortured over a period of time, blood removed through a catheter," he said, lifting his hand, "retained in that sink."

Shapiro stared down at me. I examined his haggard face, met the umber eyes as dark as forests.

"You know anything about the hunting wasp, Madson?" he asked in a haunting voice that made my skin crawl. "Its lifespan is only two months. It comes out of its egg, but in a month it's fully grown and has eggs of its own. Now the eggs need food, but only one kind: a live insect, a fly, let's say. The food must be alive because putrefaction would be fatal to the grub, yet a living, normal fly would crush the egg or eat it. But if the wasp can just *paralyze* the fly, the problem is solved, so it has to figure out exactly where to sting its prey and exactly how much venom to inject or else the fly escapes or is dead. It needs all of this medical knowledge, but soon it watches happily while its offspring consumes the fly, still alive and feeling, over a period of days, even weeks. Imagine the pain, the mental torment, Madson; imagine the horror."

"*Succinylcholine?*"

"In just the right proportion. Injected in exactly the right spot. Our killer is no ordinary man," Shapiro concluded, shaking his head side-to-side with certainty, "but a doctor or a scientist, and judging from the bite marks, he may not be a man at all. Come upstairs with us, there's something you need to see."

Again I looked into Shapiro's face, deadly serious, then to Gifford, whose gaze had never left me, until like soldiers locked in an opium nightmare, we trekked beyond the foyer, ascending single file up the wooden staircase to the landing, cramped, with low-hanging ceiling, more attic than second floor.

"The father, John Fetters, was found in the bathroom of the master bedroom in the same condition as his wife—body dismembered, blood drained, half-eaten appendages scattered around the room—internal organs stuffed into the drain of the bathtub where the killer collected his blood and the twins', who were murdered while at play in their bedroom."

"But wouldn't they have heard something—screams, cries for help coming from downstairs. Wouldn't Fetters have been alerted to what was happening while his wife was being tortured just one floor below?"

"Doc doesn't think Mrs. Fetters put up any struggle at all. More like she knew the killer, and was talking with him, when he tells her he wants to cut her to pieces and she has no problem with it. She sits down, lets him tie her up, then he does her."

"Bullshit, this is the mother of two! Do you really think she's not going to put up a fight to save her own children because she had to know he'd be coming after them next!"

"The drug was injected with a hypodermic needle, Madson. That's the only method exact enough to produce the effect he wanted. He didn't put it into her coffee, or lace a box of chocolates. Somehow, for some reason, she let him do it," Gifford argued, the horrific nature of the slaughter so surreal as to make us feel absurd even attempting to attribute a rationale to it, like someone or something very near was laughing at us, mocking our inability to fathom its mind, motives, actions.

"I can't say more about it, Tommy," I confessed, "because I can't begin to comprehend the mind of anyone who'd do something like this to another human being."

"Precisely," Shapiro observed, "you can't comprehend, but he can."

"Beg pardon?"

Shapiro's large head bowed, his gangly frame turning as Gifford and I followed him down the hallway to the twins' room. Together, the three of us loomed, mesmerized, in the doorway—white bedsheets from their bunk beds torn to shreds, matching dressers, drawers yanked out, contents strewn across the carpeting, clothes ripped to shreds, dolls mangled, desktop computer smashed to pieces—staring in disbelief at the dozens of Sirchmark outlines indicating where the children's body parts had been discovered by Uniforms responding to a neighbor's 911 call!

I cannot describe how much revulsion came to me at that moment, replaced when Shapiro raised his right hand to the bedroom walls by a feeling beyond revulsion, beyond fear.

Written in blood, floor to ceiling, on the wall nearest me were the words 'SMALL MIND, SMALL MIND, SMALL MIND'. Scrawled in blood, wild and raging, across the wall farthest from us was the name 'MADSON, MADSON, MADSON', written over and over again.

Can words describe the horror that seized me when. like a swimmer breaking water. I burst through the back door of the Princeton 'death house' that morning? The December air felt scorched, the words 'SMALL MIND' and 'MADSON' branded white hot and searing into my brain so that I couldn't shut my eyes without seeing them! For all of my efforts what had I accomplished. after all. other than to multiple Kurtz' slaughter by four, two of the victims innocent children?

Even the surge of media hounds that greeted me stirred no more than a clenched-teeth grimace as I plied my way through the riot of reporters and cameramen, long-stemmed microphones shoved into my face, one question indistinguishable from the next, until I spied a mountain of a man wearing a white Stetson approaching, felt his huge palm come to rest upon my shoulder. Then, like a jolt of electricity vaulting through my body—brain

to heart, heart to balls, balls to clenched fist—I swung the
full measure of my 190 pound frame around crashing a
thunderous right cross square into Ty Rollins' jaw before
he could mutter the words "hot damn".

The 6'4" giant toppled like a demolished high rise
onto the sidewalk in front of me.

"You're a parasite, Rollins," I seethed, standing over
him, chest heaving while reporters' cameras clicked and
videotape rolled. "You come near Coco or me again, I'll
rip your head off, grind your skull into the concrete, and
piss on it, you got that, Cowboy?"

"We need to talk, Madson," he said rubbing his jaw as
he looked up at me.

"Kiss my ass!" I answered, plowing through the morass
of faces, bodies, equipment headed for the Vette parked
curbside.

"You need me, Madson!" Rollins called out, voice
booming over the throng of reporters. "The things you
think are true, ain't. You hear me? Lies! All of what she
told you, they're lies, man!"

ABYSS

Chapter Eighteen

Elysee Hotel
Manhattan, New York

I stood in front of the door to my hotel room, inserted my card key into the lock, knowing that Amy was waiting, wondering what I'd tell her about my jaunt through the Fetters' family 'death house'. Courage is an elusive concept, but for me, seeing Amy sitting on the settee horrified as she watched CNN's 24/7 coverage of the carnage and maintaining my composure qualified hands down.

Her red-rimmed eyes lifted. She flew into my arms.

"I tried to call you on your cell!"

"Princeton police summoned me back from Germany. I left to see Gifford straight from the airport."

"I know, I been watching," she sniffled, pulling back from me. "Why? Why did they want you there? It's all they're talking about on the news."

I nodded a tight-lipped acknowledgement, "Where's my laptop?"

"On the kitchen counter . . ."

I was there before she could finish the sentence.

"Whatcha doin', Jack?" she wondered, watching me log on.

"Deep web," I answered. "See what this sick bastard may have posted."

Eyes raging, we studied the Hidden Wiki link as it swept through posts for illegal drugs, arms dealers and counterfeit banknotes, websites for assassin services, child porn and human trafficking until finally the hooded executioner 'DARK ANGEL' popped onto the screen. I could feel Amy's fingers tighten around my bicep, hear her bated breath as I entered the killer's website, saw his latest posting: a video of the Fetters' family murders, bodies dismembered with clinical precision, the eerily upbeat trilling of Theresa Brewer's 1950s hit "Playmate" blaring in the background as room-to-room he marched, immobilizing, then devouring his still-alive victims, one at a time.

"He's baiting them," I observed remotely.

"Who is he baiting, Jack?"

"The police," I said turning to her.

Amy shook her head, eyes fixed on the screen's darkening image of the wall with my name scrawled in blood across it, "No, Jack, it's not the police he's baiting," she uttered. "It's you."

I brushed her cheek with my fingertips. "Amy," I whispered and it was as if her name alone conveyed oceans of meaning, feelings, perhaps even love.

"Hold me, Jack. I'm frightened," she said, body quaking as she fell into my embrace.

I smoothed her hair and kissed her tears away, and as she subsided, I felt rising within me that most savory of emotions, a certain small affection for myself. If only it could have lasted, but it was a vista opening to all that was impossible. She slipped out of my arms, and stood with her back to me, her shoulders drawing together in an attempt to achieve composure.

"Do you remember that night in Paris, Jack, when I asked you to feel my heart? 'My heart is your heart,' I said. 'We are one and there are no boundaries between us'. Do you remember that, Jack?" She turned to me eyes lit with promise and for an instant I could not distinguish whether it was Amy, my lover, or Coco, the actress, standing there. "Well, nothing's changed, baby, despite the time we've been apart, despite these horrors, it can be like it was in Paris again. Now, I want you to say something and never ever doubt it. *Amy loves me. Amy will always love me.* Say that, Jack. Say it and believe it because it's the only thing you will ever know that is totally true."

It was near midnight when Karl at the front desk called to say that Jeremiah, Harlan, and Julianne were in the lobby to see me. Amy and I had turned in early, made love like it was the last time, before she passed out, leaving me alone to ride the elevator of my unconscious.

"Yeah, sure, send them up," I told him, tearing myself from bed, Amy still deposited in a dream world I hoped was more hospitable than my own.

I stumbled into the bathroom, threw cold water onto my face and slipped into a robe trying to pull back into this world the demons from the other so, like a marine biologist studying some creature dredged from the ocean depths, I could better understand what I'd encountered. But it was no use, I realized, padding barefooted into the kitchen because even the most grotesque sea creature was physical. One could touch it, dissect it, eat it, if one chose.

Not so with the monsters that shadowed me, I brooded, snaring the half-empty bottle of Jameson's on the counter, pouring myself a stiff one.

In the fight game, a contender often calls out the champ, center ring, after he's just vanquished a tough rival, I ruminated, savoring the *vera causa* of my angst. And that's exactly what the killer had done, called me out. "Let's play, Madson! I want to stick my hand inside you feel what kind of guts you got!" But I was no Floyd Mayweather flashing Grover Clevelands like monopoly money, pretty women lifting their skirts as I strutted by, mansion in the Hills, a Bentley parked outside. And he was a homicidal maniac, not a boxer, so if analogy held it would be a celebrity news anchor, chief of police, or attorney general, not me, he'd be wanting to put in his cross-hairs, hunt down, and wipe off the face of the planet! No, there had to be something more, *something deeper*, that bound us together, I puzzled, when like a section of polar ice cap crashing into Artic waters Jeremiah's knock on the door jarred me from my reverie.

The frail priest's face was red with embarrassment, his demeanor apologetic.

"I'm sorry, son, but if Julianne or I were going to get any peace tonight, we had to bring Harlan here to see you."

"Father's right," Julianne agreed, casting a worried glance to Harlan, "that young man just wouldn't take 'no' for an answer."

"I needed to see you," Harlan protested, facial tics working overtime. "It's about the case, Jack. The 'Princeton Slasher' c-case Julianne and I have been working on!"

I took a moment to appraise the Benedictine monk,

idiot savant, and African American caregiver hovering in my doorway and despite best efforts could not suppress a chortle.

"You're always welcome here," I said, motioning them into my parlor where Julianne and Jeremiah plopped down onto chairs leaving the sofa for Harlan while I shuffled into the kitchen to freshen my drink. "Coffee?" I called out into the adjacent room and, hearing no reply, joined the party.

"Whatever brought you here must be pretty important, Harlan, dragging these two to my apartment like this," I began.

"Mr. Madson, I don't believe I've ever seen him so worked up," Julianne fretted, handsome face ashen with worry. "So, I told Father and here we are in your living room middle of the night!"

"I did the research I p-promised, Jack," Harlan hastened to explain, rising to his feet, "and knew you'd want to hear about it!"

"We just roused Mr. Madson from bed, Harlan," Jeremiah moaned. "Maybe you ought to sit down and give the man his space."

"No! I don't want to sit down! There's a serial killer out there, Father, and we need to stop him before he kills again!"

"Har-lan," Julianne scolded, "don't be talkin' to Father like that."

"I'm sorry, but it's important . . . to our case. Remember, you're Watson and I'm Sh-Sherlock," he reminded, "and Jack needs to know about Neil Collins," the pale little man argued, brown eyes targeted up at me as Julianne, looking concerned, rose from her chair, and his body snapped rigid. "Collins, Cornelius, U.S. congressman, New Jersey's 11th District, 1958-1972; born 1926, Bayonne, New Jersey," he rattled off, staccato. "Graduated Rutgers University, 1952; Harvard Law, *summa cum laude*, 1956. Awarded three Purple Hearts, Bronze Star medal, WWII; elected U.S. Congress, 1958: Chairman Committee on Government Abuse of U.S. Citizens, 1969-1972, investigating CIA violations of Fourth Amendment. Indicted income t-tax evasion, 1971, convicted, served four years Lewiston Federal Penitentiary; released, April 1977. Indicted conspiracy to commit mail fraud, 2008; convicted, served eight years Schuylkill Correctional Facility; released, September 2016 . . ."

"Wait just a minute!" I wailed, stunned to witness Harlan's demeanor turn sudden as a light switch from machine-like robotic back to himself again.

"What, what is it, Jack?" he wondered, a child emerging from a dream.

"I know all about Neil Collins' background now, Harlan, but what does that have to do with the murders?"

"Everything," he gushed, eyes brightening. "Don't you see? They put Collins in prison to stop the Hearings! His committee uncovered t-top secret mind control experiments performed by the spooks on soldiers, prisoners, college students. Black Ops projects worth hundreds of millions to the universities, billions more to DOD contractors, exactly what you're investigating. All of it documented in congressional records still sealed after fifty years! Princeton was one of those universities, Jack, still is. S-so," he stammered, turning to Jeremiah hanging now on his every word and Julianne, who stood dumbfounded, "what do you think a them a-apples?"

"That's why you wanted to see Mr. Madson so badly," Julianne marveled, "to tell him about the congressman and those awful experiments goin' on at Forrestal."

"Last time we met you talked about Black Ops and a project involving Nazi technology and behavioral modification," Jeremiah surmised, voice rising up from the studied silence he'd entered into. "Wasn't Marjorie Kurtz murdered inside a DOD laboratory operated by ALATON? Isn't it an oddment that Fetters worked in those same laboratories on that same project?"

"In the extreme," I retorted, words knifing.

"But that's not what couldn't wait," Harlan objected, brown eyes, penetrating now, lifting to meet mine head-on. "What couldn't wait is for me to tell you that Collins is still alive and living in New Jersey. He's the link to all of this: ALATON, Mengele, the murders! You've g-got to talk to him, Jack," Harlan urged, body surging as he reached up and held my face in the flat of his hands, "you've got to go see him before they find out he's still alive!"

* * *

I didn't bother trying to sleep after Jeremiah and company decamped, excited by the prospect that the scattered shards of information strewn around me were finally converging into a pattern. Even the gaps in chronology, once seemingly unbridgeable, appeared to have linkage from Mengele's 1945 plane crash to CIA Black Ops and ALATON's applied research going on at Princeton today.

Beyond that, I had the stainless steel talon Amy managed to stash during the FBI search of my hotel suite. Lodged in the sole of my Adidas, it was presumably left by the killer and may actually have been part of his anatomy—a claw or tooth—crawling with Kurtz' skin, blood, and bone cells. Perhaps even the maniac's own DNA.

For days now I'd racked my brain trying to find someone I trusted enough to examine it. More, someone with access to the technical resources necessary to establish what it was, what it was used for, perhaps even the killer's identity. Gifford was too 'by the book', Donnolly a dunce, and to the FBI, I was more likely a suspect than an investigator trying to help solve the case.

Still, there was one name wrung from past experiences that did come to mind. No friend, to be sure. But not an enemy, either. Back three years ago while working the Kafka Society case, not only did I manage to stay out of Don Woods' way when Group 41 from Homeland was investigating Tom Dougherty, I shot the son of a bitch dead in St. Mary's chapel and let them take credit for it!

So, okay, Dougherty's demise was not without its controversy and Obama never did award me that Presidential Medal of Freedom I so rightly deserved, but Woods would remember the good turn I did him. So, I called, not totally surprised when he agreed to rendezvous at the Jackie Onassis Reservoir for a "discreet discussion" about the unsolved murders on Princeton University campus.

The mile and a half jogging track that circled the reservoir was less crowded than usual with only an occasional jogger and handful of tourists walking the track. A bone-rattling wind swept through the Park, carrying with it the sprightly voices of the Holy Trinity choir singing Christmas carols and snowflakes that barely survived the frozen ground. Woods well knew the terrain, hence his decision to meet at the no. 2 pump house planted like a concrete bunker at water's edge between Fifth Avenue and Central Park West.

It wasn't difficult to recognize Woods. He stood alone smoking a cigarette, body bunched up in a Burberry's trench coat looking every bit the aging intelligence operative he pretended not to be. Soft around the middle, with blue eyes cold as a New England forest in winter, his face was deeply etched now the way a man's countenance gets after his soul mate has passed and he's gone through months of lonely nights pining for her. He wore glasses, wire-rimmed, with thick lenses that made him look more like a retired accountant than a covert operative prowling the black seams of U.S. Intel.

"Hey, Jack, it's been a while, hasn't it?"

"Miss me?"

"There aren't many I do miss, though I had a Labrador once."

I smiled. Woods began walking, me alongside him. Beyond the cattails and elms, barren now, the El Dorado, Dakota, and Majestic hotels groped skyward into the clouds fat with impending snow.

"You look like hell, you know that, don't you?"

"If I lived your life—worked when I liked, corking anything in a skirt—guess I'd look like Brad Pitt, too. But this life of mine? It hasn't been easy. Wife died last year, cancer. Two months later, it was glaucoma for me. Hence, these Hubble Telescopes I wear; custom-made so I can see the Dark Spots on Neptune. Then, just in case I was feeling too good about myself, the Agency put me on 'garden leave'."

"Sorry?"

"A euphemism for 'don't show up to work anymore.'
They pay me. I walk around Central Park. Watch birds. Eat
a hot dog occasionally."

"Leading to . . ."

"What does one do with a blind spy? Termination, I
suppose. They're trying to unearth a legal justification.
Once accomplished, trust me. I'll sue their balls off." He
stopped walking. The sound of a Santa's bell rang clear. A
flock of geese took flight mid-reservoir. "So those are the
particulars of my dystopian existence, how 'bout yours?"

"Mind if I skip the bullshit?"

"I'm on garden leave, Madson. Flexible as Churchill's
'Boneless Wonder'."

I pulled a baggy containing the talon from the side
pocket of my pee-coat, handed it to him.

"Believe it or not, I trust you, Woods. We may not have
hit the sweetest notes last time out, but you didn't rat
me out when you had the chance, and we all lived to tell
about it."

He studied the 3" long, razor-sharp object in his open
palm.

"What is it?"

"That's where you come in."

"How'd you come upon it?"

"Marjorie Kurtz' laboratory at Forrestal," I answered.
"Found it lodged in the sole of my tennis shoe after returning to my hotel from the murder scene."

"Murder scene? Was there a murder that preceded
Fetters'?"

"Depends who you believe, but I saw her body, or what
was left of it. May have caught a glimpse of her killer . . ."

"The 'Princeton Slasher'," he said, closing his fingers

around the enveloped talon. "Anyone else know you have this?"

"Just you, me, and one other, who shall remain name-less."

"So what am I supposed to do, pack it in a Happy Meal?"

"I need you to put it through Forensics, alternate channels. Find out what it is and what it was used for, if I'm right, it's tied to Kurtz' murder. I don't know how, can't even imagine, but I'm sure of this much. There are human experiments—wild beyond comprehension—going on in the underground laboratories at Forrestal under the aegis of DARPA and the DOD. I found Kurtz' remains in one of them—body ravaged, internal organs devoured by the monster that killed her—and let me tell you: man, beast, or any-fucking-thing between, I intend to track it down, Woods. Then, I intend to kill it."

"A touch dramatic, don't you think?"

"Not if you're me," I retorted, undeterred. "Our advantage is that few know a second murder took place and no one, outside of you and me, know about that," I said, stabbing an index finger at the object he held. "Now I need your word, Don. Swear to me that you'll tell no one who turned this evidence over to you or from where it was retrieved."

"I never thought I'd say this, Madson, but I owe you one. That situation with Dougherty created a lot of turbu-lence for Group 41, but you never went public with what you knew, took the heat for it, besides. Sure, I know a lab who'll examine it, no questions asked, and you have my word it'll stay between us, but there are a couple of truths you should know first," he said, turning to me, "truths I'm telling you as a friend. Understand, I worked CIA during the Viet Nam war before coming to Homeland: Da Nang, la Drang, Dien Bien Phu, you name it. Seen some things I wish I hadn't, but nothing as consummately evil as PHOE-NIX, ever hear of it?"

I shook my head. A jogger passed. Woods' eyes, sparkling with ardor now, bore into mine from behind the thick lens of his spectacles.

"OPERATION PHOENIX was backed by DARPA with the Company picking up the pieces from their experiments: human killing machines, Madson, based on drugs, behavioral modification, and radio-hypnotic control."

"Successful?" I inquired.

"Soldiers—eighteen, twenty years old—dropped behind enemy lines for days at a time with nothing but a Colt Woodsman, machete, and index cards bearing the names of individuals they were commissioned to assassinate in the most horrendous ways possible: decapitation, dismemberment, castration, all meant to strike terror in the hearts of Charlie. Entire families massacred, scalped, body parts hung from spikes as in a butcher shop; balls sewn up in their mouths, faces scraped off so the only way victims could be identified was one of those index cards left behind, handwritten, with their name on it. So you tell me, is that 'successful'?"

A covey of Chinese tourists overtook us. Woods paid them no mind.

"Once returned from their missions, most had little or no knowledge of what they had done," he continued, blue eyes locked with mine, "and those that did showed no emotion whatsoever when confronted with the atrocities they'd committed. It was our job to debrief them once returned. But it was their eyes that threw me, Madson, and I live with those eyes even today. Black and shiny like the button eyes in a doll's head, dead while still alive, no life in them whatsoever."

Woods turned into the wind as he slid the baggy into the side pocket of his trench coat.

"Who's paying you to look into this?" he asked, bracing himself against the cold, the lilting sound of Christmas carols swirling like ghosts in the December wind around us.

"It was Kurtz," I answered, "left twenty grand moments before the killer did her."

"Twenty K," Woods said, assessing the number with a succinct nod. "Let me give you some advice, Jack. You take that money, blow it on booze, or whores, or black jack tables in Vegas, I don't give a rat's ass. But whatever you do, drop this case, and get the fuck out of Jersey. The guys we're talking about operate on a whole different level than the rest of us, Madson. Wackos most of them, programmed to kill and keep on killing until their mission is terminated, them along with it."

"Ever hear of a former Jersey Congressman named Collins?" I asked speculatively.

"Yeah, I heard of him," Woods shot back, eyes contracting to needle points as he glared at me from behind the lens of his silver-rimmed spectacles, "two time loser, crooked as a bag of snakes."

"Crazy?" I asked.

"Dangerous," he answered.

Chapter Nineteen

Collins Residence
Columbia, New Jersey

My Stingray convertible sailed west on Rt. 80 headed to the isolated cabin Neil Collins called home these long winter days and nights since his release from prison. The unbridled freedom I felt letting the Vette do what it did best had all but put my mind at ease when the Stones' *Stop Breakin' Down* ringtone blasted over the Bluetooth.

I smiled. It was Tiffany.

"Hey, babe," I greeted.

"Hi, Daddy," she answered, worriedly, a tone I'd come to expect. "I'm calling to remind you to visit Mom with me this Wednesday."

"Wild horses couldn't keep me away," I answered, still thinking of Jagger and the Stones, I suppose.

"Promise?" she asked, a wellspring of optimism rising.

"With bells," I quipped.

"It's her birthday, Dad!" she declared so that I half expected her to cry-out 'Oh, goodie!' as she might have twenty years earlier. "Nurse Keating's going to have a cake and everything!"

"Wouldn't miss it," I pledged a final time before ending our conversation, reveries not of Jennifer or Tiffany, but of CIA black ops and GRIN experiments ongoing since the 1960s, swirling like eddies through the black water of my mind.

Finally, after navigating gravel roads, one-car bridges, and enough forest to replenish the ozone, I pulled up to Collins' log cabin situated like a soldier's final redoubt in the middle of the woods.

By all accounts, Collins' early life read like an American dream, I remembered from his bio: varsity baseball and basketball in college, family man, law school valedictorian and war hero returned from Patton's Third Army with a Bronze Star and three Purple Hearts, taking enough time to open a thriving law practice, only to re-up with the onset of the Korean War.

I climbed the wooden stairs leading to a makeshift porch, knocked on the door. It was Collins, who answered. Still handsome, he looked the ghost of an Irish poet, his face ruddy with white hair swept to the back of his head to camouflage a mottle of cancer.

"Afternoon, Congressman, name's Jack Madson," I said, extending my hand.

"I know who you are," he said, eyeing the outstretched appendage. "So are you gonna stand there all day or come inside?"

I followed Collins into the living room, cramped and rustic, except for a Steinway baby grand with framed photos atop it, grim reminders of his glory days as a rising star in American politics. Posing with him was Martin Luther King; Bobby Kennedy; former Louisiana Congressman Hale Boggs; Jack Kennedy; and Malcolm Little, better known as Malcolm X.

"Quite a collection you have here," I remarked. "But do me a favor: don't put a photo of me on your piano top. It seems every one of them was murdered. Except you."

Collins tossed a log into the fireplace, flames leaping. "Yeah, I'm dead. They just didn't do it with a bullet through my head," he said, easing into a lounger. "But you didn't come here to talk about King and the Kennedys. I spoke with your pal Harlan," he noted with a chortle. "You want to know about my Government Abuse Hearings and the CIA's experiments with programmed assassins. That's the sexy stuff, but it went a lot deeper than that."

"How much deeper?"

"It started when our Committee discovered that between 1964 and 1966, 500,000 grammar school kids were forced by the Department of Education to take "personality tests". All part of a government master plan to collect psychological profiles, criminal records, medical histories — anything they could get their hands on — to create cradle-to-grave dossiers on every living American citizen."

"CIA?"

"That's right," he replied unhesitatingly.

"Why would the CIA want to get involved in domestic spying?"

"To understand 'why' you need to appreciate the hysteria that permeated the country during the Cold War," he retorted. "The Soviets had the bomb, so did we, but they also had that goddamned Sputnik satellite circling above us that American families could watch from their backyards each night. Some wondered, 'what if the Russians had, not one, but hundreds of those things circling above us?' worse, 'what if they dropped atom bombs?' So the

214 Dark Angel

gloves were off. Hoover, with his FBI, and Dulles, with the
CIA, would do anything — any fucking thing — to protect
our American way of life from the Commies," he winked,
"while furthering their agency's grip on the U.S. population! Within weeks came another bombshell: the unau-
thorized dispensing of psychotic drugs — Melleril, Ritalin,
Adderall — to 350,000 grammar school kids to track their
performance against drug free control groups."

"So, okay, these kids' rights were trampled," I persisted,
probing the logic that propelled his conspiracy theories.
"What makes you think these incidents are part of a government 'master plan'?"

"Control!" Collins shot back, sounding more ex-con
than former congressman. "Once the Committee's work
got underway, credible individuals — scientists, university
professors, military men — started coming forward with
fantastic stories about secret military programs at Stanford, Princeton, Harvard to develop biological weapons,
many without cure; gene splicing to produce chemical
weapons to wipe-out targeted ethnic populations; and,
yeah, programmed assassins, nexus to an army of genetically engineered super-killers." The wizened Irishman's
clear blue eyes searched mine for a reaction. His spidery
fingers swept a lick of white hair across the back of his
scalp. "You want to know what made them part of a government 'master plan'?" he challenged, leaning forward
in his chair. "Aside from the billions of dollars poured into
them, each started as DOD initiatives to fight Commu-
nism, but soon morphed into a CIA strategy to re-create
America based on post- World War II Nazi technologies!"

"The scientists, the ones that exported those technologies," I asked, groping for a link between the Princeton

murders and ALATON's experiments, "was Josef Mengele one of them?"

"Among others," he answered, eyes haunted as he reclined back into the lounger. "Once the Committee gained access to CIA files, we discovered that the black ops programs we uncovered during the 1970s had been going on since before the war ended: radio stimulation of the brain, stereotaxic surgery, cloning! The result was paradigm-shattering breakthroughs in genetics and radio-hypnotic intra-cerebral communication, the ability to control the behavior of others through the use of microwave transmissions."

"Silent messaging," I uttered harrowingly.

"Exactly," Collins avowed, a coiled cobra spewing its venom. "Nazi bastards called it *unterbrechung*, 'brain fracking'. Light years beyond that now, but the same core technologies the CIA used to create domestic assassins like Oswald, Ray, and Sirhan Sirhan. Hell, Mengele was experimenting with manipulation of genes as far back as the 1940s trying to create super-soldiers, *schlacht maschinen*, who like kamikaze pilots would take orders without questioning."

"Wait a minute," I interrupted, stopping him there. "Are you telling me that our own government programmed the assassins who killed King and the Kennedys?"

"That's right. Specific individuals whose backgrounds and psychological profiles made them ideal candidates for the job. Oswald, a man supposedly obsessed with celebrity, called himself a 'patsy'; Ray was a petty thief, totally non-political, and anything but a murderer; Sirhan Sirhan to this day has no recollection of ever setting foot in the Ambassador hotel, let alone firing a pistol at Robert

Kennedy. These were loners, without family or career ties, emotionally disconnected from their victims and the murders they committed, programed to kill."

"What about *das schlacht maschinen?*" I probed, jutting my frame forward. "What about Operation Phoenix and the atrocities your committee uncovered?"

"Unlike the domestic hits I told you about, Phoenix was done on a massive scale," he asserted with an 'in your face' Jersey swagger. "These were teams of manufactured assassins, brains wired to torture, kill, and mutilate enemies, real or perceived, on sight behind enemy lines during the Viet Nam war. But here," he declared handing over a transcript titled, "House Committee Hearings: Human Experimentation and Mind Control" from the end table beside him. "This is what you came here for, isn't it? Proof that these programs existed and are still going on at Princeton today!"

I paged through the document stopping at a dog-eared section marked, 'Testimony, Lt. Robert Louis Jordan, 101st Airborne, OPERATION PHOENIX, August 7, 1971'. Heart pounding with anticipation, I began reading:

>As standard equipment we carried Hush Puppies, a Mark 22, model O, which used 9mm ammo and had a five-inch barrel equipped with silencer. This weapon, along with the fact that each of us could kill with our hands, had only one other thing in common—we were insane.
>
>The most important element of the program, aside from the men, was the drugs supplied by the local Case Manager that kept us awake for days at a time, erased the deeds com-

mitted from the mind and allowed peace to enter the soul, at least for a time.

It was called the Green Hornet, a capsule containing a mixture of Benezedrine, an amphetamine which stimulated the central nervous system, Dexamil, a synthetic steroid which stimulated the adrenal gland and made a man superhuman, and Reserpine, commonly used to treat high blood pressure and mental patients.

The Green Hornet caused a man to act faster than normal. You could feel your heart speed up. Your head would throb, and it felt as if the brain was actually growing. It gave a man his own personal radar so his senses were finetuned to an extreme pitch. Every nerve end was sensitive to sound, sight, and smell, and it seemed as if a receiver was implanted in your brain. Put all this together and a man could stay awake for days, fight, function, kill, and if you were lucky, not lose your mind.

I looked up from the transcript, "Can I keep this?"

"I have no use for it. I'm dying, Madson, pancreatic cancer," he confided. "Not that I haven't been dead these past forty years anyway. Ever hear the acronym FLEAS?"

I shook my head in the negative.

"Federal Law Enforcement Agencies," he expounded. "People call them that because like fleas they work their way into everything you do, everything you are, and won't get off 'till you're dead and buried. That's what they used to kill me, not guns or bullets, FLEAS!"

Collins smiled then, eyes twinkling with guile as he

appraised me from across the room, logs in the fireplace blazing behind him.

"You're not built for this kind of work, you know that, don't you, Madson? You lack the constitution," he struggled for a better word, "the *mentality* for the brutality it entails. You feel too much to be in the game you're playing among the men you're playing it with. You should get out now while you can, cut your fucking losses."

"Says who," I snorted, "an ex-con politician living like a hermit in a log cabin in Jersey?"

"Mentality," Collins repeated, tapping his temple with his forefinger. "By the time these men, *these evil men*, are through with you there'll be nothing left but a hank of hair and some fillings," he lamented, "but I'm not your keeper. So, tell me, exactly what is it you want?"

"I need to know about DARPA's relationship with Elon Powers and ALATON," I said, unflinchingly.

"Powers," he scoffed, the tenterhook of obsession rising up, shimmering, "a spoiled, goddamned brat! His father, a banker at DeBeers, steals off in the middle of the night with a half billion in cash, bribes his way to citizenship here into the States, and Elon brags about walking out of Africa with nothing but the shirt on his back. Now there's a goddamned laugh! The little bastard was the wealthiest man in the state of California the day he set foot in this country. To him, America's a capitalist playground, and he works it like a pin-ball machine!" He sat back in his chair then, the glimmer in his eye returning. "By the way, since you're determined to go through with this, you might want to consider the pedigree of the people you spend time with."

"Are we still talking about Elon?"

"No," he barked, dismissively, "I doubt anyone will

ever know a man like Elon Powers. Too many rooms in that house, doors locked, with God knows what species of incubus lurking inside. No, I'm talking about that neo-Nazi Princeton University has been harboring for the past thirty years."

"Neo-Nazi?"

"His given name was Merckx, Loris Koiten Merckx, born 1928, Ghent, Belgium, indoctrinated into the Nazi movement while a student at the university," Collins expatiated, right hand dipping into a battered leather briefcase. "Merckx was a courier for the ex-*SS* hierarchy relocated to South America after the war," he continued, plucking a photo from a dossier, thick with news clippings, the surname 'MERCKX' inscribed upon it. "Experts, most of them Israeli, believe he changed his identity sometime around '55 as part of the CIA's OPERATION PAPERCLIP. Shielded by U.S. intelligence for decades, no one's bothered to ask him about the time he spent in the jungles outside of Sao Paulo, 1965–\68."

"Why?" I asked. "Why that particular period?"

"Because that, Mr. Madson, is when Merckx teamed up with Dr. Josef Mengele, Auschwitz' infamous 'Angel of Death'. Working in laboratories, hidden from civilization, they were able to perform experiments; all kinds of crazy projects—a race of blue-eyed babies, genetically altered embryos, early attempts at cloning—on humans kidnapped from native tribes, immune from ethical considerations, beyond the reach of international law."

"She called it the three pillars of technology," I noted, recalling my walk with Kurtz along Lake Carnegie.

"Pardon?"

"OPERATION MAYHEM, a DOD project Marjorie

Kurtz, a scientist working for ALATON told me about just before she was murdered."

"No surprise. Those projects, the ones initiated by Mengele and Merckx in Brazil, were funded by DARPA. It was that revelation, exposed by our Government Abuse Committee, that earned me two stints in federal prison! Not much more to tell, except that like so many of these Nazi vermin scrambling for cover post WWII, the name 'Merckx' became synonymous with U.S. national security; a chess piece our boys plucked from under Stalin's nose. No, not a King or Queen as coveted as Von Braun or Mengele, but a working asset with skills and knowledge we couldn't hope to acquire without access to the research he validated: crimes, associations, true identity lost forever behind the great coat of patriotism!"

I held the black and white photos at its edges, slowly raising it eye-level.

No need to look twice at the serious young man with piercing blue eyes proudly wearing his crisply pressed Nazi officers' uniform, chest thrust out, chin jutting forward with bravado, facial expression unabashedly defiant.

It was Dr. Paul Lindstrom, circa 1953.

Chapter Twenty

Mehanata
Lower East Side, NYC

That night I took Amy to *Menhanata* to let off steam, something we both desperately needed—her, harried with the stress of launching her film; me, obsessing over the Kurtz case and a serial killer at large. It was a short trip from the Elysee to the Lower East Side. We took a limo, and there were reasons for that. One was the paranoia Amy felt about the paparazzi's intrusions into her life, appetites whetted with news that the previews of *Twisted* were first rate. Another was that I, too, had become a celeb of sorts since police photos with my name plastered over the walls of the Princeton "Death House" had been leaked to the *Inquirer.* Couple that with rumors that Coco and I were an item (thank you Tyson Rollins!) and it was easy to see why we'd gone stealth, Amy dressed-down in jeans and work shirt, face hidden behind Jackie O-sized Ray Bans; me, looking pretty much as always, black 'DEMPSEY' T-shirt, leather flight jacket, Adidas.

I can't say why I chose *Mehanata*, but best guess was my pal, Johnnie Giambi, and I used to hang there once upon a time. Maybe I also liked to believe the ghost of my one-eyed, MMA-fighting friend still lingered amidst the riotous atmosphere that avalanched the place around midnight when Artic Monkeys rocked the upper level and patrons downed shots of vodka non-stop in the "ice cage" two floors below.

Sound logic, but now I need a couple of stiff ones to accompany the morphine I'd been taking for my side-wound, a quiet table, and someone with whom to share the conjectures erupting volcanic in my head. Was there, indeed, logic to them? Did any one of them make sense to someone, who unlike me, was not embroiled in the maelstrom of complexity surrounding the Kurtz case?

I said not a word to Vitali "Ruby" Rubinoff, the owner. One look told him that Amy and I needed to talk, so he deposited us on one of the swings that substituted for bar stools with a bottle of Stolichnaya, bucket of ice, no customers, no bar tender.

I dropped two cubes into a tall glass, filled it three-quarters high.

"Don't think you need the shades," I said, handing the drink to her, pouring one of my own, no ice.

Amy fidgeted with the Ray Bans as she shed them, "I'm discombobulated, Jackie! Like that director you told me about who couldn't stop filming, I don't know what's real anymore! Sure, I'm ex-totic everybody likes me in the Brolin flick, but I can't change my panties these days without paparazzi jumpin' out of a closet tryin' to catch me in some lousy situation. Then there's you, baby. You, and these murders, and this maniac everyone's saying wants to kill you next!"

"You want to know what's real?" I asked, watching as she took a long cool sip of vodka. "This is what's real,"

I said, kissing her flush on the mouth, holding her lips pressed against mine until together we savored the crisp, clean taste of the Stolichnaya tongue-on-tongue. "Don't worry, baby," I soothed, eyes melting one into the others', "we're both going to come out of this fine, you'll see."

"Are we, Jackie? 'Cause sometimes I worry," she fretted, "really I do. How did it go with Neil Collins today? Did he know all those things Harlan said?"

"He did," I answered, leaning back, rocking the swing forward. "Seems like Paul Lindstrom, VP Technology at ALATON, actually worked with Mengele in Brazil after the War. Can you guess what projects they worked to develop?"

"Something to do with genetics?" she ventured. "I know, super soldiers, like the ones Kurtz told you! Am I right, Jackie?"

"You are indeed. Proof that Kurtz had every right to be scared silly by what was happening at ALATON. Turns out, Lindstrom's real name is Merckx, Loris Koiten Merckx, a Belgian neo-Nazi relocated to Princeton, given a new identity by the CIA. What Collins handed me today is the link I needed: Nazis to CIA, CIA to ALATON, translated Mengele to Lindstrom, Lindstrom to Powers. I'm not dealing with institutions any longer, Amy. I've got names: real men with real identities who can be tried and brought to justice."

"What about the murders, Jack?" she wondered, big-eyed wary as the swing arced skyward.

"That's the piece that's still missing: is there a connection between ALATON'S experiments and the serial killer?" I brooded, Adidas brushing the floor, upward momentum stalling. "Could it be that Hitler's dream to create an army of killing machines spawned the monster stalking Princeton campus today?"

"You wanna know somethin', Jackie?" Amy declared, taking hold of my chin, turning my face to her. "I don't want to talk about this anymore. Too depressing!" Then, face alight, she slapped on her Ray Bans, grinning, "Let's go to the ice cage! Let's have some fun!"

* * *

Once returned to the hotel that night, romance permeated the room: playful and sexy, our first moments broke loose from the gravity of Princeton in weeks. Amy fired up a joint. We shared it, locked in one another's arms standing by the open window overlooking the street, partaking of it mouth-over-mouth, close and sexy.

"Did you see their faces when we got into the ice cage together?" she asked, giggling.

"I don't think it was us getting in the cage together that made people crazy," I laughed. "I think it was you taking your clothes off!"

"Well," she said indignantly, taking a hit, then inhaling, "I'll bet *Celebrity News* is going to say I had *nothing on*, but that's not true, Jackie. I had my *I-Phone on* listening to Radiohead!"

"Want a drink?" I asked, grinning.

"Champagne!" she gushed.

"Whatever pleases, mi' lady," I obliged, headed for the fridge.

"While you do that, I'll get in my PJs," I heard her call out brightly, and the sound of her voice made me happy, I thought then, simply being around her, knowing that we'd be sharing a bed that night, the air around me thickening with the tender, wise, and witty presence of this angel of sex.

I popped the cork on the bottle of Armand de Brignac, pouring. 'Jesus loves me,' she would often tell me when events turned on her, but for every indication that Amy was a spiritual orphan trapped in some never-never land of unawareness, there was Coco, mistress of that great remote female void where wonder at the comedies of men's urgencies reside, ready, willing, and able to exploit them. But thoughts so venial could not survive what waited for me, and perhaps it was the culmination of both Amy and Coco's virtues—vulnerable and hard, sensual and elusive, tender and insatiable—that left me sporting an erection bold as the Freedom Tower.

Amy watched me watch her, unabashedly. Dressed in a snow white lace-up bustier with garter belt and spike heels, I took in her every aspect—tussled blonde hair, full lips, deep-set eyes that glittered like gems—lost in a cloud of drifting senses.

I stepped forward, handing her the flute of champagne. My fingers cold from holding the chilled glass touched hers and I held them for a moment and let them go slowly as one lets go of a dream when they wake with the sun in their face and have been in an enchanted valley.

"Whatever you want," she pledged, the faintest hint of a smile crossing her cherry lips.

I'm told that on the scale of life's requirements, sex places third behind food and water, but during the moments Amy and I shared that night I doubted it could be true. We both needed sex, hungered for it, and left no stone unturned in our garden of carnal delights, some practiced, others so spontaneous that by daybreak I was sure no two people had done such things or ever thought of them.

But even in the bliss that followed, I could not afford

the luxury of sleep without first gauging the private joys and terrors that might lay waiting for me in that shit pit of unconsciousness. Perhaps, Satan, himself, or a journey back to the tranquility of better times with Tiffany as a child, Jennifer when I loved her, or Havana Spice lying on my chest amid white sheets floating on a cloud. It was a coin toss and that is what filled me with dread.

Warily I drifted — morphine absorbed tissue-to-blood, a half bottle of vodka close behind — eyelids falling like the shutters of a turn-of-the-century mansion brimming with memories, ghosts, living horrors. Finally, I fell victim to the inevitability of sleep.

Dark shadows cavorting! I feel the bane of infection plying its way into my side wound. See the silver **ID BRACELET**. *"Confianza en su corazon"*, it reads, "trust in your heart!" **FERRIS WHEELS** spinning. Scraping. Loud. A surgeon's lancet knifing through veils of static. Faces swirling: Coco Channing, Eddie Lawler, Lindstrom, Powers, Mengele laughing. THEN, total darkness. Silence so profound I can hear the thumping of my heartbeat. NOW I am in bed, Amy asleep beside me, confronted by the specter of **BILL "SALVATORE" BONANNO** standing at my bedside.

"Bill, what are you doing here?"

"To see you, Jack."

"But why?"

"We come here first. Here to wait. Dead," he explains, expressionless. "It's like a ship, a hospital, with Doctor Angels. But sometimes we come back on 'special' missions."

"Like now?"

"Yeah," he answers, "like now. The Family worked

with guys like the one you're after: special ops, trained killers, stone cold. None crazy as this motherfucker! But you're not hearin' me, are ya, Jackie?" he concludes, shaking his head from side to side. Then, staring down at me, Bonanno mutters, "Death Be Not Proud," the words inserted like poorly edited dialogue in a foreign language film. "You can't say I didn't warn you," he sniggers. "You can't say I didn't tell ya to get your ass back to Frisco!" But Bonanno is Bonanno no longer, and I watch as before my eyes he metamorphoses into **THE PREACHER**, ghoulish as he smiles, face thrust forward inches from mine, breath heavy as kerosene, voice so tremulous it seems to derive from inside, not outside, my head.

Heart stopped. Abandoned in some obscure dimension between life and death, I watch as molecule by molecule **THE PREACHER** recedes, tide pulling back from shore dragging me into the hidden enclaves of an unseen world.

NOW I am submerged, deep, in a dark universe. Human existence seen through the predator's eyes. Locked in a chamber. Constructed of steel and concrete. Snakes of contagion dart like eels unseen around me. Then there is It. Shimmering. Brute. Eminently powerful. It drifts through the cold hungry air in search of its quarry.

> *open*
> *static scraping hissing voices*
> *"silent message"*
> *bright as day*

"Oh, you are lovely," the predator admires, stroking the nipple of Julianne Johnson's bare breast, talons extended as he looms over

her. "*Yes, now you are trembling, but notice the areola darkening, nipples hard and rigid, despite the terror you're experiencing. The Negro held special allure for the Fuhrer, did you know that? You have read about it, perhaps? Seen a snippet on the History channel?*" *His eyes, turned intensely blue from the dark brown they had once been, twinkle. "No, I don't think so, but along with Gypsies and Jews, the Negro was of great importance in establishing a baseline for the Reich's genetic experiments. Unlike your friend, or is he your lover?" he asks, casting a withering stare at Harlan Haberman, pinioned to the wall not five feet from them. "Idiots among the Gypsy population were a dime a dozen back then, but the Americam gene pool, a thousand times worse! Pity," he adds, smiling gently as steel claws sprout from the shafts of his fingers, "if it weren't for fear of syphilis, I might be fucking you right now."*

Sitting naked, bound hand and foot, Julianne can only stare ahead, seeing but unable to move even an eyelash now that the succinylcholine chloride has taken effect. Desperate, she tries to convince herself that this is not real; that horror like this is reserved for the movies, the sordid kind she avoids at all costs with Jason, the maniacal killer, stalking unsuspecting lovers trysting in country cottages deep in the woods away from any semblance of society or police or parents. "God help us!" she is thinking as the predator lowers his face, breath thick with the stink of rotted meat heaving down upon her as he attempts to intercept her thoughts. "Be brave, Harlan," her eyes locked with his are saying. "Remember that God loves you!"

He turns, moves to the center of the concrete and steel chamber. He steps behind the Sony video camera set on a tripod, peers through the lens. Devoid of emotions, he experiences only need: relentless hunger for violence, overwhelming desire to sate the blood lust planted inside him. "Our studio has none of the Holly-

wood glamor an American might expect, but we do have lights and camera, sound-proofed concrete walls, floor with grated drains to collect the overflow of blood, even a sound track," he boasts, unwinding a circle of high intensity electrical wire like a long coiled serpent as the sound of the Andrew Sisters singing "Don't Sit Under The Apple Tree" cascades through the corridors, bouncing oddly room-to-room as if escaped from another time; near the tail end of World War II, Julianne Johnson is thinking, mind numb, disoriented, eyes fastened upon Harlan's. "Don't be afraid, my handsome Harlan," she implores. "Trust in Jesus! Trust in our Lord and Savior!"

> *'Don't sit un-der the apple tree with anyone else but me,*
> *Anyone el-se but me — BAH!*
> *Anyone el-se but me — BAH!*
> *No! No! No!'*

Strange, Julianne contemplates beyond the music's blare, she's been a Roman Catholic for her entire life, but suddenly cannot remember the words to the "Our Father". And no matter how hard she tries, feverishly attempts, to extricate herself from the physical and psychological grip the maniac has on her; to pretend she is on a beach, or at home reading the Bible, or tucked beneath the sheets in the warmth of her bed, finally she is forced to realize that it is all a lie. That she is, in fact, in a closet or bunker or chamber of torture with a madman obsessed with tearing her body apart!

"Our Father, who art in Heaven," the words seep up from the depths of her childhood rearing. Taught by nuns. At St. Francis. "Hallowed by Thy name. Thy kingdom come. Thy will be done,"

she prays, terror mounting riotous inside her as the monster approaches. "Oh, God, what have You done? How can you let this happen? Sweet Baby Jesus!" she begs. "How can You let him do this to me??"

> *'Don't start gazin' at the moon to-night*
> *with anyone in your arms,*
> *Anyone in yo-ur arms — BAH!*
> *Anyone in yo-ur arms — BAH!*
> *'Til I co-me mar-chin' home!'*

"There was a time I despised popular music," the predator pontificates, "but it occurred to me that music was just one more path to discovery: an insight into the zeitgeist of a culture. Wagner! I thought. Mozart and Schubert! Elvis and the Beatles! JayZ, why the hell not? Music is the clearest window into the soul of a society and therefore the individuals that comprise it, wouldn't you agree, Miss Johnson?" Then, feigning disappointment, "Oh, but that's not fair, I'd wager you're thinking," he surmises, face thrust forward, jaw distended, steel teeth bared, "expecting intelligent answers when it's clear you're just a nigger bitch too stupid to think at all!"

He stares into her eyes a long terrifying moment, then pulls away, snapping the black electrical cord taut in front of her. "But if you could speak," he says, leering down at her, "I think you'd be begging to save the Jew Boy's life!" he scowls, dangling the black cord like a hangman's noose inches from her face, touching it to her ears and nose and mouth.

Fascinated, he studies her reactions, primal, perhaps even fetal, body quaking, arms and legs twitching spasmodically, eyes still locked with Harlan's, until his icy gaze deserts her, and she watches, drawing fast, shallow breaths as he inserts the cable's three-pronged inset into a wall socket just inches above her. He turns, the fires of Hell raging in his eyes as he attaches one of three alligator clips to the nipple of her right breast then stalks toward the washtub near the steel framed door that seals the darkened concrete chamber.

In icy silence, Julianne watches, chest pounding like some living thing fluttering inside her ribcage battling to escape, eyes shining ardent now as she attempts to communicate with Harlan, body shaking uncontrollably, face soaked with tears. "Let's pray together, Darlin'" her eyes tell him. "Let's you and me pray, Harlan, for the people who won't see Heaven like you and me. Let's pray for Father Jeremiah, who we love so much, and for sinners like this man that God will forgive him!"

But with juices churning orgiastic in anticipation of the kill, the monster cannot be deterred by prayers or pleas for mercy. Trudging forward, eyes gleaming, he raises his right hand shoulder-high running his razor-sharp talons deep across Harlan's throat, blood spouting in torrents from his jugular as he marches forward, implacable, to confront her!

Steel claws receding, the predator seizes Julianne at the jaw. He forces her mouth open, attaches a second alligator clip to the tip of her tongue. Then, powerful hands sweeping downward, he spreads her legs in a violent, scissor-like motion, searches with fingers for her clitoris, snapping the third and final electrical connector onto it.

In that instant, with the clutch of the clip's teeth firm upon her, Julianne is jolted by a blinding flash brighter and hotter than the sulfurous rock that boils at the center of the sun, the muscles and tendons and molecules in her body set screaming like some savage beast has ripped the flesh from her bones, as she arches up in the wooden chair, conscious and withering, hearing the rasp. Inhuman. Totally devoid of emotion.

"Our Father who art in Heaven," he taunts as the music of

*the Andrews Sisters swirls loud and mellifluous through the con-
crete and steel torture chamber.*

> **scratch scratch**
> **woman's voice emerging**
> **through the mist electric**
> **"close silent messaging"**

I awaken, shrieking—Amy's panicked eyes set upon
me—drenched in cold sweat, phone ringing. Wordlessly,
she handed me the receiver.

"Sorry to disturb you, Mr. Madson, but there's an
urgent message here at the front desk for you."

"Huh?"

"It was Karl talked to him. Said the guy was very upset.
Want me to read it?"

"Yes, yes, go ahead."

"'Jack,'" he read from the note Karl had scribbled,
"come to Princeton Chapel now. There's been a horrible
tragedy! Jeremiah.'"

Chapter Twenty-One

Princeton Chapel
Main Campus, Princeton University

Steeped in graveyard silence, I raced the Vette south on Route 1, Amy's face ashen with dread, neither of us daring to imagine what awaited us at Princeton. One thing sure, it wasn't good, and even before we'd approached the Harrison Street exit, we could hear sirens screaming, a prelude, I suspected, to the swale of panic-laced mayhem resonating within reporters, EMTs, local, state and federal investigators converged on campus.

I parked the car beside the guard station off Nassau Street then took the short walk into the courtyard, bordered by East Pyne, the Chapel, and McCosh Hall. Together, Amy and I threaded through the tumult, beyond the crime scene demarcations, finally washing up like lost seamen upon the sandstone steps leading to the heavy oak doors of the Chapel's main entrance.

"Where do you think you're going, Madson?" a Uniform demanded.

"Reverend Jeremiah contacted Miss Channing and I. Said he needed us, urgent."

He cast a questioning glance to Gifford, conferencing with a team of FBI crime scene specialists.

"Yeah, he's all right," Gifford called back, breaking from the group, Donnolly tagging alongside.

"Just get here, or are you returning to the scene of the crime?" Donnolly inquired, contemptuously.

"Shut up, Don," Gifford warned, stomping through the throng of media as he made his way toward us. "Do you have any suspects, Gifford?" an *ABC* reporter hollered over the sea of voices. "Is it the same MO as the Fetters?" asked another. "Come on, Tommy, give us the name of the victim, anyway," pled Larry Erskin from *WNET*, "We're local, for Christ's sake!"

It was only then as Gifford approached, safe behind the cordoned-off perimeter, that I saw his face. I mean I *really saw* it: black skin gone gray, eyes glazed over with something that looked to be shock.

"What crime?" I asked, urgently. "It's not Jeremiah?"

"No," Gifford confirmed, not bothering to make eye contact. "Come with me."

Amy and I followed both men as they stormed passed the phalanx of cops and EMT personnel through the great west portal into the Chapel's narthex, its vaulting ceiling sixty feet above, the lilting voices of forensic investigators rising like rarified vapors into nowhere.

"Say, Tommy, what's going on here?" I asked, catching up with him. "This place looks like ground zero, 9/11, is it terrorism?"

Gifford ignored me. Donnolly turned, eyes fierce, raging. But raging at what? Raging at whom? *Me? God? Life, itself?*

My questions would soon be answered, I realized. Their cadenced footsteps slowed, then stopped entirely. Both turned, then parted, making way for Amy and I to pass, each drawn inexorably toward the altar, bedecked in the bright ribbons and the blossoming poinsettias I'd watched Harlan and Julianne so meticulously arrange.

Dappled remnants of sunlight spilled into the Chapel through the Great West window rendering it dark and perturbed like the light from the half-realized sun during a partial eclipse as we drifted beyond Braman Transept into the holy sanctuary where towering above the altar an eight-foot crucifix rose up from its center.

My cautious eyes traveled beyond the communion rail to a carved relief depicting the Passion of Christ, aware only then of the stream of clear liquid dripping from the crucifix onto the floor forming a shallow puddle the size of a dinner plate at my feet. I stared hard at the inscription, reaching for Amy's hand, clasping it tightly in my own. "*Christus vicit,*" I translated in a hoarse whisper, "Jesus Christ conquers all," but stopped then, compelled to follow the wending stream farther, and farther still, to something we did not want to see, a desecration that both our eyes and our minds rejected without forethought.

"Victim #1, white male, found naked at foot of cross. Throat slit, blood removed. Genitalia inserted into gullet. Mouth sewn shut with fencing wire," Donnolly read aloud from his preliminary notes, "DOA, body mutilated, disallowing visual identification."

"*Oh-my-God,*" Amy wailed, flying into my arms, "*I think that's Harlan!*"

"Victim #2, black female, found naked nailed to cross. Blood removed . . ."

"That's enough, Donnolly," I said, casting him a lethal stare.

"Body elevated above altar. Five-inch nails driven through hands and feet . . ."

"Enough," I repeated.

"Foot-long crucifix inserted into vagina," he continued, relishing every syllable. "DOA, body mutilated, crucified, disallowing visual . . ."

"Listen, you son of a bitch!" I roared, seizing him at the lapels, glaring into his swollen red countenance. *"Have you no decency? Do you see what you're doing?"* I thundered, turning to Amy, sitting Indian-style on the floor, unable to stand, Gifford rushing to her.

Donnolly stood immobile, a big Irish grin plastered over his face as one by one he removed my fingers from the blazer he wore, collar twisted tight around his bloated neck in the manner of a *jiu jitsu* choke hold.

"You know what assault on an officer gets you in Jersey? Seven years, Hot Shot." He said, toothsome grin folding back into a scowl. "Next time you lay a hand on me, I'm gonna rip your arm off and beat you to death with it."

I let the fabric of his jacket fall away, but not the fire in my eyes that blazed up at him.

"Arrest me," I muttered, "your word against mine. Besides everyone in this town, magistrate to mayor knows you're a piece of shit. Who'd believe you anyway?"

"Big man, huh?" he jeered. "You're a lucky fellow to hook up with a movie star. You must see dollar signs every time you go down on that bitch."

I glowered into his boiled green eyes with loathing, "You have a good instinct for personal details," I observed, smiling. "When did they promote you from vice squad?"

"Tell ya somethin' about your girlfriend, Madson," he said sidling up to me in the manner of a confidence. "No respectable call girl would talk to a piece of shit like Coco Channing."

"Say one more thing like that," I growled, "and see what happens."

"Hey! Knock it off, you two!" Gifford shouted, then, leaving Amy, walked toward us. "Madson, you know them?"

"The man is Harlan Haberman, works with Father Jeremiah, the Catholic chaplain here. Woman's Julianne Johnson, a private nurse assigned him," I answered turning back to Amy, who was being administered to by a paramedic.

"Let her be," Gifford advised, "I know Meredith. He'll talk, give her 10 ccs of *diazepam* to calm her. Believe me, it's worth the wait."

I considered what he said, nodded in the affirmative even as some twitching filament inside me—call it ESP—cautioned that I pay attention to Donnolly. I knew the first time I saw the him that if it ever got out of control I couldn't hope for too much. He could use his hands probably as well as me, but that would be only the beginning. Donnolly was of the stripe that didn't like to lose and would know other ways to fight. Before it was over I'd come to learn about his elbows and knees, the heel of his hand shoved into my kidneys, solar plexus, and of course other places. He looked like he'd changed more than one man's features in his life.

"Shapiro hasn't given us an ETD," he said, motioning toward the bodies, "but maybe you'd like to tell us where you been the last twenty-four hours," he challenged. "I ask since unlike everybody else, you knew both victims personal."

"Donnolly, I've got four thousand bucks in the bank.

You come on with that *CSI* bullshit, I'm gonna use it for
a lawyer. Now you just think about the hoops I'll have you
jumping through to get that information when all you
have to do is ask polite."

"Don't you just talk a lot," he sneered.

"I was with Amy Caulfield, sorry," I amended, "*Coco
Channing* last night until this very moment," I said, thinking with amazement that maybe he was a little afraid of
me, too.

"Just don't leave town," he instructed, both his eyes
and Gifford's fixed upon me.

"Tommy, you'll help, won't you?" I asked, sensing an
opportunity to stick it to Donnolly. "Was it Gary Cooper or
John Wayne used that line in those old westerns?"

Gifford nodded slowly, a 'you'll get yours' smile drawing the corners of his mouth upward as I turned my back
and strode toward Amy.

She seemed better now, and maybe Gifford was right
about Meredith. Still sobbing, hysteria subsided, she
peered up at me, then glanced to the foot of the altar
where Jeremiah knelt between the two corpses, immured
from the chaos that engulfed him.

I walked toward him understanding the pervasive
nature of evil perhaps for the first time in my life, its presence in this world as tangible as brick and mortar. The
world's foundation, I was coming to believe, was constructed upon evil. And at that moment, with the sight
of the old priest praying beside the towering crucifix and
massacred bodies of his closest friends, it seemed to me
a wonder that mothers did not consume their young at
birth, men did not walk amongst cadavers in the streets
carrying crowbars—except for Jeremiah, and the infini-

tesimal percentage like him, I surmised, feeling the reverence of a man dying of thirst approaching a clear, babbling brook run through a vast, pitiless desert.

"May God have mercy on their souls," I heard him whisper, blessing himself, "in the name of the Father, Son, and Holy Spirit."

"Harlan and Julianne?" I asked.

"No," Jeremiah answered with a sense of conviction borne of faith unyielding, "the killer's, and others like him. Harlan and Julianne are going to be just fine."

Chapter Twenty-Two

Monkey Bar
Manhattan, New York

Amy rejected the idea of heading for 'Emergency' at nearby Princeton Medical Center opting to go back to my suite in Manhattan. I watched her down the two 10 mg. tabs of Librium Meredith gave her with a glass of water, tucked her in, then decided, horrific day it'd been, I could use a nightcap. Where, after all, would wandering souls like me go without places like the Monkey Bar? I wondered, dragging my ass out of the suite onto the elevator to the hotel lobby.

An ironic simper crossed my lips as I took note of the club's bronze casting of three chimps—eyes, ears, mouth covered—as I made my entrance. Perhaps it was because I was dog-tired, or just didn't give a damn, but rather than reconnoiter my surroundings for potential bad guys, I nodded a greeting to Todd, the barkeep, never noticing Ty Rollins sitting across from me, Stetson hat on the bar top beside him, staring into his drink.

"You ain't gonna pop me again, are ya, Tough Guy?" he asked, rubbing his chin.

"Too tired, come back tomorrow," I answered, bloodshot eyes raking him over.

"Mind if I join you?"

"Yeah, but you're going to anyway."

"You knew them, didn't you? The murder victims at the Chapel tonight?" he inquired, angling his huge frame down onto the barstool.

"They were friends," I answered, downing my Glenlivet.

"Well, you may think I'm a piece of shit and not capable of it, but I feel for you, Madson." He ordered one himself, downed it, then took another. "That's why I come to see you."

My gloomy eyes lifted, "Humanitarian effort?"

"Might say that," he drawled, sipping from his double. "You read my article 'bout you and Coco?"

"You really want to go there?"

"I got no choice, not if I'm gonna help you and, trust me, you're a guy could use some help."

"I'm listening . . ."

"The paparazzi call it the 'hook'. You know the handle that grabs your reader right off? Well, the 'hook' for that article was that you and Amy, crazy in love, travel to Paris to get hitched, but 'torn between love and career ambition, small town girl Amy Channing leaves you behind, goes on to Tinsel Town stardom!', follow?" he asked, hound dog eyes reaching out to meet mine.

"I fucking lived it, Rollins, remember?"

"Well, I feel for ya, your friends bein' killed like they was, and thought you should see this," he asserted, reaching for a wad of papers tucked inside the band of his Stetson. "I came upon 'em researching that article about you and Coco rippin' through France back in '08."

I scanned the documents, copies of Amy's passport

issued 2008 stamped with dates and destinations into and out of the U.S.

"You have a source within ICE?"

"No, Bejing," he joked, rearing back on his stool with a big Texas grin.

"Maybe it was 2007 instead of 2008, maybe they forgot to stamp it. Amy and I were young and in love. What did we care about passports? Besides, for all I know, these papers were forged and you're full of shit!"

"Maybe it don't prove much by itself, but fact is, you never been to France, neither, Madson," he pressed, handing over a second set of documents. "No Paris! No Ferris wheel! The whole goddamned story fabricated!" he contended, looking me steady in the eyes, "but I got a feelin' that may be news to you."

"Where'd you get these?" I asked, fucking around no longer.

"Coco's publicist, Bianca. Paid five grand! Way I figure it, Coco showed 'em to her knowing she'd pass them to me on the QT."

"Why that?"

"I come here thinkin' you'd be the one to tell me, but that ain't true at all, is it, Madson?"

I downed the last of my Glenlivet. "You're out of your mind, you know that, Rollins?" I laughed, rising from my bar stool then whirling around to him, finger jabbed into his solar plexus. "I was there, you understand? I was with Amy Caulfield in Paris back in '08 as sure I was with her in the aftermath of that abomination at Princeton Chapel tonight! You don't know us! You don't know what the two of us have together! Now, for the last time, lay off Amy, you understand what I'm saying, Tyson? You're looking at

a son of a bitch doesn't care anymore, not about you, not
even about myself, and I promise, that makes for a fucking deadly adversary. Todd!" I called out, turning to leave.
"Bring my friend here a last whiskey and put it on my tab!"

"Fair enough," Rollins conceded, stuffing the papers
back into the band of his Stetson, "you believe what you
want, but let me make a prediction. Before this is over,
you're going to wish you listened to me."

* * *

The next morning, over coffee with Amy, I received
a text message on my iPhone from Don Woods that read,
'Meet me in front of City Hall in twenty minutes.' To make
it there, I'd have to hussle but given the most recent murders and knowing the importance of the forensics testing
Woods had promised I'd have sprinted crosstown if that's
what it took.

We linked up at City Hall then walked a block over
to the Brooklyn Bridge. Woods was either half Eskimo, or
half crazy, wearing an Irish knit pullover, slacks and street
shoes, face turned crimson as the December wind lashed
by us, standing two-hundred and seventy feet above the
East River. Looking wall-eyed paranoid behind the thick
lens of his wire-framed spectacles, he scanned our surroundings, turned to me, braced against the wind, and
began walking the pedestrian path toward Brooklyn.

"It's a kind of cutting tool," he explained, referring to
the talon I'd passed along to him, "constructed of surgi-
cal-grade platinum steel, serrated and curved inward for
maximum tearing effect like the tooth or claw of a predatory animal. Guys at the crime lab swear they've never seen
the likes of it."

"How do you mean?"

"Aside from its construct?"

I nodded.

"The DNA recovered had an equally unique pattern, genetically engineered, synthetic."

"'Synthetic'?"

Woods stopped walking. He turned to me, the two of us standing midway between shorelines. "Tell me, Madson, do you believe in the resurrection of the dead?"

"Maybe I do."

"Then this is your lucky day," he expounded, a taut smile, clinical and remote, crossing his lips, sunlight reflecting off of the lens of his spectacles. "The DNA found on the talon you gave me is a perfect match for Nazi war criminal Joseph Mengele, confirmed dead, Bertioga, Brazil, February 1979."

Chapter
Twenty-Three

The Commons
Princeton, New Jersey

After leaving Woods, it took every ounce of resolve I could summon to focus on the killer and not the carnage he'd inflicted at Princeton Chapel. Indeed, I was sickened by the indelible image of Harlan and Julianne's savaged bodies swirling like phantoms inside my head, theories about the killer's identity configuring and re-configuring like the tiles in an ever-evolving mosaic along with nagging notions of recrimination I carried around with me like a secret sharer: *had I not allowed Harlan to get involved in the Kurtz case, would both he and Julianne be alive today?*

Perhaps it was during anguished moments of consternation like I felt that afternoon—when throwing in the towel seemed the only realistic alternative—that the discipline instilled by the monks at St. Damian's proved most valuable. Predictably, I rejected the possibility of quitting. Jack Madson was not about giving up! I owed Harlan and Julianne more than that, I swore to myself, and would not rest until their killer was brought to justice.

If, prior to meeting, Woods I'd proven linkage between Mengele, the CIA, and ALATON, I reasoned stalking passed City Hall back to my Vette, but lacked the nexus between ALATON's experiments at Princeton and the killer, I believed I'd found it with the stainless steel talon bearing Mengele's DNA. Yet, like the heads of the Hydra, from out of that revelation emerged yet another.

Wasn't it Paul Lindstrom, *aka* Loris Merckx, who participated in genetic experiments on natives in the Brazilian jungles with Mengele? Wasn't it Lindstrom—Nazi background erased—who'd presided over ALATON's applied science and the DOD's black ops projects since being relocated to America by the CIA? Wasn't it Lindstrom whose high risk-high reward experiments in human directed evolution, silent messaging, and cloning provided the foundation for the radical science ongoing at Princeton today? Clearly, then, it was he—with Nazi background, expertise in genetics, position as ALATON's VP-Technology—who held the key to the Kurtz case and the identity of the 'Princeton Slasher'!

I arrived at The Commons, an upscale townhouse community where Lindstrom resided, mind a cauldron of sentiments beyond hate for a man I'd come to recognize as devoid of humanity, soul wracked with disdain for a Government I once revered, convinced now that in a Faustian trade-off the CIA had set Evil loose to flourish like plague.

I pulled into a parking space in front of the perfunctory patch of grass that marked Lindstrom's residence then stared at the red door to his townhouse until my eyes watered. The unbridled arrogance he'd demonstrated during our first encounter would be the ace I held, I strategized, understanding that if I asked the right questions, sat back, and gave him enough rope to hang himself, the information would be there for me.

The car door slammed behind me as I crossed the spate of lawn. I stood at his door, rang the bell. The former Nazi's mountainous frame filled the doorway, first ring.

"Madson," he greeted, "to what do I owe the pleasure?"

"May I come in for a moment?"

"By all means," he boomed, more gracious than I could have imagined. "In fact, I'm glad you're here!"

He stepped aside. I slipped past him with the realization that being around Lindstrom was like cohabitating with a disease.

"Maybe it's none of my business, but you don't look well, is something wrong?" He ushered me into the living room. A pile of logs blazed in the faux fireplace. The decorative lights on a miniature Christmas tree atop the mantle glimmered like flecks of diamond. "Make yourself at home," he said, gesturing toward a Windsor chair. "Like a cup of coffee?"

"Thanks," I answered, feeling as if I'd stepped back in time to Vienna, circa 1920, noticing bookshelves stuffed with scientific volumes like *Brain Children: Essays on Revolutionary Bio-Genetics by K. Erik Dressler*, *The Rise of Neo-Biological Civilization* by Dr. Wolfgang Heitbaum, *The Human Genome Project* by Horst Gehmecker, philosophical treatises by Hegel and Nietzsche, arcane histories dealing with Hitler, the Third Reich, and World War II. Open, on a mahogany table was a bottle of Divourniac brandy, a cup of half-drunk Brazilian coffee, and two open books, Lindstrom's own landmark work *Speculative Studies in Radical Evolution*; the other, the *King James Bible*.

He handed the coffee to me in a Winfield cup then

eased his strapping frame into a chair. He took a sip and looked to me, a vibration not unlike an electrical current passing between us.

"So, what brings you here, Madson?" His wizened blue eyes twinkled. "It wouldn't be those murders at the Chapel last night?"

"Yes, that's it exactly," I confirmed, recalling Fetter's comment about Lindstrom's penchant for behavioral predictability. "I was hoping that as a psychologist you might have some insight into what type of individual is capable of killing like that?"

"The work we do at Forestall is classified," he rejoined, putting coffee aside, pouring a snifter of brandy, "but if it's murder that interests you, why not talk to the police?" He downed the brandy in a single gulp. "Unless," he remarked, eyes blazing, "you think I'm involved. Could it be you've been talking to that old loon Collins, running his mouth with fantasies about my past?"

"I know all about your history with the Nazis, Lindstrom. What I want to know now is the connection between ALATON's experiments and these murders."

He nodded, the twinkle in his eyes returning. He poured himself another. "The Jew boy and his nigger girlfriend, is that your problem, Madson?"

"That 'Jew boy' and 'his nigger girlfriend' were my friends, Lindstrom, but I doubt you'd understand concepts so trifling as friendship."

He chuckled. The bluish veins that ran through his cheek and jowl more evident, face reddening, with the aftereffects of alcohol.

"Did you know that during the height of the war

Churchill had already drunk a fifth of Divourniac before
breakfast each day?" His joviality shriveled at the recognition of my stare, cold and deadly. "But that was a long
time ago and at eighty-four years of age, Churchill's appetites for both notoriety and brandy seem to me excessive."
He placed the snifter on the mahogany table beside him,
sat back in his chair. "So is this the point in time that I'm
supposed to tremble with dread, throw open Shakespear-
ean closets of remorse, poured forth unbounded? Love,
friendship, human emotions, you say! As if we in the Reich
never experienced these sentiments with our SS brothers,
wives, children, Hitler, himself! Sorry to disappoint, but I
feel no remorse," he sniggered, piercing blue eyes shoot-
ing through me like x-rays. "What I feel is vindication."

"You know, if I had a razor I'd cut your throat just to
see what ran out of it?" I marveled, suddenly aware that
more than a man, a luminous presence was sitting across
from me.

"Monster? Is that what you see? No," he admonished,
"we are the world's salvation. And you, a Jew, yes?"

"Part," I answered.

"Ah, but there is no such thing as *part* Jew," he corrected, wagging a finger in my direction, "and now because
some corrupt ex-politician tells you about my work with
Mengele fifty years ago, I'm supposed to be frightened?
No, it's you who should be frightened of me, Mr. Madson.
America is a shambles! A veritable text book of inferior
racial types: niggers rioting in the streets, yellow-skinned
mongrels infesting Silicon Valley like cockroaches, bor-
ders overrun with spics and their heroin. This is a nation
of human shit!"

"Your politics fascinate me," I observed with icy resolve, "but it was MAYHEM we were discussing."

I watched him drain the remainder of brandy realizing for the first time he'd been drinking most of the morning.

"REBIRTH is what Mengele called it," Lindstrom expatiated, the mask of arrogance suddenly dropped to expose an embittered old man, sardonic and deadly, "the blueprint for what would become the DOD's MAYHEM. The Nazis, stalemated at Stalingrad, needed a 'miracle weapon', something to turn the tide of the war and believed they'd found it in Mengele's research: 'slaughter machines' that would kill without scruple for days, even weeks at a time, with no need for sleep, food, or water.

"The early generations were crude and clumsy, 'Small Minds' we called them, incapable of thought or reason. We knew that the genetically enhanced embryos Mengele carried from Wewlesberg were spawned from his own DNA—strips of flesh surgically removed from his body and others in the Nazi hierarchy, but we didn't care. REBIRTH was Mengele's joke on a world that rejected his genius and Elon would not deny that final triumph to him; a war criminal to many, but a genius to us, brain extended in time, at least theoretically, forever!

"The process, even once we learned to accelerate it, was time consuming and unpredictable," he continued, more a rave than an explanation. "Some functioned as envisioned, others not. Elon finally abandoned REBIRTH in favor of a recombinant process that coupled microchip implantation conceived during the CIA's MKULTRA with 21st century bio-augmentation. We called it MAYHEM because that was its purpose, a non-nuclear plan B in the event of a ground war with China to destabilize entire cities, countries for that matter. The Joint Chiefs understood that US forces would be hopelessly outnumbered and, like Hitler, envisioned armies of mass murderers, *trans-humans*, dropped behind enemy lines; smart, agile, trained in the latest combat techniques to kill and keep killing until their mission was terminated. Not only did using students in place of embryos compress our timeline from decades to months, but with candidate profiles established outcomes became predictable, opening the door for subliminal control of thoughts and behavior."

"But something went wrong, didn't it?" I prodded. "With Schumann? Wilder?"

Lindstrom's malice cut a swath through the air as it knifed its way toward me. He cleared his throat with a short harsh sound as though ordering an animal to come up, then spit into his handkerchief.

"American students! It wasn't like this with Germans, those you could count on! Who could predict the instability, the thin line that separates normal behavior from insanity in your so-called 'culture'?"

My mind lurched forward. "They couldn't handle the psychological strain," I accused in a solemn whisper. "Some went berserk like Wilder; others committed suicide like Schumann; 'Small Minds' to your way of thinking, unable to cope with the microchip implants, behavioral modification, drugs and whatever else you put them through! Christ, it must have galled you and Elon, men of such large intellect and so few scruples, to see a DOD project worth trillions spiraling toward oblivion because of a handful of students, isn't that so, Doctor Lindstrom, or should I call you 'Merckx'?"

"Yes, that's right!" he lashed out at me, "and if it weren't for our dedication, our commitment to the dream, the entire project would have turned to shit!"

"But the prototypes, the *trans-humans*, they must still exist, must still be functional . . ."

"Just one, but hardly your killer!" he scoffed. "Clumsy, awkward, a 'Small Mind' soon to be terminated. Nothing fancy. A suicide gene inserted into its genomic sequence! But there is another 'special' one, indistinguishable from any other man. For all you know, he could be standing next to you on the morning train or regurgitating the nightly news on the television in your living room. Partly human, he knows, he understands himself and the consequences of his mission. That's what makes him 'special'."

"And what mission is that?"

"To kill you, Madson," the silver-haired Belgian retorted, lifting a bloody handkerchief to his mouth, a raffish grin accompanying the glint in his eye. "Call it a stroke of good fortune for you, but with self-cognition came the realization that in ending your life he, too, would be terminated."

"Me?"

"His mission once you blundered onto the scene questioning the Schumann and Wilder suicides was to hunt you down and kill you; a game for him, proof of the program's efficacy for DARPA and the military who threatened to cut off funding."

"Most games don't involve murdering people."

"That depends on your definition of fun. Elon wanted a real life challenge, so why not you? Out of work with no parents or siblings, no immediate family except an institutionalized wife, and a daughter you've been estranged from for years. To us you were the perfect candidate.

We've even given you a moniker, a pet name, so to speak," he beamed, " 'Oswald', as in Lee Harvey Oswald."

"Take me to him," I demanded.

"You still don't get it, do you?" he asked, eyes crawling up and down my face. "He's taken to a survival mode not unlike the conditions of war in which he was programed to survive. I haven't a clue whether he's deep in hiding or behind the curtain in the bedroom of my townhouse."

"Then take me to the laboratories where ALATON's experiments are conducted. One way or the other, this nightmare's coming to an end," I threatened, drawing a Walther PPK semi-automatic from the inner pocket of my jacket, leveling it at him.

He looked me over feature by feature, "You may be impulsive Madson, but you're no fool. I'm the one with the answers. Kill me and you've got nothing!"

Eyes locked and unblinking, I squeezed the trigger. A 9mm slug tore off the right upper corner of his chair, sent it flying into the air.

"You think I wouldn't do it? Blow you away to give Shitdom another martyr?"

"You're goddamned crazy!" he blustered, blue eyes raging as they lifted to meet my own lethal glower.

My lips drew back from my teeth, "Crazy? Yeah, I'm fucking crazy, but you're going to take me to those labs, or I swear I'll use the eight bullets left in this clip to remove every appendage, one at a time: ears, nose, hands, and fingers, 'til I get to that shriveled Nazi cock of yours!"

Slow and cautious, Lindstrom lifted his 6'3", 230-pound frame from the chair. Minutes later, I was passenger in his Mercedes sedan on my way to Forrestal, and soon after—with PPK jammed hard into the small of his

back—he escorted me through the network of underground passageways reserved for Powers, himself, into
the bowels of the PPL's high security Tactical Technology
laboratories.

Chapter
Twenty-Four

Tactical Technical Laboratory
Forrestal Campus
Princeton, New Jersey

L indstrom stopped at the entrance to the TT laboratories, slipped his UNIX card into the lock, glanced
into an iris scanner. The security door slid open. We
entered the hanger-sized laboratory where like a bustling
city ALATON's applied research was being carried out
full-bore, 24/7.

"You know the phrase *noblesse oblige*, Madson?" he
asked, airily. I stabbed the barrel of my Walther deeper
into his back. He smiled. "That's how I feel about our situation now. It's out of courtesy, master-to-drone, that I've
introduced you to concepts you can't possibly fathom, let
alone try to stop. Look here," he said gesturing toward
a monorail where tubes holding *trans-human* prototypes
immersed in green liquid hung from hooks some without
eyes, ears, noses; women breathing with gills instead of
lungs, electrodes implanted in their exposed brains leading to banks of Cray X-MP computers where lab-coated

scientists monitoring physical, intellectual, and emotional development, "come see the post-human future," he reveled leading me into an adjacent laboratory, "a world beyond war, beyond violence."

Mechanical doors gliding shut behind us, I stopped thunderstruck at the spectacle of male and female *trans-humans*—suspended mid-air outside their liquid environs, large eyes shining, skulls diaphanous, brains nested in wires—being interviewed by scientists while viewing holograms of murders; humans engaged in sexual intercourse; newborns crying; children at play in a school yard, laughing; soldiers battling enemy forces, AK47s blazing.

"What do you see?" the psychologist asked.

"Soldiers killing," the electronic voice resonated, translating thoughts into words.

"What do you feel?"

"Excitement," he responded, scientists monitoring telemetry, adrenalin levels, brain wave patterns.

In a 'Psych Station' beyond that, a female—fetuses clinging to the slick membrane of her upper torso, webs of wires emerging from the temporal lobe of her naked brain—dialogued with an alternate team of psychologists and neuro-surgeons.

"How old do you think you are?"

"One," she answered.

"One hour? One day? One year?" the female scientist pressed.

"I became capable of human cognition twelve months ago," she responded.

"And your babies?"

"One month."

"Do you love your babies?"

"Of course, I love them, don't you love your babies?" she asked, astonished. "Don't all mothers love their babies?"

Together Lindstrom and I made our way into an open area, Walther firmly planted into the base of his back.

"Do you know Nietzsche?" he asked.

"Not personally," I growled, nudging him forward.

"Hitler's favorite philosopher," the old Nazi observed. "It was Nietzsche who created *der Ubermensch*, literally the 'Over Man', an entity that will follow humans on the evolutionary ladder. 'Man is a rope tied between beast and Over Man—a rope over an abyss,' he once wrote, 'what is great about man is that he is a bridge and not a goal,' brilliant, yes?"

"A bridge to what? Eugenics?" I asked, shoving the gun barrel deeper into his back. "After six million murders—a million at Auschwitz alone—you're still at it, aren't you?"

"Genocide, old age, disease, plague," he rattled off, "if Mother Nature had been a real parent, she would have been put in jail for child abuse. No, what you're witnessing here, Mr. Madson, is prelude to the greatest evolutionary leap in history: the introduction of self-awareness, emotions, rationality to a new race of post-humans. We share 98 percent of our genome with chimpanzees," he lectured. "The genetic difference that makes us human is barely significant statistically. Yet chimps cannot imagine human ambition, philosophy, or the emotions we share with one another.

"Mengele correctly believed that governments could improve the human species through control of hereditary factors in mating. That belief led to the extermination of Jews, Gypsies, cripples who polluted the master race. But

GRIN technologies have handed us the ability to remake humans absent the physical and mental defects that like millstones have dragged civilizations down into the swamps of evolutionary obscurity. In the future, it won't be Nature that chooses our fate, but humans who will shape our own truth, happiness, social order. Has no one bothered to tell you, Mr. Madson? God is dead."

"Not like anyfink yer've ever seen, I'd wager," a sing-song voice, distinctly Cockney, interrupted.

I looked up to find a man with a pink, round face, longish hair and mutton chop sideburns approaching. He smiled toothily. Sans arms and legs, oversized head atop a torso no larger than that of an eight-year old, he sat in the center of a metal contraption with rotating spindles that propelled him forward.

"This is Brando Hemings. He works as a technician in Artificial Intelligence," Lindstrom informed me, accent prominent. "Brando doesn't like to hear it, but he is a reject. We keep him around despite his obvious physical handicaps. An act of tolerance that has him living on bor-rowed time, you might say, between existence and non-existence," Lindstrom was keen to remind him, "and, as Brando well knows, it's unacceptable to interrupt when I'm speaking with a guest, even if that guest happens to have a gun pointed at my back."

Brando grinned self-consciously, "No, right," he shrugged, "not 'uman, if that's watcher finkin', but not inhuman 'ither!" he added with a trill of laughter.

I studied the strange little man nested within his Big Wheels contraption rubbing my eyes in disbelief.

"Not ter worry," Brando consoled. "I cop 'at reaction all 'a time. Well, right, actually never since we rarely cop visitors," then, recalling Lindstrom's comment, "did yer say 'gun', honest guv!"

"Get back to work, Brando," Lindstrom commanded, "this is none of your concern. You see, Madson, Brando is programed to serve," he explained. "He thinks, feels, experiences emotions, even forms relationships with humans. What he cannot do is hate or envy, or even fathom acts of violence or aggression which makes him, plainly speaking, a twenty-first century slave."

My eyes traveled to Brando, who was busy making faces at him.

"Beggin' yor pardon, Boss, right, but will yer be takin' 'im to the glass house, luv? I mean, since 'e's 'ere and since . . . 'ooops!" He clamped his eyes shut. "Blimey! Brain fart . . . should not 'ave said that . . . should never 'ave said a word about that!"

"I hadn't planned on it, but perhaps it's time," Lindstrom appraised, watching as Brando glided away silent as a spider on mechanical legs, turning his attention to a square room defined by four plate-glass walls.

Visible as we approached was a bevy of scientists, heads crowned with *transcranial magnetic stimulation* headgear, feverishly collaborating as moment-to-moment they studied bio-electronic monitors, broadcasting words, images, visual scenarios into electro-magnetic radio transmission units.

"The men and women you see working inside that glass box are integral to our 'silent messaging' experiments. The 'Exceptionals'? Just one of multiple studies we've undertaken. The others involve influencing the behavior of subjects we've selected to participate in a broad spectrum of scenarios. The 'silent messages', we choose to communicate emanate from out of this very room."

"Messages like the ones Mary Linda Schumann heard before she jumped from that window ledge at Pine Hall? Like the ones that sent Dimitri Wilder hurtling into a concrete embankment before he was burned alive in a fireball on Rt. 1?"

"The very same," he sang-out blithely, striding toward the exit, "and others," he smiled, nodding, "soon there will be many others."

"And the university? The Princeton's Board?" I asked, pausing to observe the carnival of madness around me. "They know about this?"

"Don't think of what you see here as experiments," Lindstrom suggested as we deserted ALATON's TT laboratories for the daylight brilliance of the west wing corridor. "Think of them as ATMs spewing hundreds of millions of dollars each year to our most prestigious universities, carrying out projects with names like ROBUST, MUSCULAR and RAPTOR, research begun decades ago by former *SS* like Von Braun, Strunghold and yes, Mengele, who slipped into U.S. black ops like they'd never left Berlin! So it was, and so it shall be: money, power, control, the mainstays of your so-called 'free' society! You see, the Nazis were not wrong, Mr. Madson. We were simply ahead of our time."

"Kurtz and Fetters knew too much and were talking, Schumann and Wilder were out-of-control," I anguished, "but why Harlan? Why Julianne? They were no threat to anyone!"

Lindstrom coughed a skein of mucous and blood into his handkerchief.

"The predator obsesses. In many ways he is like a child. He kills because he likes to kill. That's how he was engineered, and he cannot reprogram himself to abort his mission," the old Nazi expounded. "He can't kill you because he knows that he himself will die, and yet he can't stop killing. Still, there's logic behind these murders and it's about you, Mr. Madson. Harlan Haberman and Julianne Johnson were murdered because he tied them to you!"

"Who's next?" I demanded, putting my gun to his forehead. "You know that 'thing' stalking around out there better than anyone! Hell, you and Powers created it!"

"I told you, it's taken on a life of its own. We no longer control it."

"Who?" I screamed, seizing him at the throat, pulling him close enough to see the pupils of his eyes narrow to the slits of a reptile as I shoved the Walther PPK into his mouth. "Tell me who or I swear I'll paint the ceiling with your fucking brains!"

"Your wife and your daughter!" he snarled breaking clear of my grip, reeling backward, blood-soaked handkerchief in hand. "Don't you see? He's toying with you in a game full of surprises, preying on those closest to you to let you know he's very near, yet beyond your reach, just as you are beyond his. For him, it's a chess match using humans instead of inanimate objects."

"Who's the killer?" I asked.

"'Call me Legion for we are many,'" he said quoting from the New Testament.

"Why?" I demanded.

"Because like me, Mr. Madson, he enjoys watching you squirm!"

"Give me your car keys."

"You've got to be out of your mind . . ."

"Give them to me *now*!"

Chapter
Twenty-Five

Public Safety Building
Princeton, New Jersey

L indstrom's words exploded through my brain like hurtling shrapnel. When asked about the killer's next victim, he'd answered 'your wife and daughter'. When asked to identify the killer, his answer was cryptic. 'Call me Legion for we are many'. True, neither statement put me any closer to identifying the killer, I thought barreling toward Princeton Police Headquarters, but I knew now that if the 'Slasher' was stalking Jennifer and Tiffany, I had only to find my wife and daughter, and he would come to me!

I struggled to pair my iPhone with the car's Bluetooth, finally jabbing Tiffany's cell number into the keyboard while weaving through traffic along Alexander headed for College Road. "Godamned phone!" I cursed, staring dead-eyed at the 'call failed' message. "You need to contact Tiffany, *have to contact her now*, it's a matter of life or death!" the voice inside my head raged, spirits lifting once I saw the Public Safety Building a half-block away.

I left the Mercedes, sprinting up the esplanade of

concrete steps to the landing where clusters of reporters waited like jackals for the scraps of information, TV lighting units blasting probes of white light that stretched-out into the nighttime sky.

"They got 'im!" an emerging reporter called out.

"They made an arrest. They caught the 'Slasher!' " I heard another clarion, reporters lurching toward the entrance with the single-mindedness of a mob, photo cameras flashing, anchors primping their hair for video cameras already rolling.

A Uniform pulling security in the foyer made a motion to stop me. "I've got evidence for Gifford!" I growled, flashing the phony PI badge I carried, making a B-line for Gifford's office.

Both he and Donnolly were heavy in discussion with State and FBI when I entered. The mood was celebratory which should have told me more than it did.

"I just left Lindstrom," the words gushed from my mouth, "and, Tommy, he confessed to everything: experiments begun by Josef Mengele, the Nazi scientist, decades ago now part of a black ops project at the university. The 'Slasher', a virtual killing machine, borne out of those experiments!"

If a picture is worth a thousand words, my expression must have spoken volumes to Gifford, who seemed puzzled, and Donnolly, who could not have been more pleased, when the realization came to me that I could have been talking about the land mass of Asia for all of the interest they had in the news I carried.

"Sorry to burst your bubble, Buddy Boy," Donnolly exulted, "but the killer's been caught."

"He's right. It's over, Madson. We got our man," Gifford confirmed motioning to the "holding" area where the suspect paced the length of his cell, wild-eyed insane, "Afghan Vet gone Charlie Manson crazy. We just took his confession."

About to protest a rush to judgment gone horribly wrong, I stopped short at the sound of my Stones' ringtone. Donnolly snickered. Gifford turned back to his discussion. My heart leapt at the sight of the caller "ID".

"Tiffany!"

"Where are you?" she asked, panicked. "You were supposed to be here with us. And now . . ."

"Now what, Baby?"

"The phone rang twenty minutes ago in Mom's room," she confided, an ugly menace creeping into her voice. "We thought it was you calling to say you'd be late, but there was no one on the line, Daddy, just this heavy breathing and a song playing in the background; an old one, "Paper Moon", I think, and it was really freaky but that's not all. Along with the music, there was screaming in the background. Horrible. Awful. Like a man or a woman was being torn apart, literally ripped to pieces. Then the music stopped, so did the screaming, and the only sound left was the breathing, and don't ask me how, but I knew then that whatever it was on the other end of that phone was not human!"

Then, silence.

"What? What is it?"

"All the lights just went out," she answered in a slow, hollow voice, "the entire building's gone dark . . ." Another silence. Then, *"Daaad-dy!"* I heard her screaming.

"Lock the door! Tiffany, can you hear me?" I exhorted. "Lock the door now and don't leave the room until I get there!"

Chapter
Twenty-Six

Greystone
Morris Plains, New Jersey

Wracked to my soul with foreboding, understanding the execrations the 'Slasher' was capable of, I did not want to imagine the horrors Tiffany and Jennifer might endure at his hands. Still, the images assaulted me: the decimated remains of Kurtz, the Fetters' family, Harlan and Julianne as I stabbed the gas pedal hard down onto the floor bolting toward Morristown.

Set against the brooding December sky, the Kinbridge Building came into view. I plunged the Mercedes through Greystone's wrought iron gates, beyond the condemned mansion to the complex of modern buildings, wheels screeching to a halt.

I parked, sat quiet for a moment gathering my thoughts and my courage. My eyes brushed over the silver **ID BRACELET** dangling from my right wrist. *"Confianza en su corazon,"* I whispered, a flash of light sudden as a thunderbolt cleaving through my brain. I switched the ignition 'off', the entrance to Greystone spinning like a pinwheel.

I reached for my temples, palms pressed tight against the sides of my head, wondering if that was all that prevented its content from spilling out into my hands.

NOW there is the **PREACHER**. Screaming. "Death be not proud!" Surgeons, staring down upon me. Lights, shimmering above. **FERRIS WHEEL**, Amy beside me. Father lying on bed. White sheets, turned crimson. Tiffany crying out for help. Tumbling inexorably away!

I look up. Salvatore "Bill" Bonanno stands before me. He spreads his hands with a magician's penache. Invites me into a corridor. Deep within Greystone. EOU WARD, the letters above the entrance read. "I think I am dreaming. Am I dreaming?"

> *static beyond static*
> *from out of the electric mist*
> *scientist's voice emerges*
> *"open silent messaging"*

Dark and grim, static-laced and blurry I recognize Nurse Keating alone in the deserted hospital corridor holding a boom box to her ear, grinning broadly as she peers down upon the black male teen who once owned it, his head split open with a fire axe, lying dead in a pool of blood at her feet. Giggling mischievously, she listens through dense waves of dissonance to brain-fracked commands audible only to her. "Yes, that's right, absolutely," she agrees, face aglow with enthusiasm. "Yes, I understand, entirely," she confirms a final time before marching, axe brandished above her head, toward the hospital room where Tiffany and Jennifer cower in hiding.

Heart in throat, I observe Cephus Jackson creeping up from behind about to pounce upon the surrogate killer, but quick as the swipe of a cat's paw, she turns, smiles wickedly, a Kinsey surgi-

cal blade already drawn from the side pocket of her white nurse's uniform, and plunges it into his heart.

Effortlessly the ninety-pound nurse twists the blade inside him, driving it still deeper as he staggers from her, eyes popped open with shock. Still standing, he writhes back against the wall. She pulls the blade from out of his left ventricle then sweeps it hard across his breast laying open his upper chest cavity before dropping the lancet onto the floor. Undeterred, a smile wholesome as a bucket of farm-fresh milk beams from her face as she draws the axe up above her head and begins beating the locked door down while Cephus, blood spouting from severed coronary arteries, clings to the wall then slides down onto the floor, dead.

> *clouds*
> *in tumult*
> *"close silent messaging"*
> *I am myself again*

Escaped from the dismal purgatory of brain-fracked visions, I sprung from the Mercedes into the eerie dim of Greystone's lobby acutely aware now of the deserted security stations, blank surveillance monitors, elevators rendered inoperative by the power outage. My eyes darted to the emergency staircase. I charged up the stairs to the fourth floor, flung the door open!

Perhaps fifty feet away, Laurie Keating stood, a broad axe swung over her head splintering the door to the room where Tiffany and Jennifer had retreated. Battered door hanging from its hinges, she entered, then paused seizing her quarry with the sheer force of her gaze. Incensed, I charged ahead tackling her to the ground. But not before she managed to turn halfway around slamming the blunt end of the axe onto the side of my head with a blow so powerful I heard the crack of bone shattering as my legs gave out from under me!

Lying there, I watched paralyzed as she grabbed me by the hair, then dragged me across the floor with her left hand toward Tiffany, who cowered in the corner of the room, hysterical, and Jennifer, oblivious to all that was happening, still wielding the fire axe in her right.

"Small Minds!" the nurse-turned-maniac screeched. "You dare to fuck with me? You dare to fuck with *me!*" she ranted, wild-eyed, drawing the axe over her shoulder ready to split open Tiffany's skull with her next swipe while dazed and anguished I began climbing up her frame, now rigid as steel, clawing desperately at the axe ready to drop upon my daughter when a single shot rang out and everything stopped.

Concussive within the confines of the hospital room, the air became clouded with the smoke and smell of burnt powder from the discharged Glock. The first 9 mm bullet tore through the back of Keating's skull emerging from out of her right eye socket sending the crazed murderess to her knees. The second sent her lurching forward falling onto her face, the bullet sprouting like some exotic species of fauna from out of her right breast. My head jerked up instinctively to the doorway. It was Don Woods, Homeland Security, an avenging angel materialized from out of nowhere!

Amidst the room's smoke-laced silence, Tiffany rushed sobbing into my arms. Jennifer, suddenly aware of her surroundings, began laughing inanely, perhaps out of relief, more likely at the bizarre nature of the events that had just transpired.

Woods lowered his weapon, then ambled toward Keating, body collapsed in a heap.

"She's dead," he pronounced, feeling for a pulse, "and if I were you, I'd be gone before the Locals get here with your pal Donnolly a half step behind."

"How did you . . ."

He looked up from the corpse, the lens of his spectacles reflecting the red glimmer of emergency lighting.

"I've still got the juice when it counts," he grinned darkly. "We track global terrorists, Madson. You think I can't tail a 'person of interest' like you?"

"Me? A 'person of interest', you're joking?"

"Cops think so. Now why don't you get your ass out of here, let me handle this."

"And trust you to explain?"

"Your choice, but stay here, they're going to arrest you," he pledged, eyes luminous behind the lens of his glasses as he crouched over Keating's body. "Trust me, Madson, Lindstrom's going to explain the killer's motives in a way that puts you heavy into the equation. "'Take-out Madson, the killings stop', that's what he'll tell 'em. Enticing, especially to a thug like Donnolly who already hates your guts. By the way," he drawled, the sophistication of his argument modulating, "you might consider paying Elon Powers a visit once you come to your senses and get the fuck out of here. In the final analysis, it all leads back to him, don't it?"

BEGINNING
OF
THE END

Chapter
Twenty-Seven

Fifth Avenue
Manhattan, New York

The naked air resonated electric outside of Greystone. The icy fog that shrouded the institution had thinned away, night was quickening. Now a hunted man, I drove into Morristown, abandoning the car for an Uber, then headed to Powers' Fifth Avenue penthouse understanding that Woods was right about Lindstrom and Donnolly. In the absence of nailing the real killer, there would be a fall guy and between a Nobel Laureate ensconced deep in the bosom of U.S. Intel, a billionaire genius providing the DOD with advanced weaponry, and me, it wasn't hard to predict whose profile would best fit the frame-up the Agencies were constructing.

I exited the cab corner of 93rd and Fifth praying that Don Woods, alienated super patriot that he was, would give me the space I needed to confront Powers if not by diversion then at least with his silence. I stepped into the lobby of the Cutshaw Building dogged by a prescience of disaster that clung to my back like chill wet leaves. All

277

around me I could sense vague tracks, feel menacing eyes fixed on some easy prey within me. A powerful secret calling my name in whispers; asserting, demanding. I fought it. The secret. What secret? The question rose like a fetid corpse up through swamps of outrage at the atrocities for which I held Powers accountable.

It was lunacy to believe I could penetrate the levels of security that enveloped him, so I decided to take the challenge head on. He'd remember me from our meeting at Babbo, and, despite our withering exchange, hadn't he gone out of his way to meet me? Didn't he know that I'd already made the connection between the Schumann and Wilder suicides and Marjorie Kurtz' murder? Clearly, that line of reason was anathema to him and like a bone lodged in his throat I was someone he'd want to engage, if only to ascertain what new dots I'd uncovered and if, once connected, they led to ALATON, perhaps even to him. Based on that supposition, I stalked unhesitatingly to the security desk, offered my ID and boldly proclaimed it was Elon Powers I wanted to see!

Surprised, if not amazed, I cleared lobby security, sibilant whispers still calling my name as I trundled toward Powers' private elevators — sequestered from the bank of public ones — that would rocket me seventy floors up to the ten stories he occupied when not lobbying elected officials in D.C., closing deals in Dubai, or clubbing with beautiful women for rent or for sale with his billionaire pals.

Two body-builder types dressed in black suits greeted me as I approached, the one flashed a smile, the second motioned me toward a print pad and iris scanner. I obliged, and we ascended up toward Powers' penthouse. I exited the elevator, ambled toward a second security station manned by three guards, *Gavin de Becker* logo prominent on each of their uniforms.

"Good evening," the man seated behind the desk greeted.

I nodded a curt acknowledgement, then went through the drill—ID, signature, eye scanner, metal detector—half-expecting the bastards to pull a tooth or draw a blood specimen before it was over. As expected, the third security man frisked me.

"I don't think you'll be needing this," he suggested, taking the PPK from my inside jacket pocket still smiling, an eyebrow lifting.

The officer-in-charge reviewed the outcome of my electronic inputs. Then, raising a thumbnail to a front tooth, gave me the go-ahead. "He's okay," he declared.

"Elon is expecting you, Mr. Madson," the guard behind the desk confirmed with all the aplomb of one of ALATON's robots.

"'All roads lead to Rome,' " I observed, flip and ballsy, "that's what the Italians say."

"I wouldn't know about that," the guard demurred, and at that moment I wondered if the others would repeat the sentiment, 'No, we wouldn't know about that", 'No, we wouldn't know about that.'

"*Ciao*," I bade, grinning like the wise guy I am while predatory eyes trailed me down the hallway to Powers' front door.

I stopped at the entrance to Elon's 21st century Xanadu, lifted my hand to strike the knocker, but before I did the door creaked open. I stepped into the foyer then jumped back instinctively, stunned to find—what would one call them?—gremlins, guarding the entrance—holograms with the dangerous brooding eyes and leathery faces of baboons, frolicking like deadly ADHD house pets yapping excitedly in a language I could not hope to identify. 'What kind of mess have I gotten myself into now?' I wondered, emotions like ghosts passing invisibly through the aisles of my body, hands jutting up into a fighters' stance, ready to strike.

"Don't mind them! Just showing off for the new-comer, though I would not touch them," Dieter, the but-ler, cautioned, motioning them back from me with the wave of a hand. "They are electrified, Mr. Madson, and as harmless as we want them to be," he added, summoning whatever warmth existed within him into a poultice-like smile.

Tall, lean, and dressed in formal attire, Dieter escorted me imperiously through a multitude of dimly lit hallways, finally stopping at the lip of a high-ceiling room that could only be described as Gothic. There, Elon Powers, dressed in jeans and white shirt, presided in gloaming stillness seated atop something akin to a medieval throne surrounded by bookshelves brimming with works on alchemy, theosophy, the fall of apartheid in South Africa, the rise of the Third Reich in Germany; vast battalions of books interrupted at intervals by oversized computer screens on which grue-some surgeries, hypnotic mind experiments and electro-shock therapies dating back to the 1920s played side-by-side with popular ALATON commercials, jingles sung merrily by cartoon bears, taken from boundless volumes of footage archived in Cloud data banks hovering miles above the planet.

I understood immediately that I'd walked into the middle of some kind of hearing, a trial perhaps, where standing mesmerized at the edge of the room I watched Lindstrom, flanked by what I assumed was a prototype 'slaughter machine', emotionally pleading his case to alter the predator's termination gene and extend his existence.

Could this creature standing head bowed with reptilian eyes, enormous jutting jaw, elongated arms and legs, fingers and toes clawed with razor-sharp talons be the killer I'd been stalking since the day I first arrived at Princeton? Possible, I speculated, head throbbing, side wound yowling, but equally possible was the alternate explanation that like Brando Hemings the creature was simply a mistake. Hadn't Lindstrom disparaged the clumsy 'Small Mind' that still existed within the confines of the PPL while gloating over another so sophisticated that no one would suspect it was *trans-human*? If that was true, the creature that loamed beside Lindstrom was most assuredly the former, I concluded, watching Powers wave a dismissive hand at Lindstrom, turning his attention to the predator.

"Today, you will find peace," Elon promised, eyes fixed upon it, voice brimming with an amalgam of melancholy and fatherly pride.

Torn between the poles of vaulting ambition and murderous instinct, the predator spoke in a guttural rumble.

"What is my purpose?" it asked.

"You are a prototype *trans-human* created to be destroyed and then replaced by the next generation, not unlike we humans."

"I am no man," the creature despaired.

"I can't change that. I can't change what you are."

"*I am Joseph Mengele!*" it erupted, head thrust upward, jaw jutting forward in defiance.

"That is correct, but now you are a *trans-human*," Powers clarified, "hopelessly underdeveloped for the times. A 'Small Mind' that like the others has served its purpose and must be destroyed. Your destiny is bred into the DNA sequence that created you, and in that sense, Mengele, you are no man and never will be."

"I didn't choose this body! I didn't choose this mind!" the predator groused, a petulant child, leering at Lindstrom. "How am I responsible for his ignorance?"

"Noooo!" Lindstrom bridled, unable to contain his indignation any longer. "It was *your* vision! It was *your* path forward! The three pillars! And, yes, two succeeded beyond our dreams, but this! Look in the mirror, Mengele, you are grotesque!"

"It was you who failed! You who brought me back to exist in this living Hell, neither dead nor alive, neither man nor beast!" the predator seethed, icy blue eyes meeting icy blue eyes.

Sensing the flutter of murder in its demeanor, knowing its capacity for killing, Lindstrom stepped back drawing a Sig Sauer X-Five from a holster at the small of his back, "Stay away, Mengele," he warned. "If I shoot, I shoot to kill!"

But the silver-haired Belgian never fired a shot nor uttered another word as the predator, feigning a move to his left, pivoted forward seizing Lindstrom by the skull with both of his long-fingered hands, "You are no visionary! You have no vision!" it bellowed, unabashed of its German accent, driving elongated thumbs deep into his eye sockets, Sig Sauer clanging as it dropped from his hand to the floor, the scientist's eyeballs bursting like grapes, body quaking like a man in the midst of an epileptic seizure. Blood surging from two gaping cavities that once were his eyes, Lindstrom collapsed onto the teak floor, dying, most assuredly dying!

Powers, who'd risen to his feet, inched back toward his throne-like chair then dropped into it like dead weight, stunned at the sudden virulence of the murder. When he looked up again, he was smiling benignly.

"Come to me, Joseph," he uttered, beckoning the creature to him.

Awkward and obedient, it lumbered from the writhing body kneeling at the feet of his creator; understanding its fate with no words exchanged.

"What will death be like?" it asked, voice deep and low, a quaking tremor resonating through the gloom.

"For you, it will be beautiful."

"Do I have a soul, Father?"

"Yes, a magnificent one, Josef."

"Will there be a place for me, Father?"

"In death you will find a home. A place where your genius will finally be understood and you will live there exalted with the others forever."

The predator took both of Elon's hands into his own. He looked up to him pleadingly, "And you forgive me for my failure?"

Powers gazed into the eyes of his creation, Artic blue and reptilian, bent down and brushed his lips over its forehead.

"I want you to close your eyes now, Josef," he whispered tenderly. "I want you to close them now and think back to different days and a different time. A time when you believed to your soul that the world was yours and your destiny was a shimmering path upward into the stars. Picture the *Fuhrer*," he suggested in dulcet tones, "see him in his glory, as you shall see him again, speaking at the height of his power in the Reichstag before an ocean of humanity with you there, alongside him, with Himmler and Goering, Bormann, and all of the others.

"These were the architects of the new world, Josef, the purveyors of mankind's dream to become Gods. Our vision made reality for a thousand years! Think those thoughts. See them now, Josef. Feel the magnificence of our triumph rise up like the Phoenix within you as the Reich shall rise up again!" Powers exhorted, stroking the creature's face lovingly, talons extending from the shafts of his fingertips as he reared back and with one powerful swipe, majestic in its efficiency, sliced through skin and bone and cartilage, neutrally observing the predator's head drop from its shoulders then tumble onto the teak floor, eyes still open and cognitive, until with its final gasp, its glacial blue eyes turned back in its oversized head, black, glassy, sightless!

My eyes traveled then as if in slow motion from Lindstrom's corpse, my mind numbed with astonishment as I attempted to process the disparate threads of reality spun together labyrinthine, the lilting sound of music—was it Wagner's *Song of the Valkeries?*—swirling like souls unleashed from unsanctified tombs around me.

My blank stare lifted from the carnage, focusing now upon Powers in time to see the vague and haunting smile cross his thin lips, eyes aglow, the blood lust of a rabid killer awakened as he leapt with a panther's grace—throne- to-floor—disappearing into the swarming darkness beyond the room's parameters.

I'd seen that smile before.

Effusive . . . arrogant . . . coiled with distain . . . at the PPL . . . when I looked up from Marjorie Kurtz body, slashed and torn to pieces, into the laboratory's darkened doorway.

It was the murderer's smile.

Chapter
Twenty-Eight

Fifth Avenue
Manhattan, New York

I t was the killer's smile, I knew, the dissonant screams of Powers' victims echoing through the fogbanks of my unconsciousness, carrying with them long forgotten recollections buried in the detritus of surgeries and drugs and experimentation. Disturbing images of clinicians' faces hovering over me like masks. Fragments of sentences. *'His heart!'* someone cries out with alarm. *"Notice the eyes,"* another observes. *"It is quartz crystal, smaller than a grain of rice!"* another advises. Each voice tinged by accents—New York, London, Belgium—and it is within the confines of that scintilla of time, surreal in the absolute clarity of its arrival, that I ascertained the mission I was programmed to undertake: pursue ELON POWERS, seek him out, stalk, corner, and eliminate him; whether by gun or knife or bare hands, to make him totally and profoundly dead!

I peered out onto the murder scene, eyes like shiny marbles. Dieter had rushed into the room and was kneeling over Lindstrom's protracted body.

"He's dead," the butler pronounced, as estranged from all species of emotion as his simian holograms.

"Yeah, and it was Powers who killed him! Powers, the final subject of his own experimentation, the 'special' one Lindstrom bragged about, who's killed and will kill again! But you knew that, didn't you?" I accused, my body tingling with homicidal abandon as I stomped toward him. "You and all the others responsible for MAYHEM, but you let it go on, murder after bloody murder, a meal ticket for you and a hundred thousand others at ALATON, Princeton Research Center, and the DOD! Now I'm only going to ask just once, so make it good," I threatened, glowering. "Where is he headed, Dieter? How is Elon going to make his escape, from the heliport or through the tunnels?"

The butler glanced down to Lindstrom's body, eyes lifting to meet my chilling glare and the barrel of Lindstrom's X-Five leveled mid-point at his forehead.

"The heliport on rooftop," he muttered disdainfully. "Elon has a pilot on call always in case of a robbery or attempted kidnap. But you will never get him! You will never outsmart a man like Elon Powers!" he cried out, breaking down, sobbing as he buried his face into the dead man's chest.

With Dieter's words still ringing in my ears, I charged up the spiral staircase careening through the emergency exit out onto the rooftop where Powers' Bell 201 was making its ascent. Breathless, I stanchioned myself against the gusting torque of the copter's main rotor—arms extended, both hands clutching the Sig Sauer—and fired three lightning quick rounds into the cockpit killing the pilot on impact.

The copter's reaction was instantaneous, veering like a blinded Cyclops just above the rooftop over city streets eighty stories below, reeling left and right, vertical then downward to the distance of an average man's height. Sensing an opportunity, I rushed the craft head-on grabbing hold of its landing skid, madly climbing toward the cockpit, eyes fixed on Powers struggling to jettison the pilot whose dead body brushed past me, tumbling head–over-heels toward Fifth Avenue.

Torn between his need to control the lurching copter and obsession to rip me to pieces, the billionaire serial killer swiped savagely with his left hand as I struggled to lift myself up into the cockpit, working the cyclic stick with his right and rudder pedals with his feet, desperate to steady the craft. Chest heaving, I climbed into the cockpit's passenger side where Powers and I battled for control — man versus *trans-human* above Manhattan streets — realizing with the numbing sting of his first powerful backhand that even one-handed I had no answer for his unimaginable strength. Then like an electrical impulse jumping circuits, my first impression turned to chilling reality when Powers seized my wrist. We glowered into one another's eyes, his stainless steel teeth jutting from distended jaw as he sank his fingertips deep into my forearm, puncturing skin and veins, crushing tissue and bone, until with blood gushing beyond the fingers of his wrenching grip, I groped for the X-Five tucked inside my belt, raised it, and fired five short-range shots square into Powers' face watching his mouth, jaw, and nose rip apart before my eyes.

I shoved Powers' body aside and wrangled myself into the pilot's seat knowing that I had split seconds to stabilize the copter or die trying. Already in the throes of a downward spiral, I pulled the cyclic stick back with all the power in me, feverishly working the rotor pedals to steady the craft. My mind raced. My soul cried out for survival. Perspiration streamed like hot tar from my brow down my face and the flanks of my upper torso. Finally, my lungs like heaving bellows emptied in a gasp of relief as the copter swooped hawk-like between the forest of Manhattan high rises back toward the rooftop!

I flicked a glance at Powers' body sidled up beside me. Even by *trans-human* standards, the Slasher was dead, I surmised, shoving him off of me, ready to calculate my next move, but putting together a game plan to save my ass from a prison sentence measured in lifetimes not years wasn't in the cards for me. Not then, probably not ever, I was thinking, as my harrowed gaze dropped to the rooftop heliport where—could it be?—Don Donnolly stood, head cocked skyward, bloodshot eyes transfixed, bovine lips curled upward into a sardonic smile.

Could anyone adequately describe the sense of dread and futility I felt at that moment? Whichever direction I chose seemed catastrophic. If I fled the building by copter as Elon had planned, rest assured there'd be no private jet waiting to facilitate my escape! If I acquiesced to Donnolly's beckoning toward the heliport, my odds for survival were no less daunting, I reasoned, but preferable to the extent that I'd save myself from being blown out of the sky by SWOT marksmen!

I landed the copter, climbing over Powers' corpse as the main rotor wound down, Donnolly's Glock already drawn and pointed at me. The detective approached unblinking through the draft of prop-stirred gust, frisked me with his free hand then tossed the Sig Sauer he'd discovered to the side.

"Hit the jackpot this time, didn't you, Hot Shot? You just iced one of America's greatest assets," he drawled, an ugly menace creeping into his voice. "Now put your hands on your head. You're coming with me!"

"Should be an interesting autopsy," I observed, glancing sidelong to Powers body hanging from out of the cockpit, face half blown-off, white shirt soaked in blood, "but I don't think that's what your employers have in mind."

"Shut up!" he snarled, poking his gun hard into my spine as we marched toward the ledge. "I been waitin' a long time to see you beg like a dog for mercy, Madson, or will you do your swan dive still playing the tough guy? Guess it don't matter 'cause you'll be dead soon enough; a puddle of red goo spread over Fifth Avenue that I may just decide to piss on." He paused to assess me. "What? No wise-ass remarks?" He sniggered. "I didn't think so."

"Ah, the sweet stench of money!" I observed sniffing at the air around me. "How much will they pay you to kill me, Donnolly? Ten grand? Twenty?"

"It ain't about cash," he answered, edging me further toward the ledge.

"What then?" I asked, pressing. "What would interest a thug like you other than money? Sex? Or is it blackmail?"

"It's something you wouldn't understand, Fuck Head, call it a 'world view', a vision of what the world should and shouldn't look like," he spat back like disgorging a dram of poison from his system. "You think somethin' like this just happens? You think this hasn't been planned for decades?" We stopped near the building's edge. "Now jump, you son of a bitch," he ordered, jabbing me forward with the Glock. "Jump or I'll blow your fucking brains out and throw you off myself!"

I nodded fatefully, feinted toward the ledge then whirled my body around slamming my ankle full force into his gun hand in a back kick *jiu jitsu* move that sent the Glock skittering across the rooftop.

Caught off guard, the big man's face contorted with rage. He cast a furtive glance at the gun, weighed his options, eyes darting from Glock back to me, then charged full-bore ahead. Donnolly was a powerful, hulking man with the build of a linebacker and, hand-to-hand, size and strength would be an advantage but not now, not once he'd set his course forward.

With studied anticipation, I took a step back and to the side so the impact of his body slamming into mine was negated, then seizing the one chance I had at survival, took hold of his arm using his own momentum to throw him to within inches of the ledge. The detective staggered back, waivered, barely able to maintain his balance. He cast a wary stare to the street then struck out at me again, this time anticipating my side move, hitting me low at the thighs, clutching my legs with his hands from behind, slamming me to the ground!

It was as if a number beyond measure had been struck, the cap that gauged his hatred of me blown sky-high, leaving him more beast than man as he pressed down onto me, chest forward, while I parried his blows, rolling my hips to the left and right, desperate to reverse positions. Fierce and deadly, we fought—move versus move—the detective's flaccid face tightened into a mask of contempt. He was winning and he knew it, nostrils flaring, lips stretched into a feral grin of bow-mouthed mockery. But that nano

second of complacence was all I needed. With a stab of discovery and hot-surging hope, I felt my right hip slip from
beneath his bulk. I was free. Or at least free enough for
my legs and feet to propel my lower extremities to one
side, sweeping my leg up and around his back with force
enough to throw him off of me!

Ruddy face matted in sweat, grin wiped from his lips,
Donnolly nodded grudging respect. He reached down to
his ankle drawing a Karambit combat knife from its sheath,
crouching into a fighting position. Our eyes searched one
another's. I stepped away. He edged forward to an equal
degree, circling around me. The circle tightened. He
jabbed at the air between us, smile returning, eyes lit with
anticipation. I flicked a kick out at him testing his reaction, his reflexes. It was trained. Professional. White teeth
beyond taut lips, the smile broadened. I took a chance.
Another kick at the huge man's ankle. His knife hand
would be next, I calculated. But that never happened. The
shift of my frame toward him afforded the opportunity he
needed thrusting forward the Karambit's six-inch blade
beyond my open hands!

Call it survival instinct or blind luck but he'd mis-
judged the distance between us, slashing my shirt above
the sternum with the side of the blade. Now he'd exposed
himself. Now *he* was vulnerable, I concluded, the thought
a meteoric impulse leapt through the adrenalin-spiked
filament of ten billion brain cells, shrieking. I took hold
of the detective's wrist with both hands wrenching the
blade back toward him with a surging power unknown
to me until that moment. Awkward and off balance, his
green eyes, deadened and boiled, spread wide with panic.
Yes, he knew it. I did too. My eyes, two particular pools of

Hell, told him as much as I passed my right leg behind his crumbling ankle then pushed forward, driving the combat knife deep into his heart as I dropped down on top of him to the rooftop.

Snapped out of my wanton blood lust, I lay atop Donnolly's massive chest, blood pumping through my clenched fingers wrapped around the Karambit knife. Adrenalin surged. Temples, fingertip, toes throbbed with blood excited. Breathless, I peered into the detective's panicked eyes, wide and dimming, the light shining from them bright like the trail of a falling star before fading to umber green then disappearing forever.

I climbed off Donnolly's bloody corpse and frisked him. Wallet, fifty bucks, two twenties, a ten. Drivers' license. Cop ID. Visa credit card. PPD badge. Shoulder-holster. Empty. Business card. Babbo, 110 Waverly Place. Handwritten, 'Thursday, 9 p.m.' Why that? Why Babbo? my mind—that untiring raconteur of illusion—had already started to puzzle.

Understanding that Powers' Security was about to set upon me with the frenzy of bees protecting a violated hive, I staggered to my feet already contemplating Elon's Plan B escape route through the network of tunnels leading from the Cutshaw's basement. I scanned the streets below for signs of the inevitable NYPD onslaught, my attention diverted by the heart-stopping thwomp of the Bell 201's rotor blade revving and unimaginable spectacle of Powers, with half of his face missing, piloting the copter attempting to escape!

I dove at the ground toward Donnolly's Glock simultaneous with Powers' whirling motion toward me as Uzi in hand he strafed the rooftop with a barrage of machine gun fire, Bell copter teetered precariously above the bustling Manhattan streets!

Limits. There were limits. Must be. Had to be, my mind was pounding, fearless as I rose from the ground, semiautomatic stretched out in front of me, stalking toward the copter like a fighter walking down an opponent in the ring, merciless as I emptied the full clip of 9 mm bullets into the cockpit.

The craft wobbled uncertainly, Elon still alive, trapped within, until like a game bird taken mid-air it plunged, swirling inexorably downward to Fifth Avenue where amongst cars and buses and pedestrians it erupted in a vaulting fire ball as I watch, spellbound, from eighty stories above!

Police cars raced into the dead of night. Sirens howled like mangled souls broke loose from Hell. FBI and NYPD helicopters circled like vultures overhead. But by then I was long gone, escaped through a basement portal into the serpentine tunnels run beneath the city, emerging unseen into a long-forgotten subway station two miles west of Chelsea.

How fucked am I? I pondered, attempting to piece together my descent into this maelstrom of madness beginning with Lawler's phone call, the Schumann suicide, Wilder's rampage, Kurtz' and the Fetters' slaughter and my current status as fugitive-assassin responsible for the murder of billionaire-patriot, Elon Jacobus Powers!

I sagged, weak and bleeding, back pushed against a concrete wall in the deserted underground station contemplating the series of ironies, coincidences spread like a feast of gloom before me. From out of the morass, Lee Oswald's "I am a patsy" comment post Kennedy assassination drifted ghost-like up from the patchwork of oddities buried like bones at the fringes of my consciousness. I had killed Powers. Donnolly had attempted to kill me. Was it possible that like Jack Ruby, Donnolly's function within this half-century- long conspiracy, was to assassinate Powers' assassin?

Awash in a tumult of fear and paranoia, I needed someone to gauge just how far I'd drifted. Who I'd become. What I was doing. *Had I gone mad?* The proposition was not without merit. Clearly, anyone but myself, and perhaps Amy, would believe it to a certainty!

Yes, Amy, that was it! She knew. She'd help set a course forward to vindicate me. To get me off my ass and become Jack Madson again!

I reached into my pant pocket, grabbed my cell, and began dialing. I put the phone to my ear. It was ringing. Amy, Amy, my frazzled brain repeated. Then I heard it, the voice, distant and vague.

"Donnolly?" My eyes clamped shut, the phone dropped from my hand to the concrete. *"Donnolly, is that you?"*

Chapter
Twenty-Nine

Greenwich Village
Manhattan, New York

I sloshed through the flooded subway rails accompanied by the rustling squeal of rats scurrying for cover until I reached a rusted-out emergency exit leading to the basement of Bolton's on 96th and Lex. The heart of more than one stalwart employee must have skipped a beat when feeling my way through racks of prairie skirts, polyester slacks, and designer jeans I emerged looking not unlike an unearthed corpse from "Night of the Living Dead".

"You okay, Mister?" A Puerto Rican designer stepped out from the cluster of workers to ask.

"Never better," I lied, but he wasn't buying and, good fellow that he was, led me to a dingy, closet-sized john watching the door while I cleaned up.

My heart lurched like an elephant from its stall when I saw myself in the mirror: face bruised, shirt torn, forearm wrenched purple and bleeding, side-wound oozing putrefaction.

"Chico," I barked, "you got some gear?"

"Wait here, My Darling, and I'll be back with a trous-
seau," he pledged fluttering away, then returning with
slacks, *N.Y. Mets* hoody, black leather jacket, and pair of
Tacoma work boots. "We just opened our Men's Department," he confided, hiding a giggle. "No offense, but
one week earlier and you'd be wearing a Liz Claiborne
jumper!"

"One week ago, *mi amigo*, I wouldn't be caught dead
in a shithole like this," I shot back, discarding pants, shirt,
and shoes for new ones. "No offense taken."

But clothes were the least of my problems, I calculated,
deserting Bolton's for the blaring car horns and pedestrian bustle of 96th Street. I felt as if I'd fallen out of a ten-
story window, landed in a fireman's net, and was strolling
in a glow and daze, my mind weaving images like pictures
from a grainy film along with snippets of past conversations
clear enough to have been played back on a recorder!

AMY, eyes wet, heartfelt, "Do you remember that night
in Paris, Jack, when I asked you to feel my heart? 'My heart
is your heart' I said. 'We are one and there are no boundaries between us.'" Nazi historian **ERNST MOLTER**, "Still
there are rumors, *persistent rumors*, that Mengele was on the
brink of breakthroughs based on mind control, genetic
engineering, human cloning." Medical Examiner, **JOEL
SHAPIRO**, harrowingly: "*Succinylcholine* in just the right
proportion. Injected in exactly the right spot . . . imagine the pain . . . imagine the horror!" Ex-con politician
NEIL COLLINS, "Once our guys accessed CIA files we discovered paradigm-shattering breakthroughs in radio-hypnotic communication, the ability to control the behavior
of others through the use of micro-wave transmissions."

PAUL LINDSTROM *aka* MERCKX, monstrously corrupted, "These are the 'Exceptionals' . . . The men inside that box integral to 'silent messaging' . . . We've even given you a pet name, it's 'Oswald', as in Lee Harvey Oswald." Cowboy-reporter, TY ROLLINS, shouting to me from the ground, "All of what she told you, they're lies, Madson! No Paris! No fucking Ferris wheel! The whole story a total goddamned fabrication!" FERRIS WHEEL . . . PREACHER . . . ID BRACELET! "Eyes!" Theresa Eckhart screams up from Mengele's human laboratory. "The jars were filled with human eyes!" BRIGHT LIGHTS bearing down on me now . . . SURGEONS . . . Micro-chip receivers smaller than a grain of rice . . . FADED NEWSPAPER CLIPPINGS . . . black and white photos . . . OSWALD . . . RAY . . . FBI mug shots . . . SIRHAN SIRHAN whirling up in a vortex from the depths of my subconscious! Then there is me, JACK MADSON. Alone. On a deserted playing field. Caught in the glare of stadium lights, baring his soul to friend and lover COCO CHANNING, "It's more than a diary," he anguishes, palms jammed against erupting temples. "I live with those thoughts or maybe they live with me. But they're always there, inside my head. Nightmares, entire scenarios that creep into my mind like assassins in the night, *so visual, so fucking real*, most too horrible to put into words!"

I am standing now. On corner of 96th Street. I know this. But the idea that I am still alive seems an illusion. I feel the bellows of my lungs on their rise and fall. Breathing faster, shallower now. WORDS . . . IMAGES . . . MEMORIES resonate like an ancient code tapped out by a dead man!

I open my hand. Nested in palm. A wadded white card, soaked in sweat.

"Taxi!" I call out, curbside. "Babbo," I tell the driver, "West Village *now.*"

Chapter Thirty

Babbo
West Village, New York

The cab arrived at Babbo. I handed the driver a fifty, popped a handful of Adderall for alertness then an Oxycodone to tamp down pain and took my time chewing. The bitter piquancy of the cocktail wound through me like a cobra uncoiling. I reconnoitered the terrain.

Yeah, sure, I was less than a hundred percent but back on my feet again, mind laser sharp and focused as the drugs worked their magic. This was it. My last chance to confront Coco Channing and expose the puppeteers behind the predatory evil let loose during these interminable days and nights of blood and slaughter.

I gathered my wits and my courage and marched beneath the black canopy leading to the restaurant's front door bursting into the foyer where celebrity chef Emeril lavished goodbyes on rapper Jay-Z and his oh-so-lovely bride, Beyonce Knowles.

"It's time to leave, baby," he said, nudging her out of the door. This, my first indication of just how lethal I must have appeared to those unacquainted with the horrors I'd witnessed, who had not slain demons incarnate like Donnolly and Powers, on that fateful night of reckoning. The second was Emeril, himself, whose accommodating gaze shifted to me, the blood draining from his face as I mauled my way through the knot of customers awaiting tables at the outermost edge of the bar.

I studied the room searching for Coco, a buzz like millennium insects communicating from inside its walls, barely audible beneath the spirited storytelling of inebriated patrons. The eyes of some lifted, sensing the gravity of my glare then froze upon me. No doubt I appeared nothing less than a madman, but I didn't give a damn about anyone save Coco and when Mauro, the maitre d, touched a hand to my shoulder I swung around with a slew-eyed fury that might have stopped a man's heart! His hand shriveled from me, his wary eyes searched mine, but I did not engage. Rather, my glower, riotous now with ferocity, homed in on the woman entering the ladies' lounge.

It took no measurable amount of time to start after Coco, plowing through coveys of high-tone patrons. One or two of the men trying to impress their women, or simply too quick to react and too slow to know better, even put a hand on me, but I was on a blood mission, blood was in my heart, *blood was in my eyes*, and it took no more than a fleeting glance for their flinty aggression to wilt like a flower touched by Hell fire.

I threw the door to the ladies' lounge open. Coco was already ensconced within a stall. I hit the metal door at its upper edge with the heel of my right hand. It flung open as if rocked by SemTex!

Inside, wide-eyed and loopy, Coco sat on the commode, a ten-inch strip of rubber tubing wrung tight around her bicep, a hypodermic needle in her hand.

"Jack, what are you doin' here?" She shook her head as if trying to dispel a hallucination. "I though you were . . ."

"Dead?" I inquired, jerking her to her feet so she stood facing me.

I drew Donnolly's Glock from my waistband, pulled her panties up over her crotch with my free hand. Coming to her senses, she ripped the tubing from her arm, needle dropping to the floor, and straightened the black velvet gown she was wearing.

"Are you fucking crazy?" she screamed, blood rushing to her white-as-death pallor.

I wrapped a thick, long-muscled arm around her throat, pressed the Luger to her temple.

"Now we're going to walk out into the restaurant, then back into the banquet hall you just came from and you're going to shut your mouth or die with your brains on your tits, you got that, Coco?"

Eyes bulging, she nodded woodenly. Together, we trudged, a single step at a time, out into the foyer. Desperate whispers rose up from the pockets of diners that greeted us. There was nothing subtle about what I was doing. "He's got a gun!" "Somebody stop him!" "Call 911!" the phrases knifed their way through layers of hushed apprehension.

A muscle-bound waiter shifted his bulk forward ready to pounce, but so acute were my levels of perception that even subliminal aggression did not escape me.

"Don't do that!" I warned, eyes shifting to meet his anticipatory gaze, Glock leveled mid-point at his forehead. "First bullet's for you, next one's for the bitch!"

The waiter edged backward.

"You!" I called across the hallway into the bar.

A kid in his early twenties stared back at me blankly, "*Me?*"

"Bring me that bottle!" I growled, waving the gun at a bottle of Glenlivet on the bartop.

"S-sure," the boy stammered, running it to me.

I took a greedy swill, whiskey streaming from the corners of my mouth, handed it back to him.

"I got ten bullets in this fucking clip. Someone gets brave, nine of you go down," I promised, eyes searching the faces of customers around us, arm coiled around Coco's throat, Glock pressed to the back of her skull, as we shambled like a two-headed carnival act to the edge of the banquet hall's closed doors.

I swallowed hard, swung the hall's double doors open, and was struck silent. It was as if a veil had been lifted exposing a parallel universe I could not believe existed! Perhaps one-hundred-fifty guests regaling in triumph: white-haired patricians dressed in Gucci suits, stately beauties, hair up, wearing Jovani gowns, the younger amongst them outfitted in brown para-military uniforms, white arm bands emblazoned with Nazi swastikas spun around their biceps radiating energy as dark and chilling as the death-tainted signals broadcast from an alien world!

At first the scene did not fully register, and so I plodded forward along with Coco as if entering a labyrinth of caves, my composure fast evolving into a murderous nest of feelings. From a podium staged upon an elevated platform with Nazi flag unfurled to his right, a Steinway piano to his left, and a dais of VIPs seated at a table behind him, stood Paul Lindstrom *aka* Loris Merckx, resurrected from the dead, I supposed, champagne glass hoisted about to deliver a toast.

"Meine lieben freunde, unsere heilige mission ist heute abend endlich in Reichweitte!" he boldly proclaimed, then thought better of it. "Pardon, we are in America and not all of us speak the mother tongue, *not yet,*" he joked, "and this is a night of celebration for all us all! My dear friends, our sacred mission is finally within reach, our dream to create a better world . . ."

Then, taking notice of the disturbance to the back of the hall, he stopped speaking. His hawkish blue eyes locked on Coco and I. Patiently, he waited for the buzz around us to subside.

"Mr. Madson," he boomed over Sennheiser speakers. "I see you've seen fit to join us—and brought a guest along. How nice!" Merckx smiled, depositing his glass onto the rostrum, the sound of hisses and boos spreading amongst the crowd like brush fire. "Now, now, that behavior will never do, not for a super race," he chided. "After all, none of this would be possible without Jack Madson! And you performed brilliantly," the old Nazi beamed down at me, "precisely as expected! You murdered Elon Powers and, God knows, he had to go. For the good of the project! For the glory of the Reich!" he elucidated. "Elon was a serial killer, a madman of his own making, and you killed him!" he laughed, raising his glass to the audience. "Now ALATON, the most advanced genetics research enterprise in the world, will be owned and operated by the most advanced race in the world, pioneering a new direction for human evolution. No niggers! No spics! No chinks or gypsy trash, except perhaps for our research," he mitigated, "or to mow our lawns in summer and shovel our snow when winter's chill descends upon us! The Fuhrer's dream of world domination marching inexorably toward realization right here in New York City, right now, in the United States of America!"

"Don't forget Herr Doktor Mengele!" a woman from the dais called out merrily, flute of champagne in hand. My eyes darted to Marjorie Kurtz, who'd proposed the toast, then to others seated alongside her: Woods, from Homeland; Eddie Lawler, in from St. John's; Princeton physicist, John Fetters, never more alive; ex-wife, Jennifer, passing a remark to Todd, the barkeep at the Elysse, giggling like a school girl, sitting in her wheelchair. "Mengele predicted all of this seventy years ago!" Kurtz was quick to add, Nazi audience nodding enthusiastically.

"Indeed he did, Dr. Kurtz," Merckx answered, fox-eyes glinting, "but it's such a novelty for one of his predictions to prove accurate I nearly forgot!"

A rumble of laughter emanated from the crowd and for the moment it was as if neither Coco nor I existed.

"But perhaps it's Mr. Madson and Miss Channing who should be congratulated. Miss Channing for her soon-to-be announced Golden Globe nomination! Madson for surviving long enough to be here!" he roared, glass lifted to his audience's delight.

My feral eyes prowled the swarm of bankers, businessmen, corporate lawyers, Wall Street moguls, foreign dignitaries as they emptied their glasses, unabashed.

"Donnolly was supposed to kill me, that about right?" I called out, voice tremulous and booming.

A cadre of Brown Shirts inched forward to encircle me, unnoticed by others but conspicuous as a neon sign to me, my senses operating now at hyper levels of perception. I fended them off with a lethal glower, the Luger pressed deep into Coco's right temple.

"Shoot the motherfucker!" Coco shrieked savagely as she struggled to free herself. "I just want his dirty Jew hands off of me!"

"Now, now, no need to get ahead of ourselves," Merckx assuaged, eyes tracking the Brown Shirts' tightening circle. "Yes, you're quite correct, Madson. Lt. Donnolly was assigned the role of assassin's assassin just as you were programmed to kill Powers, but not to worry since you must realize you'll never leave this room alive."

It was in that instant—my eyes catching the glimmer of anticipation in Merckx'—that I shoved Coco to the side, hitting the floor as the Brown Shirts lunged at me and a torrent of high-powered gunfire emanating from the banquet hall entrance, exits, and sky light cut my attackers down!

Stunned for a deafening moment by the awesome display of fire power, panic tore through the crowd! Merckx, who'd brandished a Sig Sauer X-Five from inside his tuxedo jacket, took a bullet to the throat that sent him reeling backward before collapsing to the floor while FBI, NYPD, and Tommy Gifford, PPD, swarmed the banquet hall supported by SWAT sharpshooters.

Awash in the erupting pandemonium, I stood, a pedestrian on the corner of universes colliding, observing Coco—teeth bared and howling—being cuffed by a team of FBI agents; Woods, shot through the head, killed instantly, while trying to escape; Lawler, wrested to the ground by NYPD, cell phone in hand, while attempting to contact his attorney; Jennifer, hauled off in her wheelchair, shrieking bloody murder! But it was the demon Merckx who obsessed me as I threaded through the mayhem where, with stage blood replaced by the real thing, he lay dying, a land-locked Ahab pinioned to his own psychotic illusions beckoning me to him.

Emotions shunted by the blunt reality of what I knew and would never know about Loris Koiten Merckx, I knelt beside him.

"Come closer," the old man whispered beyond the sound of his own breathing. I put my ear nearer to his lips. "No need for slaughter machines . . . it was the 'silent messaging' we wanted. Imagine, anyone we choose turned assassin perhaps at a movie theater triggered by Coco Channing," he uttered, blood spurting from the hole in his throat, "or in a car over the radio, or the family dinner table triggered by a message on the internet. But there's something you could never have imagined," he added, pulling me closer. "There were three pillars of technology, Madson, *three*," he confided, grip loosening, sour breath growing more faint. "It was cloning, Madson. That was the third pillar . . . that's what OPERATION REBIRTH was really . . ." Blood gurgled beyond his taut lips. He attempted to extract the words. Then, drawing up his right index finger, he tapped the silver ID bracelet on my wrist. "That bracelet is your 'trigger', Madson, '*confianza en su corazon*', he rasped smiling slyly as the images, *those images*—FERRIS WHEEL spinning, PREACHER screaming, AMY CAULFIELD laughing, silver ID BRACELET dangling from my wrist—swept through nerve end and synapse, silent messaging initiated, high-density microwave receiver implanted three years earlier at a Stanford University-based ALATON research facility more real to me now than the flailing tendrils of my own fractured identity ever could be!

static static
    initiate silent messaging
white light
    one hundred suns imploding

NOW I am perched above 50ᵗʰ Street staring down at the entrance to the Waldorf Astoria. A black Mercedes sedan, armor re-enforced with bullet-proofed windows glides curbside. An advance security detail emerges from beyond the hotel's doors, automatic weapons drawn, vigilant eyes combing rooftops, high-rise windows, passing automobiles. The Lead Agent speaks urgently into a button transmitter. The area around the hotel entrance spreads open like the Red Sea parting.

"*You know him,*" the voice of John Fetters insists inside my head. "*A new world indeed!*" Paul Lindstrom declares, a fragment of a speech delivered before thousands in a German soccer stadium. "*What? And you weren't part of it?*" the voice of Eddie Lawler confronts me. "*Loved you? I'm a fucking actress, Jack!*" Coco Channing marvels falling into a fit of laughter.

I struggle to fend off incoming transmissions like a man staving off a swarm of wasps, head jerking in spastic motions trying to escape the random voices assaulting me from one hundred directions. I stagger back from the old Nazi, head clutched in the flats of both hands, but with implants embedded the voices seep like water through leaks in my brain, a cacophony of strident whispers over-running the boundaries of my mind.

AGAIN I am observing the Waldorf's entrance. The black Mercedes comes to a halt. The engine idles. Static-laced voices screeching like sirens. "Eagle One, established," the Lead Agent confirms as a phalanx of security operatives erupt beyond the hotel doors, their air-tight configuration seamlessly enveloping a man in his mid-thirties dressed in a dark blue, double-breasted suit as he stalks panther-like toward the Mercedes. Of average height and weight, longish black hair swept over his broad forehead with truncated black mustache, he clutches a chrome briefcase in his left hand, right hand jutting up and out in a Nazi salute before being bustled into the Mercedes' back seat where he is sandwiched between a second team of operatives acting as human shields. Re-enforced steel doors slam shut like the portals to a vault. The black sedan departs with the self-contained efficiency of a well-executed military strike, radio transmissions bouncing between those left behind and the core team now headed for Kennedy International.

In pensive silence, I edged back toward Merckx. A tell-tale smile lingered across his ghostly pale countenance as he lay on the floor bleeding to death.

"It never stops, you know," he rasped, dying but somehow never looking young. "We simply morph. Today you see us as one thing, tomorrow something else altogether. It's the nature of our genius, Madson, and so we live for all times and forever until in the end we prevail."

Now, in his death throes, Merckx began making sounds. Violent sounds. At first they came like bursts of air blurted up from his lungs, beyond his perforated throat, erupting through blood-soaked lips. Then, more like a cough, thick and nagging, escalating to something more virulent—call it a hacking—that made one consider the possibility that behind those awful noises blood-laced fibroids would soon spew forth, until finally I realized it was a laugh. War criminal, Nobel Prize winning geneticist, father of the Nazi Fourth Reich, Loris Merckx *aka* Paul Lindstrom was literally laughing himself to death!

And he did, in fact, die but not before removing an earpiece receiver and attempting to pass it to me, the Lead Agent's final transmission clear as the sound of a church bell tolling.

"Position secure. Der Fuhrer established . . . Heil Hitler!" he revels, a final deviation from OPERATION REBIRTH'S protocol.

"Heil Hitler!" "Heil Hitler!" "Heil Hitler!" one by one the chorus of disembodied voices repeat over the earpiece receiver dislodged and hanging from Merckx' right ear.

After the End

Excelsior Hotel
Askanischen Platz
Berlin, Germany

S ome people claim that evil is a metaphor for the foibles of sick minds; that it doesn't really exist and may, in fact, have been created by power hungry despots, a dependable cudgel with which to beat down the swollen masses into societal conformance. But I can tell you, that is not true. I have met evil. I have seen it. I have known it. I have looked it in the eye and can swear to you that evil does exist. It lives among us as intimate as the air that we breathe, and that is why I'm back in Germany. Yeah, that's right, the Excelsior, just off Askanischen Platz, and hotels located in far flung places around the globe: Vienna, Hong Kong, Bombay, and here in Berlin, where some say the door to Hell is located. But no matter where my travels take me, the remembrance that remains most prominent in my mind is my final meeting with Jeremiah.

It was in a cluttered hospital room at St. Claire's shared with an indigent camped out on Princeton Campus. Jeremiah was ill, enlarged heart, probably discovered too late, the doctors informed me.

"Jack," he mused while I hovered over him, eyes sad

and rheumy, "we never had a chance to finish our discussion about angels."

"Oh, but we did," I laughed pitifully. "Like Christ, angels don't always know they're angels just as Jesus didn't know he was the Son of God until He was on the cross and dying."

"But I never told you how the idea, the theory, came to me," Jeremiah objected. He elbowed himself up from the mattress, his voice soft and clear. "It was you, Jack. You were the person I was contemplating when I took my Jesus theory and applied it to angels." Then, reclining once more, he smiled as if he'd just won some kind of victory over me, or himself, or something I could not identify. "In the top drawer of the nightstand there's a Bible," he instructed, motioning toward it. "Next to it is a gold medallion with the image of the archangel Michael. I want you to have it."

My eyes shifted to the nightstand then back to him, eyes now closed, resting. I reached into the drawer and retrieved it. The medal, indeed, depicted St. Michael, wings mightily unfurled, sword raised high in the act of slaying a coil of demons writhing beneath his feet trying to escape his wrath.

"It was Michael's mission to protect the sanctity of the Church. Its lifeblood. Its integrity. It was his calling to destroy the demons that infest this mortal world and contaminate the souls of humans. God chose him because Michael understood the nature of evil, Jack. God chose him because he bore the strength to battle evil and defeat it. There are, you see, two kinds of angels, but it wasn't always that way. At first there was only one, Angels of Light, but then Lucifer, the most beautiful of all of God's creations, full of pride, bloated with arrogance, challenged the God that created him for supremacy and was cast into eternal darkness. From that moment, those angels—the Dark Angels—spent their existence challenging God in a moment-to-moment battle for the eternal souls of humankind . . ."

These were Jeremiah's last words so far as I know. And today I think maybe it was his mission to communicate that equation to me because it was then that I understood my calling and my destiny with a finality that melded mind, body, and spirit into something not unlike a fiery sword.

Evil, I know now, flourishes like virus. It spreads invisible, oftentimes in the heart and marrow of the people and things most familiar to us, the man whose hand we shake each morning, the woman whom we embrace each time she approaches smiling; in words that appeal to us like 'freedom', 'dignity', and 'progress'. Such is its nature that evil hides, disguising itself so that for now, and perhaps all eternity, it appears the incarnation of all that is right in nature. But it's not that way. Not really. And so it laughs behind our back along with its legions, at our naivety, our smugness, our arrogance and pseudo-intellectual meanderings: because these are the vanities that give it life!

So maybe I know something you don't. Maybe that's my blessing and perhaps that's my curse. But this I swear to you, I will not rest, I will not divert. I will not again be human until the Dark Angel is tracked down and slaughtered, his feckless ashes scattered from the highest mountaintops in the roiling winds, I vowed, clasping the St. Michael's medallion in the palm of my left hand, PPK semiautomatic held snug and lethal in my right.

"On the chuffin' prowl again, guv?"

I swung around reflexively, Walther PPK in the ready.

It was Brando Hemings, my new best friend and partner in
crime, bounding into the living room atop his Big Wheels
contraption, eyes bright and shining, chipper as ever.

"Looks that way, pal," I answered grimly.

"Well, I thought yer could use a taste," he suggested,
motoring toward me, a double shot of whiskey and two
tabs of Benzedrine waiting atop the device's metal serving
plate. "Glenlivet, eighteen year. Yer fave as I recall, guv."

I nodded stoically, took drink in hand and downed
them, eyes fixed appraisingly on the strange man-machine
reject with pink round face, longish hair and mutton-chop
sideburns gazing fondly back at me.

"You know somethin', my brother," I said, shoving the
PPK semiautomatic into my waistband, "sometimes I don't
know what I'd do without you."